Home

Four stories of sisters who each left small-town, Amherst, Ohio. When they come home again, they find love and family as well as a chance to redeem themselves for juvenile choices.

Forever Love

Fifteen years ago, Syndie Wilder left her small hometown- Amherst, Ohio- to escape the pain of losing her best friend and boyfriend. Deciding that Chicago offered more for an up and coming jewelry designer, she enjoyed the big city life until she chooses to return and care for her father. Taking care of her father and relocating her internet business, Syndie has no time or desire for romance but fate has a way of playing with best-laid plans.

Thom Johnson broke Syndie's heart all those years ago and regrets it every day. As a firefighter, Thom sets out to protect Amherst and redeem himself for his bad choices. However, he never has forgotten Syndie and the hurt he caused her.

When a chance meeting happens, can the two former friends allow themselves the chance to become friends again, or will the sparks turn a childhood friendship into a forever love?

Beach Desires

Can a summer fling last a lifetime? Stacey Wilder escapes to the beach for a much needed vacation and meets a woman who tempts her passion. But Stacey hid her desires growing up because small town Catholic girls don't fall in love with other women.

3

Mandy Kenzie is a Southern girl who also dealt with discrimination growing up over her choice of lovers. When she meets Stacey, sparks fly and passion ignites. But will their beach fling become a forever match or just a vacation affair?

Can Stacey and Mandy make their long distance relationship work? Or will they let the prejudices of their upbringing ruin their chance at happiness?

A Christmas Accident

Expecting her first child, Sherri Wilder Davison wants nothing more than to spend time with her father over the holidays, but fate has a way of changing her best-laid plans.

Adam Davison is willing to do anything to make his pregnant wife happy. He will face hell to have her home for the holidays.

For Sherri and Adam, the holidays are a time of celebration and love, but this Christmas will be unlike any they have ever faced.

When a horrible blizzard causes an automobile accident that puts the lives of those Sherri loves on the line, can a Christmas miracle save them?

Coming Home

Shevonne Wilder returned to Amherst, Ohio battle scarred from Afghanistan. Now, she must relearn to live in the dark.

Jackson Gambish thought he wanted just another fling but fell for Shevonne's strength.

Fate threw Shevonne and Jackson together in a desperate search for her missing father. Can a blind woman and the womanizer rely on each other to rescue Mr. Wilder or will insecurities and stress cause their blossoming relationship to self-destruct?

Holiday Homecoming

Sheryl Wilder returns to Amherst, broken but not defeated. She's running from the man she thought she loved but is too afraid to reach out to her family.

Tanner Watts moved to the small town to start a restaurant and give his daughter the life she deserved. As a single dad, he grapples with juggling his job and his family.

A chance encounter provides Sheryl and Tanner with the help they desperately need. Two broken hearts mend as love blossoms, but when danger comes calling, can the two loners learn to rely on each other or will they lose all they have found?

MELISSA KEIR

Forever Love

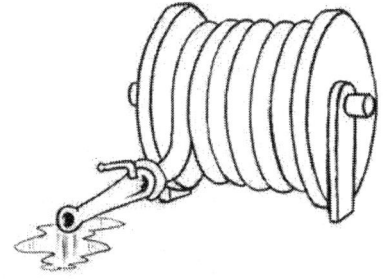

A Wilder Sisters Novella

DEDICATION

To TJ, who will always be remembered as my first kiss and to my husband, who will be my last.

CHAPTER ONE

Winding my way down the Ohio Turnpike gave me a lot of time to think. Unless you counted the many big rigs on the road, there wasn't much to look at while driving. Having left behind small-town life, I was nervous about coming home. It's funny. I've lived in Chicago for the last fifteen years, but still considered this small town, Amherst, my *home*. I don't know what scared me more—coming back to a small town after having escaped it or facing the demons that caused me to leave in the first place.

When Dad called last week, he sounded so exhausted it scared me. My memories of this robust man with a wicked sense of humor didn't fit the voice on the other end. When we were children, he would chase us around the house, trying to catch and tickle us. He taught me and my sisters how to shoot guns, ice fish, and ride our bikes. We stood on his feet as he twirled us around the room to Dean Martin songs, teaching us to dance. When I was older, Dad was the formidable bear that boyfriends had to get past in order to date us. I had only seen him cry once, at my mother's funeral. In other words, he was our first hero. No other man could measure up.

This man, who had worked in the steel mills all his life

and scared away my childhood monsters, was older now and needed me. There was no question about whether or not I would go home. That's what family is for. Of course, as the oldest, it was my job to help out, but also my career allowed me to move back to Ohio and be there for Dad. My four sisters were wrapped up in various enterprises, either trying to establish themselves in their careers or getting situated in new homes. My jewelry website and store could be run from Amherst as easily as it could from Chicago.

The urge to take a look around town before heading to Dad's hit me, so I exited the turnpike and headed left toward Lake Erie. Driving past so many memories unleashed the ghosts of my past, both good times and bad.

Amherst was already showing sad signs of the economy that many cities were currently faced with—empty storefronts, unrepaired roads and a vast sadness in the eyes of its people. Finding work was even harder in a small town than it was in a big city like Chicago. Unless you owned your own business or worked for the city government, you worked for one of the three big mega-corporations that had plants nearby.

There was an arcane quaintness about Amherst, from its brick-covered streets to its old sandstone buildings. There were churches dotting almost every corner of the town. People still gathered regularly at the small town diner right in the heart of downtown on Main Street. Nothing had really changed in the fifteen years since I left. How sad, I thought pulling into my dad's driveway. It appears I've changed more than the town. I wonder if anyone will even recognize me anymore.

Frightened, nervous, and anxious were all good words to describe how I was feeling as I grabbed my overnight bag and purse and approached the door. The first man I ever loved stood behind the screen door, watching me with a smile on his face. I gave him a big hug, then we went inside and sat down in the living room. "Gosh, I've missed you, Dad!"

"How was your drive? Did you get something to eat? Are you hungry?" Yep, that's my family, always trying to feed you as soon as you walk through the door. Food has always been a large part of our family gatherings, from the special traditional soup at Easter to the canned treats from our summer garden.

"The drive wasn't too bad once I got away from Chicago, and no thanks on the food. I stopped along the turnpike and grabbed a sandwich." I looked around the room and noted the house hadn't changed since I left. In fact, my childhood rocking chair still sat over in a corner of the living room. It felt good coming home to a comfortable place, for sure, but it was strange to do it as a grown woman who faced down things like scary spiders on her own.

"Then something to drink," he announced as he climbed out of the recliner and headed for the kitchen. From the living room, there was a straight view into the kitchen. As I watched him putter around, I noticed how *old* my father looked. He still had a full head of dark hair, although now it had more gray around the edges. My dad always was a handsome guy. The crow's feet that etched his face gave him character, as well as showing evidence of the hard life he spent working to bring home a paycheck to support our family. The lines weren't really what made him seem old, though. It was the curve of his shoulders that made him look older, like the weight of the world was on him now. I hope my being around will help.

Settling in that first night was challenging. I felt like a child again, back home with Dad. It had been awhile since I slept in a twin bed. Every little sound and noise startled me, but there was comfort in knowing that I was here in case Dad needed me.

After leaving the local steel mill, Dad had enjoyed a happy retirement, going fishing and drinking at the local Veterans of Foreign Wars club with his buddies. But in the last six months, he seemed to be forgetting things. When this first began, he would call me two to three times a day with the same piece of important information, often forgetting we'd just talked. Then, there was the frantic phone call he made from the grocery store, unable to figure out how to get home. Thank goodness his memory loss only lasted about five minutes that time. I was so far away and couldn't help him. My sisters and I didn't want to think about Alzheimer's, but our minds always came back to that possibility. One of us moving back to Amherst was our only solution, to discreetly discover the cause of my father's forgetfulness.

Dawn shone bright the next morning. I was anxious to do something, anything. I wasn't used to having time on my hands. With the change in location, I didn't have all the tools needed to begin working on my jewelry. Those boxes were coming later in the week. After putting on jeans and a T-shirt, I decided to take a drive to the local beach, which held a lot of memories for me. Hopefully walking along the shore would lead to finding some sea glass for my designs.

As I approached the beach from the road, I saw the picnic area and park where families ate and children played. My grandparents often took us to play in this park, with its giant Easter basket, beautiful fountain, and lawn-bowling court. I parked in an empty spot, watching the children playing on the sand near the water's edge and remembering my times here. This park held more than just good times with my grandparents. It held numerous memories of teenage make-out sessions behind fogged-up windows with nameless boys from my past. I was a good girl, so kissing was the most I'd do, it cost me many a boyfriend. I remembered how we would all bring our cars to the parking lot to listen to loud music and dance. It was a place to both see and be seen by everyone. It's funny how a child's playground could turn into a place for such behavior as soon as the sun goes down.

After getting out of my car, I hiked down the stairs. It was a mild September day, and the beach was fairly empty—just myself and a few seagulls. I walked slowly along the shoreline with my head down, not noticing the person swimming in the water until he began to climb out of the surf.

A dark, cropped haircut framed a face so beautiful that it could be described as the face of a Roman god. He had a strong nose and jawline that showed just a sprinkling of whisker stubble. However, it was his body that made me pause. His muscular shoulders and upper arms looked like they could carry a girl off to bed. His wet torso was covered with hair that immediately drew my eyes and tempted me to caress it. The chest hair tapered down his narrow waist and seemed to lead the way to paradise. I stopped walking and just stared. God, please let there be no drool dripping off my chin. This guy was smokin' hot! Then he smiled and I noticed his face, complete with a little dimple in his chin. He seemed familiar, but I wasn't sure where I recognized him from. When he saw that I noticed him, he winked as if he recognized me too.

"Hello! Nice day for a walk, huh? The weather has been kind to us this year." He spoke and my knees wobbled. His voice was like chocolate, smooth and delicious.

"Hi...Yes...I'm glad the weather is nice enough to get out, but isn't the water too cold for a swim?"

"Not at all. I enjoy my morning workouts after a long shift at the station. You don't remember me, do you, Syndie?"

My mind was drawing a blank. How did he know my name? Who was this hottie? "Not really. You do look familiar, but I can't place you. I'm sorry."

"It's been a long time. We grew up together, our parents were best friends. We even *went out* in high school. I'm not surprised you don't remember me, you hightailed it out of Amherst like your butt was on fire after graduation. We never saw each other again. I'm Thom Johnson, but everyone called me T.J."

Oh wow. I've got a lot on my plate and he has changed over the years, but to not know someone so connected to most of my life was baffling. This man had been my best childhood friend. I was T.J.'s girlfriend for a while, but he dumped me for someone who put out. Before we went out in high school, I grew up with images in my head of him as the ideal guy. Our families encouraged our dating, thinking we were perfect together. When he dumped me, it broke my heart. I couldn't stand watching him move on without me.

"Yes, I recognize you now, T.J. I took off because I thought that a big city had more to offer me. Well, it was nice to see you again. I had better get back to my walk, you seem busy." I took off wanting to escape this awkward moment. Having to explain to T.J. why I was back in town was the last thing on my to-do list today.

"All right, Syn. See you around." T.J. smiled. "Glad you're back!"

I began heading back to my car, no sea glass having been found. Instead, I'd discovered the one guy who broke my heart and, based upon my initial reaction to the sight of him, has the potential to do it again. I backed out of the parking spot and headed back onto the main road into town, thoughts of T.J. occupying my mind.

CHAPTER TWO

After settling in, the first order of business was to get Dad into the doctor's office and get some answers. He was still seeing the local doctor who had delivered me, handled my mom's illness, and patched up our family's many broken bones, so getting an appointment was easy. We arrived around ten o'clock and met with Dr. Freeman in his office. He shared the results of all of the tests he had already run, as well as his diagnosis. It turns out that Dad had been secretly seeing Dr. Freeman for years about the memory issues. He was trying to protect us from the diagnosis—it was Alzheimer's. My heart dropped when the doctor said those words.

What would this mean for Dad? How much would he change? It was just like him to try to keep this quiet and from worrying us. Now that I knew the truth, though, I planned on making sure Dad got the best care he could. Dr. Freeman suggested some meds that might help slow the onset of the disease, and as soon as Dad agreed to take them, I agreed to get them.

* * * *

My boxes arrived that afternoon. I unpacked everything in the workspace I'd set up in the spare room at Dad's. There was nothing like the feeling I got while creating a beautiful piece of jewelry from pieces of glass and stones. It gave me pleasure to know the jewelry I was crafting would end up as gifts of love for others. Humming to myself, I laid out my tools and begin sorting through my beads.

Dad was apparently running the vacuum in the living room, based upon the loud and annoying sound echoing through the house. I listened with half an ear, idly wondering why the vacuum was so loud. All of a sudden, a high-pitched whine came from downstairs, followed by the smell of smoke. Was that the fire alarm? What was going on?

I ran down the stairs to the living room, barely able to see through the haze of smoke. "Dad? Where are you?" I screamed over the noise of the smoke alarm and vacuum.

Hearing a coughing noise coming from the kitchen, I ran into the room to see flames coming from the oven and my father using a towel to try to put them out. "Dad, we need to go. We need to call the fire department." I pulled him toward the door and grabbed the cell phone out of my pocket.

"Hello, we have a fire at 224 West Front Street. Please send someone right away."

Within minutes, firemen arrived and set to work putting out the fire. I held on to my dad and wondered what happened. "Dad, why was there a fire in the oven? Were you trying to cook something?" Dad looked lost, like a small, frightened child. His eyes were glazed and his body was being wracked by coughing fits. The paramedics came over to take a look at him, alleviating a little of my worry. At least his cough was being treated. What was I going to do about his kitchen though?

The fire was quickly put out. When the screeching of the alarm stopped, one of the firemen came over to talk with me. As he pulled off his helmet, I noticed his familiar face. It was T.J.

Smiling at the soot on his cheek, I said, "Thank you, T.J. Is everything okay in the house now?" I wanted to run my hand over his face and brush the smudge off. Just being around him made my knees weak. You would think after sixteen years I would be over him. Maybe my mind knows, but my body doesn't yet, I thought sarcastically.

"Syn, were you trying to cook again?" His eyes sparkled, making the butterflies in my stomach flutter. "The fire is out. It was mainly contained in the oven. It appears that someone was trying to dry their laundry in there. There was minor smoke damage to the kitchen and living room areas, but I think that if you open the windows and air the place out, it should be okay in a couple hours."

I felt safer knowing someone I knew personally was here checking things over, but wished it had been someone who hadn't broken my heart. "Thanks again, T.J. It's my dad, he has Alzheimer's, and isn't himself these days. He must have thought he was being helpful. First, I heard the vacuum going. Then, the fire alarm goes off. I can't believe he put his laundry in the oven!"

"I'm sorry about your dad. He was always such a big, scary guy. Remember that time I came over to see you in high school and he wanted to show me his shotgun collection?"

We laughed together at the memory. Dad always thought it was funny to clean his guns when a boy came over to pick one of his daughters up for a date.

"You might have to keep a closer eye on him; we don't want to have to come out here for something more serious than an oven fire. Honestly, I would much rather come over and take you out to dinner than respond to a 911 call from your house."

"It's hard to see him going downhill so fast…And every guy got the same treatment in high school! No one was good enough for his daughters…Wait. Did I hear you right? Are you asking me out?"

The rest of the firemen were back at the truck, yelling for T.J. to come back so they could leave. "You bet. You were always my best gal." He grabbed my cell phone, entered his number in my contacts and headed back to the fire truck.

Shaking my head at his antics and smiling to myself, I headed over to the paramedic's ambulance to talk to them about Dad's condition. They had him huddled in a gray blanket. He looked so frail that the smile left my face. "How is he?"

"He has a slight cough from the smoke, but that's the only damage we see. He was lucky you got him out before he could inhale more of the smoke. Just have him take it easy for a few days. If the cough doesn't go away, have him see his doctor."

I pulled the paramedic aside, out of Dad's range of hearing. "My dad's been forgetful lately.

Are you sure he's okay?"

"You may want to have his dementia checked out. But really, nothing happened as a result of today's incident. He's fine."

I thanked the paramedics as we headed to the ambulance, and hugged my father tightly. Today was a close call. Losing Dad was unimaginable but in many ways, I suppose I've already begun to. As I worried about how to keep an eye on everything at all times, I put my arm around his shoulders and walked him back into the house.

After sending Dad off to shower, I opened all the windows and scrubbed the kitchen clean. The smoky smell still lingered on the air, but it was getting better. When he came back downstairs, Dad seemed more like himself.

"Syn, what do you want me to cook for dinner? Are you hungry? Why's the house all stinky? Did you try baking a pie again? You know that you forget to cover the crust every time." Opening the oven, he noticed the black remains of the fire on the inside of the door.

"Well, Dad, we need to talk." I led him over to the kitchen table, where we sat down. "Today you put your laundry in the oven instead of the dryer and started a fire," I said with what I hoped sounded like loving sincerity.

"I did what? That's crazy! I was cleaning up today, running the vacuum. I don't remember doing laundry. Are you sure?" Dad's voice broke on the last question, his eyes filling with confusion and sadness. "I'm sorry. I can't seem to remember things these days. I know that the doctor talked about memory loss with Alzheimer's, but I never thought I'd put anyone in danger, let alone you. What am I going to do?"

As his shoulders slumped, his face looked so crestfallen. This man, who had faced hot molten steel each day in the steel plant and had been burned a time or two, had just struggled to remember why he put his laundry in the oven. My heart shattered.

"Don't worry, Dad. We *will* get through this." Secretly, I wondered and worried myself about what we were going to do.

CHAPTER THREE

Life returned to our new state of normal after the fire. Dad had mostly good days. He was more like the man I'd always known, alert and engaging, but the fear of leaving him alone was always present in my mind. I worked on my jewelry in the kitchen from the day of the fire on, where I could be close by in case he tried to do laundry in the oven again.

Deciding to get out of the house, we headed out for dinner at a popular local restaurant. The Armors Diner was located in an old home that had been converted into a homey place to eat. They had a full menu, containing anything that might tickle your fancy, but they had the best Coney dogs and fries. The Armors was a favorite hangout for the high school crowd, so the walls were covered with photos from all the sports stories covered by the local newspaper. The place was packed, but we found a spot at a small table near the large front window.

The Armors held a lot of fond memories from my time in high school. I used to come to the restaurant as much as I could to hang out and visit with my friends. We would always order the large fries and talk about the boys we liked. The restaurant also had its share of sad memories too—mostly surrounding T.J. and our time together. As if just thinking about him caused him to appear, I looked up to find him walking through the door, alone, and heading directly over to our table.

"Hi Syn, Mr. Wilder. Do you mind if I join you? This place is packed, and I hate to eat alone."

"Hello Thom. Nice to see you. What have you been up to lately? I haven't seen you since you dated Syn, here. I must have scared you off good," Dad replied with a grin.

"Mr. Wilder, you didn't scare me off. Syn decided to run away to the big city and leave this small town behind." T.J. winked at me, so I stuck my tongue out at him.

I felt like an idiot while they spoke about me, and a little shocked that Dad didn't remember

T.J. being at the recent fire. "Hello—I am sitting right here. You shouldn't talk about me like I'm invisible." They continued to ignore me, in favor of the conversation. I took the moment to look at T.J. He certainly had grown up. I studied his profile, trying to find a small part of that little boy who was my best friend growing up. His strong jawline and full lips were new to me. His baby fat was gone, but his strong nose was the same. The aquiline had a bump that always looked like he had broken it, which earned him the nickname Rocky. I loved his smile. It was a full grin that lit up his whole face and made his eyes twinkle. I wish I could go back and have a chat with my teenage self. I would share with her just how sexy T.J. was today. Of course, I would probably also have a few words to say to teenage T.J. too. After all, I wasn't the only one in that relationship.

My ears perked up when I heard Dad invite T.J. over for dinner tomorrow night. It will be nice to give Dad something to do, but another evening with T.J...can my heart handle it?

The Armors provided a nice dinner among friends. Dad seemed to enjoy talking with T.J. about guns, hunting, and his job at the fire station. Sitting there in the background watching them interact was a treat. Dad was animated, reminding me more of the guy I grew up with than the pale version of himself he had become since my return. He hasn't been so upbeat in a long time. I don't think I've felt so upbeat in a while, as well. T.J. had many fun stories of life in the station that made us laugh. I was getting reacquainted with the guy I left behind, as he was filling in the missing years.

T.J. had been my best friend growing up. We were childhood playmates. Then, in high school, we turned into a *couple.* He became my boyfriend. We used to spend a lot of time hanging out at the train depot and talking about our future, but that didn't last. T.J. was looking for a girl who was sexually active, which wasn't me. He broke up with me and went on to date other girls who were more physical with him. It was hard watching him move on, but I was going to leave our small town for bigger pastures when I graduated, so I didn't need to be tied down. Now that I was back, though, would we try to make it work?

* * * *

Dad was in high spirits the next day as he was getting ready for our dinner company. He decided to make some perch that he had caught last year, so he pulled it from the freezer and set about getting things ready. I watched him while I worked on my jewelry at the kitchen table, listening to him share stories about his fishing trips with friends. My stomach was bothering me. Every part of my body was nervous about hanging out with T.J. Was I still feeling something for T.J.? Was I still in love with him?

Around six o'clock, T.J. arrived with a six-pack of green bottled beer. "I remembered that your dad loved this brand." As he wrapped me in a tight bear hug, my body responded to his hard, muscular body.

"Thank you. Can I take your coat?"

As he stripped off his dark canvas jacket, the light blue

denim shirt stretching across his chest drew my attention. His shoulders filled out the shirt and made me want to caress them. I couldn't help but notice that his dark blue jeans hugged tight to his butt and legs, as if the denim was painted on, as he walked into the kitchen to say hello to Dad. The cowboy boots he wore looked well-used and gave him a sexy walk. My mouth watered not from what we were having for dinner, but who we were having it with.

The meal was a memorable event filled with reminiscing and laughter. After cleaning up the dishes so that the guys could continue their conversation, I rejoined them. Dad was sharing his story about his turkey hunting trip that ended in a car fire. I'd heard that story a million times, but it was nice to enjoy the night without worrying about having to always be on guard with Dad. "Well, I'm an old man here, so I'm gonna hit the sheets. You guys enjoy the rest of the evening. Just remember T.J., I still have that shotgun collection," Dad said with a snicker as he left the living room and climbed the stairs.

"It's a beautiful night. Would you like to sit outside on the deck? We won't bother Dad with our voices that way." I handed T.J. the last beer and grabbed myself a soda, and we walked outside.

The night was dark, revealing a million stars in the sky. Looking up at them, I realized how many more stars I saw here than I ever did in Chicago. The air smelled fantastic, the scent of lilacs filling my nose. It was the guy sitting next to me, however, that made my heart soar. I hadn't enjoyed myself as much as I had tonight in a long time. That was all because of T.J. I felt that I could relax and be myself with him. I loved that we challenged each other with our sarcastic wit, that we shared a history together. This was dangerous territory, though. I hadn't been with anyone in ten years. No one had ever made me feel the way I felt about him. He was the one man who I never got over, even after all those years.

Breaking the silence, T.J. asked, "So, how was the big city? What was life like there?"

"I enjoyed being able to see the museums and always find something to do, no matter what time of night it was. It was an exciting place."

A look of pain crossed T.J.'s face. Is he worried my life in the big city is what I still wanted?

Small town life had some definite perks, like the guy sitting here with me.

"But there are benefits to small towns too. Since I've gotten back, I am beginning to see just what I missed out on by running to the big city right after high school. Like these stars, for example, and the smell of flowers on the air. Chicago was bright lights and delicious food aromas, but there is something about a night like this…What has life been like for you?"

"I've enjoyed being in Amherst and taking care of the people I grew up with and the town I grew up in. I get to see many of the people we went to school with. I even play baseball on a summer league team with Steve Newman and Mike Stevens, remember them? In many ways, nothing about my life has changed, and yet…" his voice wandered off.

"I remember your best friends. They loved to torment me in high school. I think their nickname for me was inaccurate, Sinful Syndie. Too bad I wasn't sinful, I might have had more dates," I added sarcastically.

"I missed that—your sense of humor and possessive nature. No one was like you. Do you remember the night of your big sleepover? When you got so jealous that you froze that girl's bra because she came on to me? I wish I could have seen her face! Syn, there were times you were hell on wheels." I gave him a shove. He started to laugh as my face warmed from embarrassment, and continued talking. "I'm glad you're back. I missed you."

"I missed you too. You were my best friend. I'm sure if my mom was alive today she would've already had out

27

those old photos of us in the sandbox and been rambling on about how cute we were."

"I visited the funeral home when your mom died, even though we hadn't seen each other in five years, but I couldn't face you, so I hid and watched you grieve. I was too upset to even face you when I had the chance to make amends for my behavior. I wanted to comfort you, but I knew how angry you must have been at me. I felt so bad about breaking up with you for those other girls in high school. You shut me out of your life and I didn't notice. I lost my best friend for a little tail. I realized my mistake when I joined the fire department and we had training about trusting each other. In a fire, each firefighter relies on the others to protect him. I have to count on these guys so we all make it out alive. During the training, it occurred to me that I treated you badly. Best friends don't do that…and neither do people in love." T.J. looked in my eyes and grabbed my hand. "I'm sorry."

Stunned, I sat there for a moment, watching him hold my hand. His words sounded sincere, like they came from a place deep inside his heart.

"Love?" My voice came out in a whisper.

"Yes. I have been in love with you since we were kids. In high school, I let my hormones rule my head and made the worst mistake of my life. I let go of my best friend and my heart at the same time. I love you, Syn. I don't know how you feel about me but I had to tell you."

I held my breath, not knowing what to say. "T.J., I want to tell you that I love you too, but I don't know if I do love you romantically at this moment. I care about you as a friend. I've missed having you in my life. You were the one person I could share things with, who understood everything about me. But sixteen years is a long time. How do you know that you still love me? That what you're feeling isn't just sex? After all, I'm the one that got away."

He pulled me close and kissed me. The kiss started out chaste, but then he put his hands on my face and deepened it. His tongue ran over my bottom lip as if trying to tease my mouth open. Our tongues intertwined as I granted him access. My breath caught in my chest and a whimper escaped. I pushed back on his chest to catch my breath, and he grabbed my hands.

"At least you're honest. But I'm going to prove to you not only that I love you, but also that your love for me is deeper than you think. Thank your dad for dinner. I will see you tomorrow."

I was in shock. I could only nod.

CHAPTER FOUR

After waking up from a highly erotic dream involving T.J., my body felt languid and spent. I wish I could just stay in bed and dream all day, but T.J. was coming over. I jumped out from under the covers and into the shower, then spent a little more time on my makeup and clothes than I usually did. I felt like I was back in high school again, waiting for a date. Dad was still asleep, so I got to work on some jewelry pieces that were ordered. I was so caught up in my work that I didn't hear Dad come down to the kitchen.

"Susan, why aren't you at work?" he asked, looking confused.

Oh, no. It looked like today wasn't going to be one of his better days. Dad had me confused with my mom. Getting up from my chair, I walked over to him and kissed him on the cheek. "Dad, it's Syndie, your daughter, not Susan, your wife. I live here with you, remember?"

"Oh. Good morning, Syn. I was just a little confused. You look so much like your mom."

I didn't trust that he was okay. I kept one eye on Dad and the other on the clock. When was he coming over? Because of Dad's issues in greeting me this morning, I decided to put away the jewelry and help him with the yard work today in order to continue to look after him. For as long as I can remember, Dad always had a garden. He loved growing vegetables for our family. His pride and joy were the grapevines he grew from clippings that he gathered from my grandfather's vines.

Later, while Dad made sandwiches for lunch, I finished up the jewelry I had been working on. We enjoyed a quiet meal, talking about the garden. We decided to make Dilly Beans and Sun Pickles when the green beans and cucumbers came in. After cleaning up the kitchen, I looked at the clock again. Would T.J. ever be here? What if he changed his mind?

A knock sounded on the door, followed by the door opening and a booming voice shouting out, "Hello…anyone home?" Heading to the front door, I told Dad that I would get it. T.J. was standing in the entryway with a petite older woman. He took her coat off and put her arm through his. "Hey Syn, do you remember my mom? Mom, you remember Syn. She's back in Amherst living with her dad."

I gave the woman a hug. "It is wonderful to see you, Mrs. Johnson. Thank you for visiting us. Dad! T.J and his mom are here."

We all went into the living room and sat down. Dad came in from the kitchen and smiled at Mrs. Johnson. "Hello T.J., Elizabeth! It is nice to see you. Beautiful as ever, I see, Elizabeth. Can I get you something to drink?"

T.J. was the one who answered. "No, thanks. Mom and I were hoping that you and Syn would like to go with us to the VFW for some drinks and dancing. They have an early bird happy hour with a local band that plays the oldies."

Dad answered for us. "Sure! I love the VFW, haven't been there since Syn has been back in town. We would love to go. Give me a moment to get changed, I didn't plan on going out today and have my gardening clothes on." As Dad rushed upstairs to change, looking spry for a man of his age, I sat in the living room, catching up with Mrs. Johnson. It was fun to hear about all the things that I missed while in Chicago.

When Dad arrived back downstairs, his hair was slicked back and he had on a nice button- down shirt and tan slacks. He looked very handsome, as if he was trying to impress someone.

At the VFW, the band was just beginning to set up. We picked a table near the dance floor, but not too close to the band so that we could still talk to each other. As the guys went to get us something to drink, Mrs. Johnson and I had a longer chance to talk.

"It's nice to see you back in Amherst. I sure have missed you. I've kept up with your jewelry business. In fact, I've bought a few pieces myself for gifts over the years."

"Thank you, Mrs. Johnson. I'm glad to be back in Amherst, but I'm worried about my dad.

He has Alzheimer's. Some days are good, others aren't so good."

"Call me Elizabeth, please. I was sorry to hear about your mom. She was such a nice lady, and a good friend. When you left for Chicago, it devastated T.J. I think he'd come to his senses about how he treated you and realized what he messed up. He missed your friendship too and, well, I always thought you two would marry," she replied sincerely.

"I don't know what T.J. told you, but our breakup wasn't easy for me. I felt like I lost my best friend because he wouldn't give me the time a day. His girlfriends were always more important than I was. I'd have been happy being T.J.'s wife a long time ago, but I don't know my feelings right now. We're friends, but I don't know if there's something more."

When the guys came back, Dad began to monopolize Mrs. Johnson's time as the two of them talked about their past and shared stories of their children. It gave T.J. and I a chance to talk ourselves. He looked gorgeous in his blue jeans and dark blue sweater, which brought out his eyes.

"So, have you decided you love me yet?" T.J. asked with a smirk. "I think bringing my mom was a brilliant idea. Ever since my dad passed away three years ago, Mom has missed getting out. I thought she would enjoy tonight's music. I thought you might as well. To be honest, she's also here to run interference for me and to help convince you that I'm the man for you."

"You had me convinced many years ago, but then you blew it. Now you'll have to really impress me with your dance skills. Do you remember that high school dance we went to when we were dating? I can't believe we slow danced to *Stairway to Heaven*! What a bad choice."

"Hey, it wasn't a bad choice as long as I got to hold you tight. But I'll warn you, I have learned a few things about dancing—and other things—since then, and I can't wait to show you," he said, wiggling his eyebrows.

As the band started to play, he took my hand and pulled me to the dance floor. As he twirled me around and dipped me, I could tell that he had learned some killer moves. Looking over my shoulder, I saw my dad and T.J.'s mom dancing as well. They looked like they were having a good time. How sweet he thought of his mom and my dad. They seemed to get along well. He did this for me.

Out of breath, we sat back down after the song ended. T.J. ran his fingers over my hand, causing goose bumps to appear on my arm. Picking up my hand and moving it to his mouth, he kissed each fingertip, then pulled me close and put his arm around me. I leaned into him and enjoyed the music.

Then in my ear, he whispered, "What's not to love about a guy like me? I've got a decent job, I'm a momma's boy, and I'm sexy as sin. Besides, I get your jokes. See? You have to love me."

"You have a point. You are smokin' hot and we're good friends. I just want more than a one night stand, though. I want a forever love, like my parents had. And I'm just not sure if you're serious or playing," I replied sadly.

T.J. pulled me off my chair and out the door, a wild look in his eyes. He walked me outside by the parking lot, then pushed me up against the wall and put his hands next to my face. He leaned into me and in an angry tone said, "I'm not lying about my love. I want your body, but I also want you to love me. I'm fighting myself every day to not take you to bed like I want to and prove that I love you." With that, he kissed me, pressing his body against mine, pinning me to the wall. His rock hard body touching mine made me dizzy with passion. I couldn't think straight. At that moment, I wanted him more than I wanted anything else in the world. A car door slammed, pulling us from our sexual haze.

As I tried to focus my gaze on his face, he spoke softly. "Wow, sex is going to be explosive with you…I get it, you need time, but I've lost fifteen years with you and I'm not a patient man. I'm telling you my intentions now."

I couldn't answer—both my mind and my body were still experiencing the passion. We silently walked back into the building, hand in hand, and sat back down with our parents. They were sipping their drinks and talking about gardens. It was nice to see them both looking so happy.

T.J. broke into their conversation. "It's getting late, and I should be getting everyone home. Tomorrow is a long day at the station. This was nice, we should do it again."

"Thanks for thinking of it. Elizabeth and I had a blast. I'd love to cut the rug with such a beautiful woman anytime," Dad said with a smile.

* * * *

It had been two days since I heard from T.J. I couldn't get my mind off him and what he'd said. Thoughts of him filled my head and fantasies of us together took over my

35

dreams. What does it mean to love someone? Together, we had passion and friendship. We shared a past and a deep love for our families. What more was there? Could I already love him and not realize it? All of these deliberations kept my mind active.

Deciding I needed some advice, I turned to the one man who was everything to me. Sitting with Dad over breakfast that morning, I asked him about mom and his relationship with her.

"How did you know you loved Mom? That she was your *one*? That it would work out with you two forever?"

"I couldn't get your mom off my mind. I was always thinking about her, wanting her to be happy...Also, I couldn't keep my hands off her."

"Ewww...I don't know that I want to know that!" I squealed while giggling.

"Okay, then. Most of all, I could see myself sharing my life with her. I could see myself talking and sharing my burdens with her, and wanting to do it each and every day." He said this with a mixture of sadness and happiness in his voice.

"But, you *were* taking a chance. So many marriages aren't forever."

"You're right, but love is about taking a chance. It's about risking your heart for happiness. Sometimes, it's about being angry and forgiving. Other times, it's about that mushy stuff you don't want to hear about. I want you to have a *forever love* like I did with your mom, to have someone you can lean on when things are tough and have children with, but you have to take the risk. I can't do it for you." As Dad hugged me tightly, tears fell down my face. He made everything so clear. All at once, my heart wasn't in question anymore.

Grabbing my phone, I texted T. J.

Dinner, tonight. My treat.

CHAPTER FIVE

Seducing a man was outside my range of experience. I'd had only a few simple lovers feeling that my virginity was more of a hindrance than a blessing. After arranging for Dad to have dinner with T.J.'s mom, I ran to the local grocery for the ingredients to my famous chicken piccata. Packing my picnic basket with everything we might need from food to beer, I hoped tonight would be perfect even while I deliberated if I'd be able to go through with my plan.

With the basket in my hands and a smile on my face, I jumped into T.J.'s truck when he arrived after dusk.

"Where to pretty lady?"

"Let's go back to where it started. Let's go to the beach."

Watching his face throughout the drive thrilled me with the excitement I had over finally acknowledging my feelings. Longing to run my fingers over his jaw and lips, I sat on my hands in order to keep from reaching for him.

"Why are you looking like the cat that swallowed the canary?"

"I had a long talk with Dad. He enjoyed your visit and the dinner with your mom at the VFW. I haven't seen his spirits that high since I returned to Amherst. That's because of you. Thanks."

"I always liked your dad. He was cool even with playing all *mean* and all. I'd have loved to spent time fishing or hunting with him. My own dad was gone a lot so we weren't close. I felt like I could be that way with your dad."

"I didn't realize. But I'm glad you and Dad get along. He seems to have *eyes* for your mom."

"Eww. Stop that! No pictures of parents and sex."

I laughed at the look on his face. "So you don't want to be brother and sister?"

"No, I have other plans for you and your basket! It was nice to be asked to dinner. I can smell your famous chicken. I haven't had it in ages. No one makes it like you do."

"I have cherry pie for dessert too."

Another of his full smiles crossed his face as he leaned over and kissed me on the cheek. "Hey, eyes on the road. We're almost there." The banter comfortable was between us.

Knowing he was the one for me, my nervousness evaporated.

The beach parking lot was relatively empty because of the recent chill to Ohio's weather.

T.J. walked over to my door and opened it for me, pulling the basket into his hands.

"Let me help with this. Do you remember when we used to come here on the weekends and sit watching the sun set? We'd talk about our dreams."

Turning toward T.J. and pulling the basket from his hands, I set it on the ground before looking him in the eye. "Yes. Those were my favorite times—sharing my plans with you for my life. I've thought of you but never took the chance of thinking we could go back to what we had. However, Amherst is my home again and you've earned that second chance."

I pulled his body close to mine and devoured his lips,

breathing nor the chicken was important. So stepping away from T.J. was the hardest thing I've ever done. I want to take my time with him, with this. I needed to cool down.

"Catch me." Running with the basket was harder than I realized. T.J. quickly caught up to me on the soft Erie sand.

"You're mine." He growled before lowering me to the sand, kissing me with passion.

Pulling his shirt from the waistband of his jeans, I ran my hands over his stomach. Another growl escaped his lips, which made me daring. I gripped the bottom edge of my dress and pulled off my underwear and waved them in his face. He jerked his shirt off over his head. This time the groan left my lips. I reached out and ran my hands over his nipples. Watching each bud peak, I leaned forward and lightly licked them, before sucking gently.

"Stop. I want to taste you." T.J.'s hands began to climb my legs, lifting my dress's hem.

Dropping kisses along my legs, he started first with my knees, then the insides of my thighs.

My body vibrated with need and my pussy dampened. "Please touch me T.J."

He complied sending me into my first orgasm. Not allowing me to catch my breath, T.J. lifted my dress off my body, sending chills down my skin. My nipples peaked. Feeling embarrassed, I used my hands to cover my breasts.

"Don't hide yourself. You're so beautiful. I'm so grateful you're giving me a chance to show you my love."

A tear escaped my eye. "I love you too T.J. I always have."

After escaping his jeans, T.J. laid down and pulled me in his arms, kissing me ardently. "I'm the luckiest guy."

"Stop talking and love me."

* * * *

The evening ended with us wrapped in the blanket and

eating pie with our fingers. "This was wonderful. I'm so glad we finally are together."

"I need to go." Feeling like Cinderella, my clock had struck midnight. "I need to get back to dad. He's hanging out with your mom, but they have to be getting tired. I can't have him alone. I want to see you again, but Dad's going to have to come first. Do you understand?"

"Of course I do. I wouldn't want it any other way."

CHAPTER SIX

Life entered a predictable pattern. On nights when T.J. wasn't working, he often came over for dinner or a visit. Sometimes we'd go out on a double date with dad and Elizabeth. Theirs was a romance, we hadn't expected. The more we were together, the more T.J. tended to bring up our future, and I'd end up biting my lip. I couldn't commit to forever when I was taking care of my dad. One night a fight ensued.

"Don't you understand? I can't leave my dad. He's always been my hero, the way he's taken care of us. He worked overtime in the mill on swing shift, never home for holidays or performances at school, just to put food on the table. I can't leave him when he needs me so much. What if something happened? I'd never forgive myself."

"I'm not asking you to leave your dad, just make room for me."

"I'm scared. Right now taking care of Dad rests on my shoulders. I don't want to burden anyone else with this. I have to be on guard at all times. Ever since the fire, I'm afraid to leave him alone, even to take a shower."

"But I love you and want to be with you. I'm willing to help you with your fears."

"I can't ask you to live like this." Tears silently fall from my eyes. "You have a job you love and I don't want you to be tied down. I don't want you to have to give up the things you love to take care of us. He's only going to get worse. I couldn't take it if you resented me. And you will. Maybe not now but years down the road, you will. Losing you years ago was hard enough."

T.J. reached out to wipe the tears from my face. "What can I do to convince you?"

"I don't know. I can't think about the future right now with the uncertainty of my dad's life in my focus. Losing you because of my dad, would kill me. I can't risk you hating me."

Running up into the house, I slammed the door and watched T.J. leave from outside my window before crying myself to sleep.

* * * *

"Syn, can you come down here?" Dad's stern voice made me jump awake. Anxious to see what the problem was, I washed my face before going to see what he needed.

"You're going to lose that boy. You've got to quit pushing him away." "But—"

"Don't interrupt me, missy. He's a wonderful guy, always has been. You deserve a partner, someone to help with all the responsibilities you're shouldering. Don't wait on a perfect time. Grab love when it happens and don't let go. Mostly, I want you to be happy like your mother and I were. You deserve a forever love. Give him a chance."

"Dad, I don't want him to resent me because I'm putting you first."

Grabbing my hands, Dad looked me straight in the eyes. "Time isn't limitless. You never know how long you have. Your mom's death showed me that. And I'm not willing for you to give up your future happiness for me."

Listening to him and watching the emotions play across

his face, Dad convinced me to give

T.J. a chance. "How did you get to be so wise?" "Just being a dad to all you wonderful girls."

Kissing Dad on the cheek, I then settled into his soothing embrace, determined to call T.J. and apologize for my overreaction.

A siren started screeching off in the distance. It sounded like the siren attached to a fire truck. There must be a fire somewhere. I hope that everyone is okay. The sound was getting closer and closer. Quickly, Dad and I rushed to the front window just in time to see a fire engine pull into our driveway.

"What's going on?"

As we ran out onto the lawn, I held onto Dad's hand. The whole neighborhood had turned out to watch the scene. I saw firemen begin to get out of the truck, so I asked, "Why are you here? Is there a fire?"

Dad pulled me close to him as one of the firemen approached us. The fireman kneeled down and pulled what looked like a jewelry box out of his pocket. Tears streamed down my face as the fireman took his helmet off and T.J.'s smiling face looked up at me. He opened the box, and I could see a ruby and diamond engagement ring sitting inside.

"Syn, will you marry me and be my *forever love*? I promise to love, protect, and always cherish you. I pledge that together we will support your dad and family. That's one of the values I learned from being a firefighter. You rely on your family, they will take care of you. A burden shared is an easier load. You've been my best friend. I don't want to spend my life with anyone but you. Please say *yes*."

The neighbors and firefighters began chanting, "Say yes!"

I looked down into the face that I quickly realized I've loved forever and who was willing to prove his love by sharing my burdens. "Yes! I'll marry you." He grabbed me and kissed me in front of my dad, the neighborhood, and heaven.

THE END

Beach Desires

A Wilder Sister Novella

DEDICATION

To my dad and sisters for seeing the best in me

To my children for making me laugh ☺

To Mark for keeping me sane- xoxo

CHAPTER ONE

I packed my bag, including my bikini, workout clothes and sunscreen, also a few other things just right for a five day work-free vacation in the sunshine. Those late nights finishing my numerous projects were worth the two weeks of stress. Wanting to spend as much time on the beach as I could get, I booked a direct flight from Baltimore's Thurgood Marshall Airport to Myrtle Beach Airport. One of the benefits of being a frequent traveler, I snagged a seat in first class and brought my ereader to enjoy on the plane. I'd already downloaded the latest romance novel by Liz Crowe, excited to read what my favorite bar characters were up to. When we finally touched down in Myrtle Beach, my trip was near its end. After an hour or so drive, I'd be on the beach, lying in the sand.

Clutching my bag, I stepped off the airplane into the warm, humid temperature at Myrtle Beach's airport. After picking up my rental car, I would be on my way to my own slice of heaven. Garden City, South Carolina nestled away on a peninsula only one road wide suited every beach lover's dream. Nearby, Myrtle Beach resembled a beacon for those who liked to dance or party. Depending on where you stayed, you could see the beautiful ocean or the calm peaceful serenity of the inlet. Fishing boats went out daily from the marina to catch the local seafood for the restaurants in the area.

A two-bedroom condo on the inlet at Marlin Quay Marina awaited me. The brochure for the room boasted not only a view of the inlet but also of the ocean. While I longed to rush to the condominium then hit the beach, I realized without food and drinks, I wouldn't survive long. I had planned to try some of the local restaurants but eating alone wasn't fun. Would I ever find someone to share my life with?

The sun just began to set as I pulled into the parking lot of the tall white stucco building. Grabbing the bellman's trolley, I unloaded my rental car then started up to my new home for the next five days. Taking the elevator to the fifth floor, I could see the expansive beach beckoning me. I felt eager for a run along the pristine shoreline.

With impatience, I unlocked the door of condo five-oh-two. I quickly stored the groceries away, then threw on my running shorts and a T-shirt. The door locked behind me, as I decided to take the stairs rather than the elevator. The stairs were a superb warmup for my muscles as I crossed Waccamaw Drive before navigating the dunes to the beach. With the sun slowly sinking below the horizon, I began to head north, listening to the churning of the waves.

The beach was peacefully quiet with only a few other couples walking along the shore where the waves crested against the sand. The warm, muggy weather caressed my skin but felt exhilarating. It's always more fun to run in a real environment than on the treadmill at home. After running for about thirty minutes, I turned back. The sun had fully set, bathing the beach in the soft glow of the moon. Delicious smells coming from some of the homes on the dunes told me it was dinnertime. Occasionally the sounds of children laughing or music playing drifted down to me. Heading back toward my condo, I waited for cars on the road.

This was a busy time of night as people headed out for dinner or parties. Heavy traffic flowed into the restaurant next to the marina. People got out of the cars laughing journeying in for dinner. Looking at everyone enjoying a wonderful time, I felt a little lonely without someone to share my vacation.

Should I call Jasmine or invite her to visit? No, that's not a good idea. As much as I miss her, we broke up for a reason. It's better for us to go our separate ways.

My stomach rumbled. I remembered I had beer and shrimp waiting for me back in the condo. The pang in my stomach urged me to skip the stairs and settle for the elevator. Pushing the button, I noticed a car pulling into the parking area. I stared with envy at one of the sweetest muscle machines known to humankind—a dark red Camaro convertible. I'd love to have a gorgeous Camaro like that, I thought with a smile on my face.

The car parked. A striking petite blonde opened the door and climbed out. Tanned like she spent all day in the sun, her short hair stuck up from her head in a way which made me think she'd just climbed out of bed after an amazing night of sex. Her full and pouty lips had a smile on them, showing brilliant white teeth. Wearing a pink T-shirt and blue jean shorts, she looked innocent until you got a glimpse of her eyes. Her passionate gaze sparkled with secret knowledge.

Feeling like a desert had begun to grow in my throat, I licked my lips. She must have noticed I was staring, because she waved at me. I returned the gesture, embarrassed to be caught ogling.

"Hello. That's an amazing car! What year is it?"

"A '68. I got it for graduation from college from my dad. She's my baby," she replied as she patted the back end. She opened the trunk and lifted out a wheeled suitcase. Then she grabbed another bag, setting it on top of the suitcase. Finally, after three more trips into the trunk, she had quite a pile of luggage sitting next to her magnificent Camaro.

"Do you want some help?" I hollered. "Looks like you have more things than you can carry.

I'd be happy to help."

"Sure. I could use a hand." She stretched out her left hand, introducing herself. "I'm Mandy Kenzie. I'm staying in my family's condo this week. Of course I packed up my whole closet for this trip." Her eyes twinkled with her joke.

Taking her hand in mine, electricity sizzled up my arm. "Ouch. Must've picked up some static electricity. I'm Stacey. I'm staying here on vacation for the next four days." I grabbed some of her bags and caught a whiff of her perfume. Recognizing the smell of my favorite cologne, the one Jasmine wears, my heart sped up. I headed toward the elevator, trying to ignore the seductive thoughts running through my head. "What condo are you staying in?"

"I'm in five-oh-three. The condo has been in my family for years. Usually everyone comes down during the summer for a week or two but I've been so busy with work in Raleigh, I couldn't get away then. Luckily things slowed down, so I elected to come down and enjoy some of the lingering warm days."

"We're neighbors then. I'm across the hall from you in five-oh-two."

Watching her butt as she walked, I wished I could test the firmness. Obviously, she worked out as well. When we reached her condo, I waited for her to unlock the door before bringing in her luggage.

Swallowing back a sigh, I called out, "Where do you want this?" She pointed to the main bedroom.

I took her suitcases and put them on her bed, then bent down to catch one last smell of her scent.

"All done. Meeting you was a pleasure. I'm sure I'll see you around. Let me know if you need anything."

"Thanks. I'd love to take you for a drive in my car to repay you for your help," she said as she walked me to the door.

"I'd love a ride. See you around."

Back in my condo, I couldn't get my new neighbor out of my mind while eating dinner. Mandy was a beautiful woman, someone I'd like to spend more time with. Sitting in the living room, I watched the lights of the boats on the inlet and thought about Mandy as I nursed my third beer. Definitely hot looking, but was she interested in women?

CHAPTER TWO

Thinking back to the day my sister's wedding invitation arrived in the mail, I couldn't help but remember the frustration I felt over my imminent return to Amherst in addition to facing my past.

The invitation's ivory paper with the fancy black trim was tasteful but had filled me with dread. Looking at my sister's name in flowery script crushed my dream about this whole event being just a joke.

No matter she'd shared her news with me on the phone a month ago, I still hoped something would happen to change her mind about having the wedding in our hometown.

I remember our conversation.

"Congrats Syn. I'm so happy for you. Of course I remember TJ. I thought you guys were perfect, but why Amherst? Why do you want me to be a part of special day? You know how I feel about that place." Thinking of going back left a bitter taste in my mouth.

"I understand Stacey. I felt the same way about coming back to Amherst. But the town's different now. The high school bullies don't have a say in our lives anymore. We love you, no matter who you

love. And we want you to be here to celebrate with us. Really Stacey, I wouldn't ask this of you, but Dad can't handle the travel. Please. This might be the last time we can all be together," Syndie pleaded.

She tugged at my heartstrings. I wanted my sister to be happy, but the horrifying thought of facing my past sent shivers down my spine. Like Syndie who escaped immediately following graduation, I also fled the small town with my diploma in hand for a larger city, but for a different reason.

Amherst was a 'white-bread' town. A small town with small town morals. The town wasn't welcoming to people who were different than the norm. High school made things even harder. There were all the regular cliques growing up—the popular crowd, the athletes, the geeks, and the druggies. I may have looked normal but I spent a lot of time hiding parts of myself from everyone in order to not have my secret exposed to the gossipy masses.

Growing up, I noticed there was something different about me. The difference wasn't in my looks but my feelings. So to keep others from guessing the truth, I dated the town football star and pretended to ogle the guys at Lakeview Beach with my friends. But my cravings were for my best friend, the girl I shared my high school years with. Though even then, she didn't really know me. I'd always been attracted to other women—their softness, their scent and their passion.

However, homosexuality was way outside the standard of my hometown. I managed to come out to my family, which was hard enough. Could you imagine explaining to your church-going parents about your different desires? It might be okay for celebrities to experiment, but not small town Catholic girls.

My parents struggled to understand and accept me. Relationships strained. I never blamed them. Society labeled my feelings *unholy*, even *immoral*. I hadn't even been sure I'd be welcomed back for my mother's funeral.

Nonetheless, my family stood by my side, embraced my choice as well as protected me from the old biddies who saw me as a blight on the face of society, or someone who just needed the right guy to fix her. Syn really does have a fierce but frightening attitude when she defends those she loves. The shouting match at the funeral made the local paper, and became the main reason for my fear of being at Syn's wedding.

With the invitation's arrival, I knew I'd have to put on a silly dress Syn picked out for the four of us—her bridesmaids, her sisters—then stand in the church before God and some of the same people who wouldn't understand my choices. Syndie was marrying the guy of her dreams, Thom Johnson. As her younger sister, I needed to be there for her.

* * * *

Pulling on my running gear, I decided to hit the beach once again to get the frustration out of my thoughts. Running allowed my thoughts to travel and burn off my nervous energy. Grabbing my MP3 player, I headed off to the beach and let my mind wander back to growing up in Amherst.

Growing up in a small town was a lot of fun. Our house was outside of town on a dead-end road with a quarry excavation site across the street. I was the fourth of five girls and often Syndie's, the oldest, partner in crime. We once got caught for throwing acorns at the cars driving down our road. I guess we didn't think things through because with our road being a dead-end, the only people going down it would know us. Those were some good times, playing in the dirt, creating forts and chasing the imaginary bad guys. My sisters were important to me. If they had asked me to walk naked through town, I would have done it for them.

The waves soothed my soul as I cranked my MP3

player on high and ran to escape the past. Sweat trickled in rivers down my back as 80's punk rock music blared in my ears. I pushed my body but settled my mind.

Back at the condo, my mind calmer, I climbed into the steamy shower. The scalding hot water hammering my body felt like heaven after the grueling workout. I loved the feeling of the water on my body. Swimming was a summer passion of mine that never really went away. Mom used to take us for swimming lessons at the YWCA as children, making a day of it with lunch at the park.

As a sales manager for an international fitness organization, I often traveled throughout the world to reach my customer base, which allows me to facilitate sales with other companies and small retailers for our products. Like the magnificent treadmill I work out on. My toned, fit body has created the perfect advertisement for our products plus it helped promote me to Top United States Sales Person, an award I worked hard to earn.

My job also provides me many opportunities to meet delightful people as well. Recently, I'd ended a three year committed relationship with Jasmine, who works out of the European sales branch. It was time for us to move our own separate ways. The distance and competitiveness of our jobs had gotten in the way of our romance. We ended things before our feelings were hurt and remain friends to this day. Now Mandy has piqued my interest. She's cute, sexy and full of energy. Spending time with her and getting to know her seemed like a perfect diversion from my negative thoughts of Syndie's wedding.

As I put on my silk nightgown then climbed into bed, I put the thoughts of Amherst from my mind. I fantasized about Mandy, kissing her soft lips and running my hands on her exquisite body. Touching myself, I gave into my dreams of seducing her, and climaxed, calling out her name. Satiated, I fell asleep dreaming of Mandy.

CHAPTER THREE

The next morning, I got up at dawn for a run on the beach. The seagulls and the sounds of the waves were the music I needed to soothe my desires for Mandy. I itched to see her again. However, I tried to be patient but found it challenging. There was something about her outgoing personality that drew me to her like a moth to a flame. I longed to spend more time with her, but was afraid to rush her. The exhaustion from long workout felt good and helped me deal with my pent up desires to feel her skin on mine.

After my run I decided to use the pool to help my body and mind cool off. Quickly I changed into my bikini, grabbed a towel, then headed down to the condo's pool. The beautifully clear pool overlooked the inlet and marina. I jumped into the water and did laps to calm my mind, then decided to rest for a bit on the side of the pool, soaking in the sun's rays.

"Hello, neighbor." Mandy's voice penetrated my lust-filled mind. "How's the water?"

"Hi, Mandy. The pool's wonderfully cool today. I needed the cool off after my run. How are you doing?"

"I'm good. I'm impressed with your determination. I

can't seem to get motivated to work out on vacation. My lacking incentive's why I decided to try the pool today."

"I work for a fitness supply company and working out is a passion of mine. The beach beats my treadmill any day. Are you a runner?"

"No. Unfortunately, I'm not. Although I enjoyed watching you run this morning. I sat on the balcony with my coffee taking in the view."

Now it was my turn to be embarrassed. I wasn't sure how I felt knowing she had been watching me. "So you liked what you saw?" I teased.

"You're beautiful, but you probably already knew that. I can only imagine all the guys you must have asking you out," she said with a smile.

"Actually, I play for the other team. I recently ended a relationship with a woman who worked for my company's European sales division. Our relationship couldn't survive the distance," I said sadly.

"Your admission makes things easier for me. I'm also into women. There's something about their softness and sexuality which makes me melt. I've been having fantasies about you, but I didn't want to offend you so I didn't say anything, in case. Would you like to go to dinner with me tonight? I'd love a chance to get to know you more," Mandy asked breathlessly.

"Sure. What time?" My stomach clenched at the thought of this beautiful woman possibly being into me. After dreaming about her, my fantasy might actually come true.

"How about you stop by my condo at six-thirty? I'll drive. We can head over to DJ's for dinner. The restaurant is one of my favorite places. Their seafood casserole is delicious."

"That sounds great. I've always enjoyed their food and the view from the dining room is beautiful at sunset. The inlet seems to shine with a million colors." My heart pounded so loud I swear she could hear. "I can't wait to get a ride in that marvelous car of yours. I'll see you at six-thirty."

* * * *

Dinner with Mandy was perfect. We had a lot in common, finding that we both shared a passion for muscle cars. Most of our discussion was innocent, yet the desire for each other simmered under the surface.

"When did you realize you were a lesbian?" she inquired as she reached over to put her hand on top of mine.

The touch of her skin on mine caused my pussy to clench. Her full lips drew my gaze. I thought about kissing them, running my tongue along them before nibbling on her bottom lip. Focusing on her question, I knew she would understand my thoughts and fears.

"I've known since I was a teenager. I left my hometown after graduation, never looking back. Now my sister is getting married. She asked me to be a part of her wedding party. I really don't want to go back to Amherst to face my past, but since my dad has Alzheimer's, I'm afraid if I don't go back for the wedding, I won't see him again in this lifetime."

"I understand. Living in the South, being different was frowned upon. I hid my desires as well. Luckily times have changed. I'm able to express my needs now, rather than hide them. Why are you so afraid to go back to your hometown?"

Speaking to Mandy about my past and my life was easy. I felt an instant connection to her in addition to the desire I had for her body.

"My town was very small. The people were small minded. If you didn't have a boyfriend, you were teased. So I pretended to like guys, even "dated" some to keep my secret. Even with my family's support, I'm nervous about going back and facing the people I knew. I'm worried

61

about what they will think of me."

"I understand your fears. However, you shouldn't worry about them. You are a successful, caring person. Who you love doesn't have anything to do with what kind of person you are. Let's get out of here. Would you like to take a walk on the beach? I love the beach at night."

"I'd love to. There is something about the waves crashing and the feeling of being alone in the world that I love," I answered with a smile. "This has been a wonderful dinner. I'm enjoying getting to know you."

The drive back to the condominium was quiet as we were each lost in our own thoughts. Anxious to get Mandy alone on the beach, I wanted to steal a kiss. I'd been fantasizing of her lips all night and couldn't wait to see if they felt as soft as they looked.

After parking in the lot, we walked across Waccamaw Drive. The tide was low and the moon was full, illuminating the sand and waves. Each of us was still lost in our own thoughts and hadn't spoken since we left the restaurant. As we walked on the beach, Mandy took my hand in hers. A tingle climbed my spine at the contact.

Walking for about fifteen minutes in silence, I stopped to pull Mandy into my arms. I couldn't wait to kiss her any longer. Gently I kissed her mouth and ran my tongue on her bottom lip. She moaned before pulling me closer to her body. With our arms wrapped around each other, we explored our mouths, teasing with our tongues. My breath came quicker as my body responded to her touch.

Mandy ran her hands along my back down to my butt, giving it a little squeeze and pulling me closer to her. I gripped her face in my hands, biting gently on her lips, eliciting another groan of passion from her.

I pulled away from her with difficulty going back to holding her hand. As we walked on the beach, we spoke about our childhoods and families. Mandy's family wasn't as big as mine but they were just as close. I felt very close to her emotionally, yet was nervous about whether our time together would be only a vacation fling or the beginning of something more.

* * * *

Back in the condo, I decided to call Syndie. I needed to share my feelings with someone and that's what a big sister is for.

"Hi stranger. How are things with the wedding plans?"

"Hi Stacey. The wedding plans are coming along. Dad has been having good days. He's excited about the plans. I think the medicine has been helping. T.J and him are enjoying some guy bonding over fishing. Dad has also been seeing more of T.J.'s mom. I think they're serious. Are you enjoying your vacation? How's the weather been?"

"The weather has been beautiful. I wanted to call because I met someone. I needed to share. I couldn't think of someone I'd rather tell than you. I know you'd understand those giddy feelings of meeting someone, then falling for them."

"I'm happy for you. You deserve someone to love. I became worried about you when Jasmine and you broke up. She wasn't the right person for you. So tell me about your new crush."

I shared with Syn about Mandy and our times together. Putting my thoughts out there to someone, sharing my feelings really helped me. Syn accepted my choices and always supported me. I knew I could count on her because she understood and cared about me.

"So are you serious about Mandy?" Syn asked with trepidation.

"I really think so. She makes me happy. I feel like I can be myself around her."

"I'm happy for you. You'll have to bring her home to meet everyone. I look forward to getting to know her better. After all, if you care about her, then she must be someone special."

Saying our goodbyes, we knew we would talk again soon.

CHAPTER FOUR

The next few days passed in idyllic wonder as Mandy and I spent as much time together as possible. We hit the outlet mall for some shopping, cooked at home and enjoyed our time poolside. While we were out shopping, we held hands, and later kissing over the dinner table. I was falling hard for this amazing woman. But I wasn't sure if she had the same feelings for me as I had for her. It's probably time for us to have that conversation, I thought. We need to see where things are between us. Is this only a vacation fling? Because my heart is involved and my vacation is almost over.

I called Mandy on the phone to arrange for a dinner date. "I can't believe I've got to go back to the real world in two more days. Let's go out to dinner tonight to celebrate a wonderful vacation."

"That sounds terrific," she said enthusiastically. "Where do you want to go?"

"Let's go to the Inlet View for a romantic dinner. The restaurant's got a wonderful view of the inlet and since it's within walking distance, we can enjoy some drinks without worrying about driving."

"I'll meet you at your place at seven. See you then!"

Mandy's phone clicked off.

Nervous about how to broach the subject of my feelings, I hopped into the bathtub for a long soak to relax. I thought about Mandy and our time together. I don't know how we could make things work with us living in two different states. After all, things didn't work for Jasmine and me. I'd love to be able to make this work, Mandy stirred something in me that made me want to commit. Letting the worries float away, I stayed in the tub until the water turned frigid. Getting out and drying off, I took extra care with my outfit tonight. It wasn't every day I spoke to someone about my feelings for them. I never felt this way toward anyone, including Jasmine. I only hope Mandy feels the same way.

When the knock sounded on my door shortly before seven, I pulled the condo's door open without looking. Jasmine was standing in the hallway with a smile on her face. Her petite figure and long black hair framing her pixie-like face revealed her Asian ancestry. As my eyes widened, to say I was stunned would be an understatement. "Hi Jasmine. What are you doing here?"

"I heard you were on vacation and twisted some arms to find out where you were. I've missed you, Stacey. I want to be with you again," she pleaded.

The sound of a throat clearing caused her to jump. Mandy stood behind Jasmine hearing everything she'd said. "I'm sorry. Am I interrupting something?"

Mandy looked upset. A crease crossed her forehead and a frown passed over her mouth.

I grabbed her hand and pulled her into the condo, kissing her full on the lips. "Nope, you are just in time, sweetie. This is Jasmine. I told you about her. She decided to surprise me."

"As you can see, Jasmine, you've interrupted my dinner plans. I'm sorry, but I don't have the same feelings for you that you have for me. I thought I made things clear when we broke up. This just isn't going to work for us. Besides, as you can see, I have someone in my life who means the world to me."

Mandy gasped as my words sank in. Glancing at her, I saw a dazed look on her face. So I pulled her into my arms and kissed her cheek.

Jasmine spoke with sorrow in her voice. "I'm glad for you, Stacey. You deserve the best. I guess I'll head to a hotel for the night. I hope we can be friends." To Mandy she said, "I hope you realize what a wonderful woman you have in Stacey."

"Thank you, Jasmine. I'm sorry things didn't work out for us. I wish you the best. Being friends in the future would be wonderful." I did really want to be friends with her, but my heart belonged to Mandy. Now to convince Mandy.

Shutting the door, I pulled Mandy over to the couch. "We'll be late for dinner but we need to talk. I was honest about what I said to Jasmine. I have strong feelings for you. I don't know how you feel, but I'm in love with you. I know things happened between us quickly. I don't want you to say anything now, and I don't expect you to feel the same way. However, I needed to tell you. My vacation is almost over, but I can't bear the thought of never seeing you again. Let's go to dinner and enjoy our night. We can talk later."

"Wait," Mandy said, "I want to talk now. I've been trying to find a way to tell you about my feelings as well. Seeing Jasmine in the hallway just now upset me. I was jealous and wanted to hurt her. But when you told her about your feelings for me, my heart soared. I know we've only just met, but like you, I'd like this to continue. I just don't know how to make our relationship work with our jobs in different states," she stated sadly.

Pulling her close in my arms, I kissed her lips. "We will figure something out. Love makes anything possible. Let's go enjoy dinner."

* * * *

Dinner was a somber affair for two people who recently declared their love. I was thinking about how to make our relationship work across the miles and was sure she had to be thinking about the same thing. Ordering a piece of chocolate truffle cheesecake for dessert, we fed pieces of the chocolate concoction to each other. The sensuous act of placing the scrumptious treat in our mouths made me long for her body. I wanted to show her with my body how much I loved her.

"I'm not ready for our night to end. Let's go for a walk on the beach. The moon is beautiful.

I want to be alone with you," I whispered into her ear.

When the bill arrived, I placed a one hundred dollar bill on the table and pulled Mandy out into the cool night air. We ran all the way to the beach, laughing like children with the urgency of our desires heightening our senses. Knowing we only had one more night together, I couldn't wait to undress her and have her begging for my touch. We didn't even make it to the beach before she pulled me into a lustful kiss. Her hands roamed over my back before beginning to grab at my clothes.

I was anxious to show her my love and couldn't wait to consummate it. As our clothes fell to the sand, I kneeled in front of Mandy's body. Running my tongue up her legs caused her to shiver and open her legs for me. I sucked gently on the inside of her thighs leaving little red marks, showing my possession of her body. When I finally ran my tongue along her slit, her pussy was dripping wet. Using my teeth, I teased her swollen clit and heard her moan passionately.

Mandy pulled my face up to hers. She kissed me with a furor that made me ache. Our tongues danced in each other's mouths. She nibbled her way down to my breasts lavishing attention on first one, then the other, drawing a groan from my lips.

"Oh Mandy, you're making me so hot. I can't wait to put my fingers inside you." Taking her hand, I pulled her down on the sand and lay on top of her body. I kissed her face, neck, then collarbone before moving to her breasts to tease her nipple with my lips, tongue and teeth. Mandy's breath came quicker as she ground her pussy into my own. Her hands dug into the sand as she closed her eyes before calling out my name. Bending my head to her pussy, I licked the length of her slit, then nibbled on her clit.

Mandy groaned again.

I continued to lick her engorged nub while gently inserting two fingers into her pussy. Her cunt was so tight. I felt it grip me tighter as she found pleasure in my touch. Slowly pumping my fingers into her wetness, I could tell she was lost in her desires. With another flick of my tongue on her clit, she came, squeezing my fingers as her muscles contracted with her passion.

Climbing up her body, I kissed her mouth so she could taste her juices on my lips. "You are delicious. I could eat you all day long," I uttered breathlessly.

"I want to taste you now," she declared as she laid me down on the sand.

Opening wide for her, my anticipation of her touch left me lightheaded. "Please touch me," I called out softly. "I want you."

First one, then two fingers were inserted into my soaking wet pussy, filling me. But Mandy didn't make a move to pleasure me. She just held still as I began to wiggle, begging her to end her torture. Smiling, she pulled her fingers from my body, then licked them while keeping her gaze locked on mine.

"You are so yummy, Stacey. Your pussy is so tight. Taste your juices," she demanded as she stuck her fingers in my mouth.

Licking her fingers made me even hotter as I tasted my own passion.

Mandy lifted my butt off the sand pulling my pussy to

her lips. Sticking her tongue into my cleft, she pushed it in and out like a small penis. I thrust my hips up to reach her mouth. "No Stacey, I don't want you to come yet," she said laying my bottom down back on the sand before turning her attention to my breasts. She lavished them with kisses, then took the nipple into her mouth and sucked gently on them, causing a whimper to escape my mouth.

"Please Mandy," I begged. "I need you so badly. I want to come all over your lips. Fuck me with your mouth." I groaned.

Mandy took my plea to heart, attacking my pussy like an expert, driving my delight higher and higher with passion until I exploded in an earth shattering orgasm. Pulling me close to her body, we lay intertwined on the sand as our heartbeats returned to normal.

"Let's go back to my place to continue this," Mandy uttered. "I want to explore your body in a million more different ways."

Grabbing our clothes, we kissed feverishly as we dressed. We still couldn't keep our hands off each other walking hand in hand back to her place.

"Let's grab a shower. I want to wash your body," I told Mandy with a smirk. "I'm sure there's sand everywhere."

The shower led to another round of lovemaking. Finally we headed to her bed for a third round. We were insatiable, unable to keep our hands or mouths off each other. "I love you, Mandy Kenzie. We will make this work. I can't see myself without you," I whispered in her ear. Spent from our passion we curled up under the covers before falling asleep, blissful in each other's arms.

CHAPTER FIVE

We spent every last moment of our time together, sharing loving touches and sexy interludes. I knew it had to be obvious to anyone who saw us that we were in love. I felt like crying because my vacation was over and it was time to go. When time came for me to catch my flight that late afternoon, I was sure of Mandy's love for me and determined to make our relationship work. With the promise to call as soon as I got back to Baltimore, leaving her was the hardest thing I'd ever done.

The flight back was uneventful, but sad because of missing Mandy. When the plane landed, I called her from the airport to let her know I'd arrived safely. When she didn't pick up I left a message. "Hi, sweetie. I'm back in Baltimore. The weather is a lot colder than South Carolina. I miss you."

As I was filling up at a gas station, my cell beeped. Mandy had left me a message.

"I miss you too. I was walking on the beach after you left, remembering the night we spent making love on the sand. I'll call you tomorrow when I get back to Raleigh. I love you."

Back at home, every room felt empty and lonely.

Glancing at Syndie's invitation on my kitchen counter, I felt compelled to call her to update her on how things went. She always supported me. Syn would understand how I felt as well as what I was going through. That was the best thing about big sisters, they were great sounding boards.

"Hey, Syn. I just got back from vacation and could use my big sister. How are things with you?"

"Things are good. I've gotten my dress all picked out and have decided on dresses for you all. Don't worry though. They aren't some pink confectionary nightmare. I went with black yet elegant. I'm glad you called. I've been thinking about you since we last talked. How are things with Mandy?"

"Things were wonderful. We really connected and both want something more permanent.

But she lives in Raleigh and long distance relationships are tough."

"Congrats. I'm so happy for you. I know the distance will be hard. Hopefully you can work something out. You have to bring her home before the wedding. We'd love to meet her."

"I don't know," I said hesitantly. "Amherst is such a small town. Do you think they are ready for a couple of women in love?"

"Stacey, what others think doesn't matter. The only thing that matters is what you guys feel for each other. We love you no matter what. Besides, I think you'd be surprised by how much Amherst has changed. I couldn't believe it when I came back. The world is very different than when we were in high school."

"We'll talk and set up a visit. Thanks, Syn. You're the best big sister!" I said with laughter in my voice.

"While it's nice of you to say, but I'm not your only big sister. Maybe just the smartest, or the most beautiful or…well you get the idea, but I'm sure the rest of our sisters would agree with me. Talk to you soon!"

With one single phone call to Syn, the weight of my worries lightened. I knew my family would support my relationship. They were happy for me and wanted Mandy to be a part of our lives. Now to work on the distance part.

* * * *

Mandy and I spoke every night for a month before she decided she would fly up to meet my family. After arranging to meet Mandy at Cleveland Metro Airport, I drove to Ohio to pick her up. Excited and nervous about seeing her again, my stomach felt like it held a million butterflies. Would our visit live up to our time in South Carolina? Would her feelings still be the same?

When I saw her at the baggage area, my heart skipped a beat. I couldn't believe such a beautiful woman loved me. Smiling, I ran to her and hugged her tightly. She smiled at me while she grabbed her bags. "I'm so glad you're here," I told her. "I've missed you so much."

"I've missed you too. I have some news to tell you, which I couldn't do over the phone.

Let's get out of here so we can talk."

Nervous about her news, I worried all the way back to my dad's home. We talked small talk in the car but my mind wasn't on our conversation. She could've been speaking in French for all I knew. Caught up in what her news might be, my stomach did cartwheels as I drove.

The traffic on the Ohio Turnpike was congested. The drive felt like a lifetime passed before we got to my dad's home in Amherst. Nervous about Mandy meeting my family and her big news, my heart raced but my nerves tingled.

"My family is going to love you. My sister Syndie lives here with my dad because of his Alzheimer's. I've told her all about you. She's excited to meet you."

"Honestly, I'm a little nervous. I'm so happy to spend time with you but since your family is important to you, they are important to me."

Pulling into the driveway, I turned the engine off and sat with Mandy in the now quiet car. "Thanks. I'm sorry but I can't get your news out of my mind. I'm worried that it's bad. Can you just tell me now?" I uttered with fear making my voice quiver.

She pulled me into her arms, kissing me passionately. "My feelings for you haven't changed. My news is...I've arranged for a transfer to the Washington D.C. area, so we can be together," she said with excitement in her voice. "I love you and want to be with you forever."

With tears in my eyes, I kissed her again. "I love you too. I'm so glad you could arrange it.

When can you move in?"

"In about a month. Then I'm all yours, forever and ever."

"Great, I wouldn't have it any other way," I avowed with desire in my voice.

A knock sounded on the window and I jumped out of embarrassment. Here I was, caught making out in my dad's driveway. My face was flushed and burning. After opening the door, I hugged Syn while watching Mandy come over to us.

"Hi. You must be Mandy. I'm Syn. How wonderful to meet you. I've heard so much about you. I feel like you are a part of the family already," my sister shared as she pulled Mandy into a hug.

"Hello, Syn. It's nice to meet you too. Stacey has told me a lot about you too. I'm looking forward to meeting everyone. Thank you for having me over to visit."

Grabbing Mandy's and my hands, Syn dragged us into the house.

Seeing my dad looking frail, I ran to hug him. It had been almost a year since I last visited him. In that time, he'd aged quite a bit. Turning back to Mandy, I grabbed her hand, then pulled her over to introduce her to my father.

"Dad, this is Mandy Kenzie. Mandy, this is my dad, Jack Winters." "It's nice to meet you, sir. I've heard a lot of good things about you."

"I hope Stacey hasn't been telling you fibs," Dad said as he pulled Mandy into a hug. "Welcome to the family. I'm glad to see my baby girl so happy. Thank you for making that possible."

"Thanks for embarrassing me, Dad. Why don't you just get out the baby pictures and tell her about all my misadventures growing up?"

"We'll save those tales for after dinner!" Dad retorted with a chuckle.

Smiling back at my dad, I realized I'd always been accepted by him for who I was. I couldn't wait a moment longer to share my good news. "Dad, Syn. Mandy just told me she was transferred to the Washington D.C. area. She's going to move in with me. We've found a way to make our summer fling last a lifetime."

Hugs and smiles abounded as my family welcomed Mandy into their hearts. It was at that moment I realized I had always been accepted by them for who I was, no matter who I loved. All in all, I was fortunate to have the approval and love of my family.

MELISSA KEIR

EPILOGUE

Syndie and Thom's wedding turned out to be a beautiful event. The small church was filled to the rafters with family and friends. Standing in the front next to Syn, I looked back at the church pews and caught my sweetheart Mandy's eye. Coming back wasn't as nerve wracking as I thought the whole thing would be because I had her by my side. I was confident in my desires and myself. The small town had changed for the better. Everyone, especially my family, accepted our love, which pleased me because we were planning our own commitment ceremony to take place in this very church before the year ended.

The End

MELISSA KEIR

A Christmas Accident

A Wilder Sisters
Novella

DEDICATION

To the sister of my heart, Becky, for all your help, to my own peanut and pumpkin for making my life worthwhile, and to Mark—just because. *I love you all.*

CHAPTER ONE

The evening sky turned dark with snow clouds as the weather took a turn for the worse. My husband, Adam, drove our green SUV through the deteriorating weather as we headed south on Interstate 23 toward the Ohio border.

Adam and I had been having the same discussion for weeks. We'd been looking forward to the holidays and with them finally here we were ready to deck the halls. Christmas always held a special meaning for us as we celebrated our anniversary, our special time together.

Last year we'd spent a peaceful evening at home with a delicious dinner followed by a marathon of old holiday movies. We both loved the classics like Miracle on 34th Street and It's a Wonderful Life. Now that we were joyously awaiting the birth of our little peanut, our movie choices might have to change. Not to mention those quiet nights, with just the two of us. However, with our impending parenthood, we longed to find ourselves among family rather than celebrating alone this holiday season.

Looking over at Adam, I'm amazed that such a handsome man could love me. Stubble showed on Adam's rugged face. I liked the way the short growth of beard rubbed on my face when he nibbled on my ears. Adam's dark brown hair was cut short, emphasizing his deep blue eyes and strong nose. The small dimple on his chin made him seem more approachable and much less serious. His tall stature and muscular body always made me feel precious yet delicate, like a porcelain doll, but Adam never treated me like anything other than a desirable woman.

"How are the roads? Do you think we can stop so I can use the bathroom? Your son is pushing on my bladder." Wiggling in my seat, I tried to alleviate the uneasy pressure.

Adam looked over at me with a dreamy expression on his face. His gaze settled on my stomach as it undulated. "Sure, I could use some coffee. How are you feeling? Little Pea looks active tonight."

"I'm okay except for the kicks to the bladder. I swear he's practicing his temper tantrums so he has them right when he comes out. Oh Ricky, we are in so much trouble," I replied with a silly high pitched whiney Lucille Ball-type voice, then smiled.

I am thankfully in the third trimester of my pregnancy. I'd passed the dangerous stage where many women miscarry as well as the dreaded morning sickness phase that sucks the very life out of a body. Now I had abundant energy and looked forward to finally getting ready to meet our son. We still had two more months to go but I already felt like a beached whale, not to mention the walking with a waddle. Adam loved talking to my stomach, he'd even been reading storybooks to our peanut each night.

Adam and I had eloped to Hawaii five years ago during our Christmas vacation. We'd kept our wedding private, only us. Today we are closer than most married couples, enjoying the same things, especially our cottage home on the Huron River, old movies, television shows, and snuggling up with a blanket on those cold Michigan nights.

While we both loved our families, neither one of us enjoyed traveling which became the basis for the fight. I'd won the the argument after the announcement of my father's recent diagnosis. I'd spent hours on the phone with my sister, then on the internet gathering information on Alzheimer's. The dementia had already begun to kick in when Dad accidentally set fire to his home. Luckily, Syndie had already moved in with Dad and got him out of the house in time. My need for family had only become stronger since I'd learned about my pregnancy and the arrival of the first grandson.. I didn't want my baby to miss out on his remaining grandparent.

Fear about my father never getting to meet or know my little peanut became a constant in my mind. Adam and I had distanced ourselves from our families over the years. We were always so happy spending time with just each other, we'd just never considered what those choices did to others. Having a baby changes things. My sister's wedding invitation plus my dad's diagnosis, well, both convinced me that we needed to get back to Ohio. Christmas seemed like a perfect excuse.

After pulling into the gas station, Adam stopped the car next to the pump. I grabbed my purse. "I'm going to use the bathroom, grab your coffee, then get a snack while you fill up. Is there anything else you want?" I walked over to Adam's door as he let himself out.

Adam bent down to kiss my belly, making my muscles clench. How does such a beefy man do that yet still look so masculine?

"Why don't you also grab me some pretzels. I don't know if the coffee will be good on my empty stomach. But with the way the snow has been falling, I want to make sure we can take the turnpike rather than Route 2."

Route 2 is known as Death's Highway. The area of Route 2 between Bono and Sandusky claimed dozens of lives due to the large semi-trucks in addition to the awkward two lane road. People couldn't see what was coming around the next bend so head-on collisions were frequent. The horrible blizzard-like conditions from Lake Erie only made the road more treacherous.

After grabbing the coffee, pretzels and some crackers for myself, then paying for them, I headed back to the car. The snow made the car hard to see from the door of the gas station. Driving in this mess wasn't a comforting thought.

"Adam, the weather looks really bad. Maybe we should turn on a local radio station to check on the road conditions."

Making slow progress, we listened to the bleak weather bulletin. Little did we know one single radio announcement would change our lives forever.

"A crash has closed down part of the Ohio Turnpike just past the Route 53 exit. It's recommended travelers take an alternate route."

Adam's voice sounded bleak as he responded to the news. "I guess we have to take Route 2, probably adding some time to our drive. Maybe you had better call Syn and tell her we're still on our way but running late. We don't want them to worry." As he shifted the car into four-wheel drive, I pulled out my cell phone and made the call.

CHAPTER TWO

The arctic blast of freezing snow turned Route 2 into a sheet of ice, making travel almost impossible. The drive from Michigan shouldn't have taken more than three or four hours, but the harsh winter weather increased our time. We'd passed through Sandusky and were almost to Amherst, however, the conditions were continuing to worsen. Peanut was quiet in my tummy as if he too, sensed our terror at the horrible circumstances.

Looking over at Adam, I could see the strain etched on his face. His normally bright eyes were focused intently on the road, never wavering. His hands clenched the steering wheel tightly. Not wanting to add to his stress, I didn't speak. The silence in the car was deafening. The only sound came from the windshield wipers swishing against the blizzard conditions.

I couldn't keep quiet any longer. My fear climbed as my heart raced with each pass of the wipers across window. The smell of stale coffee made my stomach clench.

"Adam, maybe we should stop. You know, wait the storm out. I don't want to put our lives on the line to get to my dad's."

"We're almost there. Just a little farther."

Suddenly, out of the blizzard, two red lights appeared in front of us. A stopped car stood on the freeway in front of us. The taillights' bright glare mocked the whiteness of the snowstorm. Adam slammed on the brakes to avoid hitting the car, only to have our SUV fishtail before sliding toward the median guardrail. Even in four-wheel drive, the car wasn't a match for the icy conditions.

Adam screamed, "Oh God! Hold on!"

Dread filled my chest, as I gripped the armrests and braced my feet flat against the floor. Please let us be okay. Prayers filled my mind as snow whipped past the windshield. The screeching became the last sound I heard as the car's body skidded against the metal guardrail before flipping, rolling over and over.

* * * *

I awoke to the sound of beeping and the smell of antiseptic. The pain in my shoulder felt like a jackhammer had been trying to break the bone. Thinking back, the last thing I remembered was Adam driving in that blinding snowstorm. Something else whispered just out of reach in my mind, though.

What had happened? Putting everything together I recognized the sounds and smells as belonging to a hospital. My heart started to race as I remembered the sound of crunching metal and the feeling of weightlessness as the car rolled.

Oh my God! Our car, Adam, our baby! Frantically I tried to sit up, but quickly lay back down when the pain in my shoulder was too much.

What was going on? Was the baby okay? Placing my hand on my stomach, I felt the familiar roundness of my pregnant belly. Holding my breath, I waited what seemed like an eternity. There…the familiar fluttering of our little peanut moving. As if he knew my fear, peanut pushed his foot against my hand. I could feel the outline of his toes. Relief filled my heart. Peanut was fine. Everything was fine.

"Sherri, are you awake?"

Hearing my sister's voice, I turned toward the curtain as she pulled it back. "Syn, what are you doing here? What's going on? Where is Adam?"

The oldest of the five of us, when Syndie had recently moved back to Amherst to take care of our father, she'd found love again with her high school boyfriend, Thom. They were planning to get married in the fall. Syn's brow furrowed as she pulled the chair over to my bedside before taking my hand.

"Sherri, you're at Amherst Hospital. You've been here since last night. There was a multi- car accident on Route 2. The medics had to airlift you and Adam. Your cell phone had me listed as an in case of emergency contact. They called me to let me know. I rushed right over. Your baby is fine. The seatbelt pulled on your right shoulder, keeping you safe, but the force of the accident caused a dislocation. The doctor has your shoulder stabilized. However, they couldn't give you any pain meds except for some Tylenol because of the baby, which is why you hurt. The doctor said you were lucky but doing fine. You should be able to be released in a few hours when they get the latest MRI of your shoulder back. They just want to be careful. You've been asleep since they brought you in. The doctors said something about the trauma and needing the rest."

Ignoring her comment about the airlift, anxiety made my voice squeak. "Syn, thanks for coming. You didn't have to. I'll be fine. I'm glad to be getting out of here. You know how much I hate hospitals. When Mom died, I vowed to avoid them. I even went so far as to consider having my baby at home, but I want to do what's best for the baby, you know. What if something went wrong? I'd want help just in case. Let me get Adam and we can leave."

Syn's face remained a mixture of seriousness and fear. I remember her look from the day Mom died. She'd worn that horrible look on her face the night in the hospital. I knew what it meant. There was something she wasn't telling me.

"Syn, why isn't Adam here? When can he leave?" A shadow crossed Syn's eyes.

"Syn, you're scaring me. Adam's fine, right? The doctors are just running tests?" I pleaded with her to answer me.

Swallowing loudly, then clearing her throat, she finally spoke. "Sherri, Adam won't be leaving right now. He's in bad shape."

My heart seized and I began to silently weep. Tears fell down my cheeks as I looked at my big sister holding my hand. Pulling together some inner reserve of strength, I look up at Syn's face.

"Tell me everything. I need to know."

"The medics brought Adam in first when you were in the medivac helicopter. He'd hit his head numerous times on the side window as the car rolled, cracking his skull. He also had a broken collarbone along with a dislocated shoulder. The head wound is the big concern. The flight nurse said he stopped breathing twice on the flight to the hospital so he needed to be put on a ventilator when he arrived. Sherri, his heart stopped. They had to shock him to get his heart beating again. The doctors ordered a full CT scan and MRI of his head to assess the damage. There were numerous contusions to the brain in addition to the cracked skull. He's currently in a coma which the doctors feel is best for him so they can bring the swelling down in the brain. Hopefully he'll be able to recover. Adam's in the ICU where they can keep a close eye on him. But Sherri, I want to prepare you…the doctors aren't optimistic. They think there is permanent damage to his brain. Adam might not ever come out of the coma."

Syn pulled me into her arms and held me while I cried.

CHAPTER THREE

My first thought was to see Adam. But I needed to be released first. I wanted to make sure our son remained fine before heading up to the ICU. Girding myself after wiping away my tears and splashing water on my face, I glanced into the bathroom mirror. My eyes were red and puffy, hiding their beautiful amber color. Running my hand through my light brown curly hair, I tried to see what it was about me that had attracted Adam in the first place. My lips were pulled down in a frown. Erasing a misspelled word on a chalkboard would be easier than rubbing away the permanent worry lines creasing my forehead. Taking a deep breath, I headed out of the bathroom and toward the ICU.

Although Syndie volunteered to come with me, my first visit with Adam needed to be alone. I wasn't sure what to expect. Running my hands over my belly for comfort, I silently pleaded with myself to wake up, finding this whole tragedy to be only a nightmare.

The third floor of the hospital held the ICU ward, with a family waiting room outside of the cloudy glass doors which stood as sentinels to the patients and nurses inside. The visiting hours were listed in large lettering above a red call button on the wall to the left of those doors. Taking a deep breath, I advanced on the doors and pushed the button.

"Yes," a voice responded.

"I'm Adam Davison's wife. I'm here to see him."

"The doctor's in with Adam right now. He wants to talk to you. Please wait in the family waiting room. He'll be right out."

The sound of the local Cleveland news station filled the empty waiting room. The decor appeared comforting, like a home. Overstuffed couches as well as reclining chairs were positioned for family members who wanted to rest while magazines littered the coffee tables.

Blankets and pillows were neatly stacked on a wooden shelf. Fresh flowers filled the area with the smell of carnations and lilies. Soft lighting completed the mood. The waiting room could have been any friend's living room except for the voice on the hospital pager that spoiled the effect. *How many families waited in these chairs for answers that they didn't want to hear? What will the doctor tell me?*

Along with my shoulder, my back hurt. Rubbing my good hand along my lower spine, I eased myself into a reclining chair, keeping my bandaged shoulder close to my body. A sigh escaped my lips as the baby turned under my right hand.

"It's okay, pea. We'll see Dad in a minute. I can't wait to tell him we're both fine. I'm sure he's worried."

The whoosh of the doors alerted me to the doctor's presence before I saw him. Tall, with lightly graying hair, the man approached me with caution. He looked afraid I would break down, then as a consequence he wouldn't know what to do with a weeping pregnant woman. Extending his hand, he introduced himself. "Hello Mrs. Davison, I'm Doctor Ramsey. I'm sorry we have to meet under these circumstances."

"I understand Dr. Ramsey. I am as well. I had hoped you were going to tell me everything was fine, just a misunderstanding but I can see by the weary look in your eyes that I'm going to need to be strong to hear what you have to say."

"Your husband is in a coma right now. The skull was fractured in two places from hitting the window. His brain is swelling due to the jostling from the rollover. There is also a subarachnoid bleed. This bleed is between the brain and the tissues covering it. We have a drainage tube in place to help minimize any swelling, which will eventually have to be stopped. Right now though, our main concern is your husband's heart, which went into ventricular fibrillation twice, before being immediately defibrillated while en route.

"We have Mr. Davison hooked up to many different machines. The cardiac monitor lets the medical team screen his heart rate and rhythm, blood pressure, mean arterial pressure and oxygen saturation. We have his blood pressure and temperature constantly observed to watch for changes that could indicate an infection as well as the ventilator which is breathing for him." The doctor watched my face like a judge watches prisoners for clues to their guilt. I swallowed before beginning to rub my hand across my belly in a nervous reaction.

He took a breath, as if I'd passed the test thus far, and continued, "We are monitoring his troponin levels. Troponin is a cardiac protein which is released when there is heart damage and its level is monitored to assess cardiac damage. The more damage to the heart, the higher the troponin level. These levels are generally checked three times over a twelve to sixteen hour period. The cause of the increased levels could be from his body being in shock, lack of oxygen or cardiac damage from the accident due to something such as blunt trauma from hitting the steering wheel. Besides the ventilator and the cardiac monitor, your husband has many other machines monitoring him. Not to mention he has a central line, multiple IV's and an arterial line. The arterial lines are the way to get the most accurate blood pressures as well as a method of getting blood specimens and monitoring blood gases. He is being given intravenous medications to prevent seizures, keep his blood pressure down and maintenance drugs."

Will I even recognize my husband? "Doctor Ramsey, there seems to be a lot you're watching. When will you know the extent of the damage?"

"Your husband has suffered a major trauma. We won't have a better understanding of his condition for days or even weeks. His collarbone and his shoulder are injured as well as his face but the brain injury is the worst. He may not even be recognizable with the swelling and bruising but we are doing everything we can for him. When his head hit the window, he suffered major facial fractures but thankfully these LeFort Fractures are classified as a level one. His face may need some surgery but we will assess that when the swelling goes down. For now, the coma is a good thing because his unconsciousness will allow him to heal without dealing with the stress of pain. However, we don't know whether or not he will come out of the coma. We're carefully monitoring MRI's and CT scans of his brain to watch for changes. You're welcome to visit the ICU at any time, but we are limiting other visitors. Are Mr. Davison's parents able to visit? The severity of his condition makes it important for anyone who cares about him to be here."

"Adam's parents live in Florida. I'll give them a call. My family lives in Amherst. They'll want to be here for me because I have an issue with hospitals since my mother's death years ago. Thank you for sharing all this information, doctor. Please keep me updated."

Before the doctor could turn or walk away, I blurted out the question plaguing my mind "Do you think Adam is going to survive? Will he be the man I married once again?"

A pitying look crossed the doctor's face, twisting my heart. "Mrs. Davison...there is a lot doctors don't know.

Faith plays a huge part in a patient's recovery. I don't want to destroy your hope, but I just don't know. Go visit your husband—talk to him, sing to him, let him know you're there. Studies have shown that some coma patients do hear familiar voices and sounds. Your husband has a lot to live for, remind him of those things." Doctor Ramsey looked at my large rounded belly, then shook my hand again before he left.

Rising from the recliner, I took a deep breath and walked over to the cloudy glass doors that would lead me to my husband.

CHAPTER FOUR

Adam was hardly recognizable with the bandage wrapped around his head and the swelling on his face. His lips were amazingly undamaged, the same ones that had kissed my belly not that long before. I longed to kiss those lips. All the wires and machines made it hard to know where to sit or how to touch him. I didn't want to make things worse. However, the need to touch him was overwhelming. Reaching out with my fingers, I ran them over his mouth and around the ventilator tubing, imagining kissing his lips and waking him up like the prince woke Sleeping Beauty. Seeing Adam lying there in the bed, I finally accepted that the accident wasn't a dream. Tears silently fell down my face.

Determined not to let him know my pain, I put a cheerful but fake smile on my face, then looked for a way to be close to him. Glimpsing a gray chair sitting off to the side by the curtain, I pulled it toward the bed and reached out to hold onto Adam's hand. Sitting in the chair, I studied him. The swoosh of the breathing machine and the beeping of his heart monitor were the only sounds in the room.

"Adam, sweetheart...I don't know if you can hear me

but peanut and I are fine. We are here to see you. Can you open your eyes for us? Please Adam, let us know you can hear us." My voice squeaked as I spoke, breaking with the realization that this wasn't a problem I could fix with a kiss or a band-aid.

Anger began to take over my feelings. Frustrated over the fact I wasn't in this bed but Adam was, I couldn't help the bite of my voice. "I'm not giving up on you or us. You are going to get better Adam, so you can hold your child in your arms. Do you hear me? I'm not going to let you leave me. We have too much to live for. I'll be here to see you every day. I'm going to bug you and annoy you until you wake up and tell me to stop. Do you understand, Adam? We love you! We aren't going to let you go!"

Putting my head down on Adam's hand, I fell asleep to the sound of the machines that kept my love breathing.

* * * *

Standing outside in the snow, my feet didn't feel the cold. Where am I? Peeking into a window, I saw a Christmas tree in a living room. A man sat in the middle of the couch illuminated by the sparkling glow from the tree. Shadow covered his face but the small squirming bundle in his arms was plain to see. Pushing closer to the window, I could hear him singing a song.

The man's voice sounded familiar. Silent Night flowed melodiously from his mouth. Who is he? Why am I outside this home? I heard another voice. A woman called out. The man looked up but didn't stop singing. When the woman entered the room, she walked over with a bottle in her hand. Taking the infant from his arms, she pulled the newborn close to her chest then began to feed the baby. At that point, the man turned from the shadows toward them. As his face came into the light, I recognized him. The man was Adam!

* * * *

"Mrs. Davison...Mrs. Davison. Can I get you a pillow?"

Startled, I awoke to find a woman dressed in hospital scrubs standing over me. She had smile lines around her mouth and eyes, indicating her love of laughter.

"No, thanks. Have there been any changes?" When she shook her head and patted my hand, I remembered the dream. That's what the image must have been—only a dream. I saw us with our baby at Christmastime. Could God grant such a miracle? Is it even possible? Returning the nurse's smile, I held tightly on to the kernel of hope that the dream gave me. I wasn't going to give up on Adam.

"I think I'm going to go home. Will you call me if there's any change?"

"Of course. We will take good care of Mr. Davison. Get your rest. I remember my pregnancy. All that baby weight takes a toll on you. You look like you're having a holiday baby."

"Yes, we are. I will see you tomorrow. Thanks again."

I smiled, then rubbed my belly as I walked through the ICU doors. The baby responded by rolling over and kicking me in the ribs. With a twinge of déjà vu, I noticed a man standing in the shadows of the waiting room. This man, while slightly stooped with age, still had a commanding presence about him.

"Daddy!"

"Come here, Sherri. Let's get you home."

Running into the safety of my father's arms, a measure of peace entered my soul. I let him guide me to the car where Syn waited to take me back to the house I grew up in.

CHAPTER FIVE

Amherst, Ohio is a small town which brags it's the Sandstone Capital of the World. Sandstone, once a precious commodity in Amherst, was mined by the families living there. Some of my own great grandparents worked for the quarry. But, over time, other companies came to Amherst. The outskirts expanded to include many other city staples like fast food restaurants, chain retail stores, and large grocery chains. However, the downtown area remained quaint yet quiet with many beautiful sandstone buildings and architecture.

Dad's home stood south of the downtown area, off one of the main roads just down the street from the Catholic church. Dad was a devout Catholic who went to Mass each week so the location suited his life. More so, since the death of my mother and his own illness. Dad seemed to rely on the rituals, taking comfort in his church.

Wiping the sleep from my eyes, I took a look around the room. Sunlight streamed in the window. Strange was the only word to describe sleeping once again in the same room you grew up in. Syn had been using the room for her jewelry business but when she found out we were coming to visit she moved a full-sized bed into the room. No matter the differences in the bed or the paint on the walls, the room remained the place I'd spent so many nights giggling with my sisters over boys or working on my school work. While I wasn't sleeping next to Adam, at least the room was a place I knew very well.

Sleep had come easy last night despite the different bed and the fear on my mind. My shoulder was still sore and would probably need some medicine today, but I felt refreshed and hopeful. Maybe the hope was going to end up hurting me more if things didn't turn out well, but I had to hold onto something or else I wouldn't be able to put one foot in front of the other. Hope was all that kept me going.

Smelling bacon cooking on the stove, I wrapped a robe around my bulging waistline, then headed over to the bathroom before venturing down to fill my hungry belly. Using the bathroom had become my favorite pastime over the last few weeks as the baby's weight pushed more and more on my bladder. So, a visit to the bathroom always took precedence over the need for food.

Walking toward the kitchen, you would hardly know there had been a fire in here just a few short months ago. The onset of Dementia had caused Dad to put his clothes in the oven instead of the clothes dryer. They quickly caught on fire, the fire department arrived, and no one suffered any injuries. Dad and Syn had spent some time cleaning and re-doing the kitchen. Luckily, Syn's fiancé is handy and helped out with much of the work.

My dad stood over the stove, like a maestro conducting an orchestra. There were three pans going on the stove. One had bacon frying. The other had hashbrowns cooking and the final pan had scrambled eggs. Toast already sat on the plates. He looked happy to be cooking and taking care of someone.

I watched him for a moment. It had been a long time since I'd seen my dad. Thankfully, the Dementia hadn't worsened yet. Age certainly had taken its toll on him but he would always be my first hero. Thinking about all the times he used to chase us girls around the house or play horsey with us, I couldn't have asked for a better father. Touching my belly, I thought about Adam lying in the hospital bed. *Would he be a father for our baby? Will Adam be alive to see the baby born?*

Banishing those thoughts, I stepped over by the stove. "Hi Dad. How are you?" I asked, kissing his cheek. "You didn't have to go to all this trouble for me. I'm happy with a bagel in the morning."

"Naw...you need to keep your energy up. Especially now, since you're eating for two. I have another dang doctor's appointment, just a checkup, but I can drop you off at the hospital around nine if that's okay with you. Syn said she would stop by to check on you around lunch, maybe you two could grab something to eat. In other words, we're at your disposal. I know we don't know Adam real well but you love him and that's enough for us."

Blinking back tears, I hugged Dad tightly. "All that you and Syn are doing for me means a lot. I couldn't do this alone. I'm just not strong enough. Right now I don't even want to think about the worst case scenario. Thank you for letting me lean on you."

As I sat down at the kitchen table, Dad brought the plate over to me. Hungrier than I'd thought, I ate all the food put in front of me. Dad fetched a glass of orange juice for me. Downing two glasses, my stomach felt stuffed.

"Thanks for breakfast, Dad. And for taking care of the little things while I stay with Adam. This would've been so much harder without you and Syn. It's nice having our suitcases here, but where's the SUV?"

"The police let us get your luggage. They also towed the car to the Jones' Body Shop. I don't think the thing is reparable. You'll have to talk to them, but that heap looked like a total loss. The body shop guy couldn't believe anyone had walked away from the accident. I wasn't sure of your insurance company but I do have a copy of the police report. You should call your insurance carrier today to file the claim to get things started. We also didn't have your medical information when you were taken to the hospital so I urge you to stop by there as well with your information so they can make sure to bill your insurance. We really wanted to do more but were more worried about you, the baby and Adam."

"Thanks again, Dad. I don't know what I would've done without you guys being there. I will make those calls while I'm at the hospital. I'm going to get ready. Hopefully, there's been some improvement in Adam's condition."

CHAPTER SIX

The days passed in much the same way. I talked to Adam about the baby as well as how things were at Dad's. I shared with him my excitement about the baby's movement. Sometimes I even read him articles from the local paper and as Christmas approached, I told him all about the preparations going on at Dad's house.

Each day, Doctor Ramsey came in to talk with me about Adam's condition but other than the bruising on his face clearing and the swelling in his brain going down, there hadn't been any change in his condition.

"Why hasn't he woken up, if the swelling is down? I thought the pressure on the brain was the reason behind the coma?"

"Mrs. Davison, we don't always know why some patients stay in comas while others regain consciousness. The troponin levels have remained normal, so we know your husband didn't suffer a heart attack. His CT scans and MRIs aren't showing any brain damage or evidence of a stroke. His brainwaves are normal. Even the bleeding is subsiding. He should have begun to show signs of coming around or a response to pain, but nothing is happening like we'd expect. We need to begin thinking about long term care. We must consider that he may not come out of the coma. There are many wonderful care facilities that specialize in patients who have needs such as your husband's."

"I'm not ready to give up on Adam, it's only been a week since the accident. I won't even consider the worst case scenario yet." My voice came out louder than I planned as anger took over my feelings.

"We're not giving up, just trying to help you make those choices that will need to be made. Please think about what I said."

As Doctor Ramsey walked away, I looked over at Adam and rubbed my belly. "I'm not giving up on your daddy, peanut. We have to find a way to get through to him. If what I saw in the dream is real, we will be a family."

* * * *

That night, I dreamt of Adam making love to me. We were in the dream home where I'd seen him with the baby.

Adam's arms encircled my waist as I stood in front of the Christmas tree. Leaning back on his body, I relaxed into his strength, staring at the ornaments. My body tingled when he began kissing my neck. I love his arms around me...makes me feel protected and loved.

"You have too many clothes on," Adam whispered into my ear as he nibbled on the lobe.

He pulled my shirt over my head, then tossed the garment on the couch. Turning in his arms, I unhooked my bra before it also went flying. Adam began working on my belt and jeans, quickly getting them unfastened, then pulled down. Stepping out of the jeans, I stood before him in only my panties with the twinkling lights of the tree highlighting my body.

Feeling a little self-conscious about my post-baby body, I folded my arms in front of my chest.

"No, don't." Adam's voice came out husky and deeper than usual. "I love your body, especially how it looks now that you've had our son." Kneeling down, Adam pulled my panties off, then kissed my belly and ran his tongue around my belly button.

Dampness trickled down between my legs. I couldn't seem to breathe as I waited for what would come next.

Adam pulled me down to the carpet before he laid his body over mine, kissing my mouth like a man starving for water on a hot summer's day. His kiss was hard and demanding, leaving me breathless yet wanting more.

"Now you're the one with too many clothes," I said as I grabbed at his shirt.

Adam quickly stood up, then peeled off his clothes. Watching his body in the soft light, I couldn't wait to finally touch those hard abs and his highly sensitive nipples.

"Come here," I demanded, patting the carpet.

Adam lay next to me on his back as I began kissing his neck. He started to touch me.

"No, put your hands behind your head. I want to do this for you without you driving me to distraction."

Running my hands over the light dusting of hair on his chest, my fingers lingered over his nipples, gently rolling them. Adam groaned, lifting his hips.

"Not yet." I lowered my mouth to his left nipple to gently suck on it. I loved his sensitive chest and how much he enjoyed it when I touched him. As I softly bit down on his nipple, Adam groaned again. Running my tongue lower along his stomach, I used my hand to caress his cock as I gently rubbed the liquid from the head. Bending lower, I took his shaft into my mouth deeply. I loved the way Adam responded to my touch. I've always been self-conscious about sex, but with Adam, I feel like a porn star. Everything I do makes him hot and bothered.

"Oh, God. You feel so good." Adam's breathing became harsher as his passion built. Pulling his hands out from behind his head, he grabbed my body and rolled me under him. "I can't wait any longer." Adam kissed me passionately as he ran his left hand down my waist to my hip. Moving his hand into the curls at the junction of my legs, he inserted a finger inside me.

"You're so wet. I want to feel you wrapped around me."

With his finger still inside me, he ran his thumb along my clit, making me moan. I wanted him as much as he wanted me.

"Please, Adam. I want you now." But he wouldn't listen to my pleas as he kept playing with my clit. With a force like a tornado, I came, screaming his name. Before I could even recover, he poised his body above mine and rammed his cock inside me, burying himself deep. He filled me completely as I could feel a second climax building. Adam began a quick pounding rhythm that sent me over the top. His climax followed mine before he collapsed on top of me, both of us spent with passion.

"I love you, Sherri. I couldn't ask for a better wife." Kissing me again, he turned over before pulling me into his arms as we cuddled under the Christmas tree.

When I awoke from the dream, I wasn't sure if I could take it as a splendid sign that we were meant to work things out or if I had been only wishing for a life that would never be. Quietly, I curled up on the bed and watched the sunrise as I replayed the dream in my head, searching for clues.

CHAPTER SEVEN

Christmas was just around the corner. Dad and Syn had decorated the house. They'd gone out, bought a live tree and decorated it. The beautiful twinkling lights were a constant reminder of my dream from that first day in the hospital. Looking at my family's tree, I noticed many of the same ornaments from when we were children. Even the angel perched on top of the tree was the one Mom used to put on.

Seeing all the familiar ornaments tugged at my heart. Christmas was Adam's and my special time. We were married on Christmas and had always spent the day together. It was my fault that Adam was in the hospital. I had wanted to come back to Ohio to visit my family. If only I hadn't urged him to come. If only we had stayed in Michigan, nothing like this would have happened. 'If only' are the two vilest words. My hope was beginning to slowly slip away.

Even the hospital started getting into the holiday spirit. A small artificial Christmas tree rested at the nurses' station in the ICU. A larger tree filled up the family waiting area. Somehow, seeing all the decorations made me more melancholy. I didn't want to celebrate Christmas or our anniversary without Adam, but there hadn't been any changes. Each day I talked to him about the future, our baby, and had even begun to put his hand on my belly to encourage him to feel peanut moving. But nothing appeared to get through to him. He stayed unresponsive.

Syn and Dad were worried about me. Although they were my rocks of support, I began to withdraw more into myself, trying to protect my heart. I could tell they had given up hope. They were tiptoeing around me, afraid to say the wrong thing. I felt bad for them because they weren't sure how to act.

"Sherri, I've been going to church each day to say a prayer and light a candle for Adam. I know God sometimes works in mysterious ways, but I thought if maybe I had a little talk with Him, it would help."

"Thanks, Dad. That means a lot to me. Adam will really appreciate the prayer too. I wish you could spend more time with him and get to know him better. He is such a great person. I know he is going to be a great dad, just like you."

"Aww, thanks sweetie…I did talk to Father MacKenzie as well. He said he will also say an extra prayer each night for Adam. God doesn't take people who have so much left to live for. But since God doesn't talk to Father MacKenzie directly, he can only interpret what he's read and seen."

"That's really nice of him. I know having an extra prayer is sure to help."

* * * *

Christmas Eve had arrived. The sounds of holiday music could be heard on every radio station. Even the television in the family waiting room played the old holiday movies. When I saw Miracle of 34th Street was on, tears came to my eyes. I remembered watching the movie with Adam in our bed last Christmas Eve. This year happened to be so very different.

Dad and Syn had gone to evening mass, while I stayed at the hospital with Adam. There wasn't anywhere else I wanted to be. Tomorrow would be our anniversary and I was hoping desperately for a miracle.

Adam's parents had arrived yesterday and spent some time with us at the hospital. But seeing Adam with all the machines and tubes pained his mom. However, the sight didn't faze me anymore. Had I just gotten used to seeing him like that? Would this be the way he always was?

I worried about Adam's mom. She seemed really devastated by the accident as well as his coma. Just seeing him made her age another ten years. Her body slumped and her face became drawn. Thank goodness, Adam's dad was there to take care of her. They were at their hotel room now. Hopefully she would handle things better tomorrow. The shock when I first saw him will always stay with me but that day seemed like such a lifetime ago.

Suddenly, a big disturbance was going on outside Adam's cubicle. There was an urgency to the voices and I could hear some crying. Not wanting to intrude, I continued to sit, holding onto Adam's hand. I'd brought in a CD player with some holiday music to play for Adam, reminding him of the season. Often, I would sing along with the songs. Adam always had the better voice, but I loved to sing anyway.

When Adam's curtain moved, I jumped. In the doorway stood Syn and Dad. Their faces were crestfallen.

"Hi, what's going on? I didn't expect to see you here. I thought you were at church. I'm not ready to leave yet."

Dad spoke first while Syn looked like she might collapse. Standing up, I motioned her to the chair.

"Father MacKenzie was just brought in. It appears he'd had a heart attack before the Christmas Eve mass, then collapsed during the service. They rushed him here by ambulance. Luckily, his family is here with him. I can't believe this could happen."

"I'm sorry, Dad. I know you and he are close. You've always spoken so highly of him. Are you okay? What have the doctors said?"

"Of course, because we aren't family, they won't say anything to us but his sister told me they aren't expecting him to survive. His heart is too badly damaged. They moved him into ICU quickly from the ER so his family could be with him during his last moments. I don't know if they expect him to live through the night."

I reached out and grabbed Syn's hand, then pulled my dad into a hug. I knew that sinking feeling. So much pain at this time of year. I couldn't believe that a family friend lay in a bed right across the ICU from Adam. Looking across the unit, I sent a silent prayer off to the heavens for Father MacKenzie.

* * * *

Dad and Syn decided to wait in the family waiting room. Secretly, I believed they were hoping to talk with Father MacKenzie's family. I wondered if more church members were also outside waiting or if they had all stayed at the church to continue praying for the dear priest. I glanced over at the family sitting around the bedside of Father MacKenzie. They seemed to be a close family, all of them holding hands and hugging each other. Father MacKenzie appeared asleep, under the watchful eyes of his family. Hopefully *they are* getting a chance to say goodbye

I hate the idea of people dying. When my mom passed away, her death hurt more than anything. Even today the feelings still get to me because there are times when I want her advice or to share something with her. I wish I'd had the chance with my mom that Father MacKenzie is having. I also want Adam to have that chance with our baby. Life just isn't fair sometimes.

Crying rang out across the hall, drowning out the voices of the nurses and machines. I turned toward Father

MacKenzie's cubicle. Medical staff was rushing into the compartment, urging the family to step back. I could tell by the looks on their faces that Father MacKenzie had passed. His family hugged each other as they sought comfort from the pain.

Unexpectedly, I heard a noise from behind me. Turning toward the bed, I noticed Adam's eyes were open. He was gazing at me as his hand lifted in my direction. My heartbeat sped up as I called out to the nurses.

"Help me. Adam's awake. Someone come quickly."

Doctor Ramsey and a nurse came into the room. The nurse checked the monitors, then shared the medical information with Doctor Ramsey as he shined a flashlight in Adam's eyes. It looked like Adam was trying to talk but with the tube in his mouth, it was impossible to tell for sure. Doctor Ramsey pulled me aside then.

"It looks like you have your miracle. Mr. Davison has just woken up from his coma. The monitors are showing normal rhythms for his heart. His breathing is just fine as well. We need to do some more testing but everything looks like he is responsive and able to communicate. We're going to take the breathing tube out and run a couple of tests. Can you wait in the waiting room while we get him settled, then you can come back in to see him?"

"Sure, just let me explain to Adam. I don't want him to think I'm leaving him." I approached Adam's bed and leaned over to whisper in his ear. "I love you. You're fine. The doctor is going to do some tests. I'll be right outside, but I'm coming right back in to see you as soon as they're done. Don't worry. Everything is fine." I kissed his ear, relieved yet amazed this was happening. With tears in my eyes, I passed through the cloudy doors to the waiting room.

Leaving Adam behind had to be the most difficult thing I've ever had to do. I didn't want spend a second apart, still afraid his regaining consciousness was all just a dream. As I entered the waiting room, I noticed Dad talking with Father MacKenzie's family. Walking over to them, I planned on expressing my condolences when the smiles on their faces stopped me dead in my tracks. *Why were these people smiling?*

Setting my feet in motion, I continued over to Father MacKenzie's family members. "Hello. I'm Mr. Wilder's daughter, Sherri. I'm so sorry to hear about Father MacKenzie. My dad spoke highly of him."

"Thank you, Sherri. I'm Dawne, Father MacKenzie's sister. Your father also speaks highly of you. We wanted to share some good news with you. Father MacKenzie is in Heaven." I must have looked shocked or stunned because she continued. "When Earl was brought into the ICU, we knew his passing was only a matter of time. He certainly deserves to be in Heaven for all his good works. But there are always times when we doubt the truth that Heaven really exists."

"Yes, I know those feelings. When I first saw my husband hurt, I became angry at God. I still don't see why He let the accident happen.."

The most beautiful smile lit up her face. "Then you understand. Tonight when my brother lay dying, I asked Earl to give us a sign he'd arrived in Heaven, something tangible we could see and know it was from him." Nodding my head, I'd become enthralled with her words.

"Within moments of his heart stopping, we heard another commotion. We heard you, dear." Not comprehending her words, I tried to think about what had happened earlier in the ICU when Father MacKenzie died.

"See, your father had been speaking with my brother over the last few days, asking him for those extra prayers on your husband's behalf. The whole church knew about your husband's accident. We wanted nothing more than to see him recover. When Earl passed, your husband woke up. We know they were connected. Your husband's recovery was the sign we were looking for. My brother always looked out for his friends. I can imagine him doing everything within his power to fix your husband. Once he was in Heaven, he had the opportunity to help."

At that precise moment, the television in the waiting room grew very loud. Everyone turned toward the screen as the final scene from It's a Wonderful Life caught their attention.

Look Daddy, Teacher says every time a bell rings an angel gets his wings.

Then the television shut off abruptly. We all looked at each other with smiles on our faces. Everyone began talking at once, creating more of a party atmosphere in the waiting room than a wake.

"Thank you Father MacKenzie. You really are an angel." I looked over at the Christmas tree but turned when I heard the ICU doors whoosh open. Doctor Ramsey took a second to watch the unusual celebration. As he approached me, I noticed the relief in his eyes. However, I already knew the truth about my husband. After all Father MacKenzie had done, there wasn't any doubt a miracle had happened. Just as Doctor Ramsey stepped in front of me, a pain ripped through my body while a stream of liquid gushed down my leg. Looking at the floor, I noticed the wet spot. Then in a booming voice Doctor Ramsey announced the obvious.

"Well, it looks like we are going to have two miracles tonight. Mrs. Davison, you're having your baby. Why don't we set you up in the ICU next to your husband so he can be there with you when the new addition to your family arrives?"

* * * *

After my water broke, things moved very quickly. Wheeling another bed into the ICU happened to be the easy part. Convincing Adam we were having our baby right now was another story. We hadn't even had a chance to talk about what had happened yet and here we were dealing with my rapidly increasing contractions and breathing. Next an IV was started. When the doctor from the obstetrics unit came down, she brought a labor monitor. We were able to see the baby's heart rate to anticipate the next contraction.

Father MacKenzie's family continued to wait in the ICU family waiting room. They considered this a part of their holiday miracle, and wanted to be there when the baby arrived. Dad and Syn were standing by my side.

"Come on Sherri. You can do it. Breathe!" My dad happened to be an expert on baby delivery after having five daughters but my sister looked a little green around the gills. She seemed like she might be reconsidering her dream of having a large family. Adam remained lying in his bed hooked up to the heart monitor and IV, just in case. He'd only been conscious for under an hour so no-one wanted to take a chance that something would go wrong. My IV bag hung next to his as he held onto my hand.

Doctor Ramsey asked his friend, Doctor Muldoon, to come down to deliver the baby. Doctor Muldoon was a caring woman with dark blonde hair and a no nonsense attitude. I was very glad to have someone whom Doctor Ramsey recommended by my side. When she first checked my cervix, she told us that I was only at two inches dilation. But after an hour of strong contractions, I was ready to deliver our baby.

"Okay, Mrs. Davison, you're fully dilated. The baby is crowning. I'm going to tell you when to push through the next contraction. Then we need to hold off until I can get the baby's mouth and nose cleaned out. Are you ready to meet your son?"

As the next contraction squeezed my body, I pushed with all my might. While my body handled the pain, I glanced over Doctor Muldoon's shoulder. A man who appeared to be transparent stood behind her. When Adam squeezed my hand I knew he saw the man as well. He wore a priest's collar and had the most beautiful smile on his face as he looked at us. The ghost must be Father MacKenzie! Just as our baby cried, he waved at us and disappeared.

Looking over at Adam, I noticed tears filling his eyes as he smiled at me, then turned his gaze to our son.

"Do you want to hold your son, Mr. Davison?" Doctor Muldoon asked Adam. "You have a beautiful baby boy. Merry Christmas! It is officially Christmas since we just passed midnight."

As she put the baby in Adam's arms, I thought I felt the brush of wings across my face. "Thank you again, Father MacKenzie."

EPILOGUE

Christmas has always been a special day for our family. The holiday was our anniversary as well as the birthday of our son, MacKenzie. But more importantly, Christmas is the day we celebrate the miracle of Adam's recovery. After the accident plus the seven days in a coma, Adam regained consciousness without any problems. His fractured skull and face healed without any brain damage. The whole event truly was a miracle. We always celebrate the holiday by putting a special angel-shaped bell on our Christmas tree to remember and recognize Father MacKenzie's intervention in our lives.

THE END

Coming Home

A Wilder Sister Novella

DEDICATION

Family is where your heart is….

May it be a town,
A home, or
A person…

MELISSA KEIR

CHAPTER ONE

April 2016

Stepping from the cab, she handed him two twenties. Shevonne could tell they were twenties because of how they'd been folded. "Keep the change." She creased her remaining money and stuffed it back into the duffel bag hanging from her shoulder. Returning to Amherst, Ohio— small town middle-America and the place she'd escaped from right after high school had her feeling like she was eating crow. But you always come home, especially when the going gets tough.

Squinting, she tried to see the house. Darkness filled her vision. Her heartbeat sped up at the thought of coming home. Slowly, she walked toward the front of the house. Shevonne ran her hands over the rail and touched the porch step cautiously with her foot. She reached toward the left, searching for the old crock. She knocked it with her hand, and it fell with a thud off the porch. She searched through the gravel for the key. *Yes. It's here. Now I won't wake anyone by knocking.*

With the door unlocked, she slipped the key into her pocket. *I'll put it away later. Too dark to find things again.* The door squeaked open. Only shadows filled her vision.

"Stop. Put your hands in the air. Don't move." A tall, muscular man with sandy-brown hair, wearing a T-shirt and shorts, stood tall, clutching a bat. While Shevonne could admire his fuzzy physical attributes, she knew he was probably her sister's fiancé. She hadn't heard of any cat burglars who broke in to threaten other people sneaking into a house.

"What's it going to be? Put my hands in the air or don't move? I can't do both." Slowly, Shevonne dropped her bag and raised her arms.

Mom always said trouble followed her like no other. If predicaments happened, she was in the midst of them, which was why Shevonne now stood with her hands up in her dad's living room at 2:00 a.m., with a bat-wielding guy standing over her. She inhaled the musky scent of sweat and the underlying smell of her childhood home...her sanctuary.

Shevonne's arms hurt from keeping her hands where he could see them as she tried to appear small and harmless. "I live here." The house was too dark to see anything clearly. She tried to focus on the guy. Reaching out with her other senses, she studied the man in front of her. His voice was deeper and younger, too. Racking her brain, she tried to remember her sister's fiancé's name... Tim? Ted? Tom?

She sat very still, not wanting him any more riled up or taking a swing at her. *Another blow to the head is just what I need.* She smiled. *I know I can take him out. Even if I'm not 100 percent. After all, this is what the Army trained me for. But I'm sure Syn won't want me hurting her future hubby.*

Waiting patiently and listening for a telltale movement, she almost missed the whispered sound to her left. Afraid to turn and give the guy a clean shot, she held her breath.

"Stop, TJ. That's my baby sister," the shadowy figure at the top of the stairs shouted. "Shevonne, what are you doing here at this hour? Don't you know how to use a phone? Call ahead? Let someone know you're stopping by...even during the middle of the night? I thought you were in Kuwait." Syn had always been like a second mom to her and her sisters. Often their babysitter, shoulder to cry on, and fiercest defender rolled into one. She also had been the first person to suggest the shenanigans but never got caught. When she'd suggested they try to slide down the stairs at Grandma's house, it wasn't her head stuck in the banister. Hearing her sister's voice, after all she'd faced over the last few months, lifted a weight off Shevonne's shoulders. Tears threatened to fall, but she quickly blinked them away.

Reaching out slowly toward the man with the bat, she sat up straighter. "You must be TJ. I bet you're so happy to be a part of this zoo. I'm the troublemaker. Can we get some coffee? This is going to be a long story."

TJ's hand felt strong in hers as he pulled her to her feet. Shevonne flexed her shoulders, trying to release the tension or maybe strengthening her resolve before facing the firing squad. She touched her boot against her bag, knowing its location before she bent down to retrieve it.

Grabbing it off the floor where it fell, Shevonne headed toward the kitchen with her bag leading the way. She was sure nothing in her childhood home had changed since she'd enlisted. Dad wasn't one for throwing out the old or buying new. She walked over the refrigerator and ran her hand over the small dent from where she'd run into it after a game of rocking-chair races. Oh, the ass whooping they'd gotten. A small grin cracked her face.

"What are you doing home?" Syn's voice had a sharp edge to it that brooked no defiance.

"I'm home for good." She turned and faced her sister. Their gazes didn't quite meet. She could hear her clearly but saw only a shadow where her sister stood. "The Army doesn't want to arm a blind person." Her voice hitched. Damn, I didn't want to show Syn how much this bothered me.

"What do you mean blind?" She could hear her sister approach and the brush of breath on her cheek as she stood toe-to-toe with her.

"Oh, sweetie." Pulled into her sister's embrace, Shevonne brushed the tears from her cheeks. Her sister's tight hug released some of the pain from holding everything inside. "It'll be okay. Come tell me what happened."

"I don't like talking about it." She straightened her shoulders and lifted her chin in an act of stubborn defiance.

"Nope. You aren't pulling that with me. You're going to tell me, now." Syn had always been the bossiest of her sisters. But then, as the oldest, she'd needed to take over when Mom became busy or caught up in her volunteer work at the schools.

Syn pulled her sister toward the kitchen table and tugged a chair out. Knowing it was a losing battle, Shevonne sat down and took a deep breath before beginning.

"Six months ago, I jumped into a truck heading off to help in town. The Afghan women are more comfortable having American women around. They open up to us in ways they won't to the military men. On our way to meet the group, our Humvee ran over a mine, sending it flying. I wasn't wearing goggles because I was in a hurry. Not thinking again. Wasn't Mom always yelling at me for not being prepared?" She smiled at Syn.

Unable to see her expression clearly put her at a disadvantage. Pressing on, she needed to get this out before her emotions overwhelmed her. "Exploding debris coated my eyes as I hit my head when the vehicle turned over. Luckily, no one was killed. But my injuries were thought to be minor until I couldn't see clearly." Tears welled up in her eyes. *This is harder than I thought it would be.* "Long story...short. I took the medical discharge and came home."

"Why didn't you tell us? Call us? We'd have been there for you." She could hear the anger in her voice.

"That's the whole reason I didn't call you. You gave up

so much to take care of Dad, and I didn't want to add to your stress." She glanced toward the dark shape of the man. "And you have TJ to help, but you don't need to add me to your list of responsibilities."

A loud crash sounded upstairs. "What's going on? Why is everyone awake?" Hearing his footsteps approaching, Shevonne stood to greet her dad.

She hadn't seen or spoken to him in over five years. He had believed the military was no place for a woman or maybe just for his baby, and harsh words were said on the day she left. Afraid her presence would hurt him, Shevonne took a step back behind the chair.

"Who's that?" Alzheimer's may have stolen much of her dad's memory but not his compelling voice. It was a voice she'd heard many times when she was in trouble. Forcing her knees not to quake at the memories, she longed to see his face clearly. Would he welcome or disown her? Eyes clearly were the most effective tool for communication, and here she was walking blind.

"Peanut, is that you? You're home?" His voice quivered with emotion.

Shevonne longed to run into his arms and have everything made okay again, just as he'd done when she was little. Her dad was her hero, squashing the spiders, playing catch with her, and teaching her to drive. She stood and stared at how much he'd changed.

Dad appeared smaller than she remembered, his figure shadowed. She noticed she was taller than him, now. When had that happened? He'd always been such a big man in her mind. However, time aged him. The slump of his shoulders reminded her of her grandfather.

"Yes, Dad. I'm home." His arms opened, and she ran those three huge steps into them. At the warmth of his hug, tears fell down her cheeks. She quickly wiped the wetness from her face then ran her thumb over his jawline. Her fingers committed his face to her memory once again. Still the strong face she remembered.

"Glad to have you home for a visit. Why's everyone up at this hour? Sounded like a ruckus going on here."

She pulled out of Dad's arms. "I'm sorry. I didn't want to wake everyone, but I suppose I did. I'm home for good. The Army kicked me out."

"Glad you're home. But why'd they kick you out?"

"I'm blind. An accident with a landmine. I can see only shadows." Her dad's fingers caressed her brow. "The doctors hoped it would improve over time, yet they wouldn't rule out it getting worse, either. But, so far, there's been no change. I couldn't think of anyplace I'd rather be than home. While I left Amherst in a hurry to escape small town life, this is the home of my heart."

"You need a second opinion. Make an appointment with Dr. Allsop. He's been our family doctor for years. Remember when all five of you had chicken pox? I thought we'd go crazy with the oatmeal baths. If things don't improve, don't worry about anything. We'll always be here for you." He hugged her tight again. Taking a deep breath, she felt a load lift off her shoulders.

"Now, it's too early for everyone to be up. Get to bed. We can talk more in the morning." Dad still had the last word.

CHAPTER TWO

Shevonne lay in her childhood twin bed and stared at the fuzzy outline of the old dresser where her softball trophies had stood. Those were long gone; she had packed them up before she left for boot camp, determined to put away her childish things. But lying in bed, she wished she hadn't taken those bold steps. Each choice she'd made had brought her back to her bedroom, crippled and unable to work. *Who'll hire a blind girl with weapons' training?* While she didn't need her eyes to dismantle and put her gun back together, she couldn't tell if the money people handed her was a ten or a twenty without asking. *Quit feeling sorry for yourself. At least, I have family I can count on.*

After the fiasco last night, she'd done little more than fall into bed. Maybe putting things away would help her depressive mood. Shevonne dumped her few clothes and toiletries into the top dresser drawer. She looked at the camo pants, jeans, and T-shirts that had been her wardrobe. *Guess I'd better get some shopping in. They say dress for the job you want. Suit? Cape?* She chuckled. *The Catwoman's black spandex? A blind-ish burglar, almost blind robber, squinting thief, or is the correct term not quite blind yet? Give me a week or six years and maybe then I'll be totally blind. How do I explain this to others when I can't explain it to myself? I'm sorta handicapped?*

She shook her head. At least her sarcasm worked just fine. Although nothing in her dad's house had changed in the five years she'd been gone, she didn't want to ask for help or rely on her family. Stubborn to the core, just like her father, Shevonne stood on her own two feet, with or without being able to see them. Only she called it determination, not being bullheaded.

She grabbed a T-shirt and jeans out of the drawer and dressed. Everything went with jeans, so she knew her outfit matched. Shevonne tugged her hair into a ponytail then headed down the five stairs to the main floor. Six steps diagonally, she found herself in the galley-style kitchen. She closed her eyes, slipping back into her memories of ruckus-filled holiday dinners and late-night gab sessions with her mom and sisters around the table. She swallowed past the knot in her throat as she recalled the first time she'd walked into the kitchen after her mother's death. The warmth of the room had fled, as she collapsed in the high-back wooden chair and sobbed for hours. This time, the pain didn't immobilize her. More like a nagging sore tooth. You only felt the pain when you poked at it.

Shevonne shook her head, sending the memories back to the storage locker in her heart. Determined never to feel that overwhelming sense of loss again, she raised her chin and locked her jaw. "Push through it," she whispered to herself. "Move on."

She spent the next two hours memorizing the layout of the house, counting steps, feeling for walls and bumping into a few, too. All it took were a few big bruises to remind her how challenging living was without vision. She rubbed her sore leg, causing her breath to hitch. *Damn stair.* She'd learned some coping strategies at the VA hospital, but applying them in her day-to-day life proved to be a challenge.

Thirsty, she opened the fridge and stuck her hands

inside, feeling around for a beer or soda. A clinking sound met her ears as her fingers knocked into a jar. *Nope, not a can. Where is it?* Frantic now, her hands moved along the edge of the shelf. She squinted. *Don't these people have anything to drink? Is that it on the bottom shelf?* She reached down and connected with the cool metal. *But is it a beer or something else?* She honestly didn't care at this point. Pulling the tap, no fizz met her ears. *So it's not a soda.* She brought the can to her nose. Tomato smell wafted from it. *Yuck, probably tomato juice. No, thank you. I won't have a V8.* Dad liked to use these to make a Bloody Mary now and again. She poured the juice into the sink.

"What are you searching for, Shevonne?" She hadn't heard her sister enter the kitchen.

"I wanted a beer or soda. Will you find one?" She turned toward her with the now-empty can. "I found only this in the fridge."

"Do you think a beer first thing in the morning is a good idea?"

"Who does it hurt? So where are you hiding the beer?"

"I'm not in your shoes, but today's the only day I'll let you play this sorry game. Dad now keeps the beer in the garage fridge. I'll get one for you." This time, she heard her leave the kitchen and walk out the back door into the garage. She felt the slightly cooler air caress her skin as her sister opened the door again, returning to the kitchen.

"Here." Syn waited for her to take the beer. She squinted again, stepping slightly to the side to see the shadow of her sister's arm. She reached out. Her hand connected with the cold can. Pulling the top, she immediately smelled the sweet smell of beer. Lifting it to her lips, she drank deeply.

"Ahh." She licked her lips. "I needed that. I hate not being able to find things."

"I'm sure it's a challenge." Her voice sounded sympathetic, but her sister had never been overly caring.

"You can't imagine. You've always been the

responsible one, taking care of all of us and now overseeing Dad. I hate having to rely on others. I'd rather be independent and with this—she waved her hand at her face—"I'm not."

She collapsed in one of the kitchen chairs and felt Syn's hand on her back. Clenching her teeth to keep from hollering, crying, or giving up, she forced her back, ramrod straight.

"I'm willing to help. Just tell me what you need." Syn grabbed her sister's hands and squatted down in front, her voice sincere.

"I need to know where things are. One piece of advice they gave me at the VA hospital was about having specific places for everything. Will you help organize Dad's fridge so I can find things?"

"Sure. Just tell me how you want it set up."

"First, tell me what's in the fridge then we sort it. And I'll need you to put some soda and beer in here for me. I don't know if I can memorize two fridges, in addition to the house layout." Shevonne sat at the table and listened to Syn itemize the contents and return them to specific places in the fridge. Painting a picture in her head, she visualized the layout. She heard the front door open and turned toward the sound. "Someone's home."

Footsteps padded on the carpet. "Hey. How's your day been?" TJ strolled into the kitchen.

"I'm organizing the fridge for Shea. Be sure to put things back where you find them, unlike what you do with your dirty clothes, mister. Else Shea will end up with ketchup instead of lemon in her drink."

Shevonne smiled at her sister's tone. She'd have made a good drill sergeant, standing at the front of the line of soldiers, bossing them around, go here, do that... Shevonne chuckled. "You sounded just like you did when we were kids and wanted to play in the quarries. You made us each pack a snack and then we had to each find our own 'fort' and follow your rules."

The shadow that was her sister leaned in close. She could have stuck her tongue out and touched Syn's nose. "Are you saying I'm bossy?" Syn's voice rose.

TJ's laughter stifled, turning into a cough.

Shevonne tried to defuse the situation. Obviously, the joke had gotten out of hand. "Not bossy…authoritative. But you had to be to keep all four of us in line. I'm sure it helps with Dad, now."

Her sister batted her shoulder then backed away. "It does help with him." Her voice softened, the pain evident in her tone.

Shea's stomach clenched, and her heart sped up. Thoughts of losing her father crashed through her mind. Questions fired rapidly from her mouth. "What's been going on? Has he been getting worse? Have you talked to his doctor?" It hurt to imagine the strong man who'd carried her on his shoulders as weak and feeble. Then her thoughts turned to her own situation. She hadn't wanted anyone to think of her as damaged, but pain sparked each time she considered his health crisis.

Syn sighed. "The dementia has been getting worse. He has good days and bad, but the bad days are outweighing the good." Syn reached over and hugged Shevonne. "I'm glad you're home. Dad recognizing you was a big deal. The last time Sheri was in town, he thought she was Aunt Kelly. It hurt her feelings. Even when you expect episodes like that to happen, witnessing it firsthand is hard."

TJ reached over and wrapped his arm around Syn's shoulder.

She smiled at him and went on. "The doctors have given him a prescription to help with the memory loss and encouraged Dad to do mind activities like word searches, crosswords, or puzzles. But none of those interest him. TJ found Dad's old coin collection, and they've been sorting and categorizing them, which seems to be doing him some good."

"Thanks, TJ. I know you didn't sign up for babysitting

duty when you agreed to marry Syn." She smiled at her future brother-in-law.

"I'm glad to do it. I remember your dad from when I dated your sister. He used to sit on the porch and clean his guns when I came over. He wanted to warn me not to hurt her." TJ kissed his wife's cheek. "Sadly, I did anyway. But, seriously, your dad's always been so full of life and such a character. If there's anything I can do to help him...I'm going to do it. Without him, I wouldn't have your sister."

"Aww. You guys are too cute. Do you have a brother you can fix me up with?" Shevonne joked.

"Only fifteen."

Shevonne's eyes widened. "Really?" She wasn't sure if TJ was joking. Surely her sister would have mentioned fifteen hot, sexy brothers.

"My brothers at the fire station. I'm an only child."

"No thanks. I don't want to offend you but no firefighter. You're great for Syn." She brushed aside his brothers. "But, I don't need another bossy 'law and order' guy. I had one of those while I was overseas. He dumped me when I got hurt. Another reason I didn't fight the discharge."

"Oh, Shea. I'm so sorry. He obviously didn't deserve you." Her sister enveloped her in her arms, holding her tightly.

Shevonne shrugged out of her embrace and put on her poker face. "No biggie. Better to see it end now, before marriage or kids. It'd kill me to have to rip a family apart, but if a man can't stand beside me...for better or worse...he ain't the man for me." She stood and opened the fridge then reached in but found an empty spot where the beer should have been. "No more beers?"

TJ leaned over her shoulder and peered in. "Nope. All out. How about if we head to the Veterans of Foreign Wars hall tonight? We can take your dad and meet up with some guys from the station. Make it a night out."

Shevonne closed the door and leaned against the fridge.

"Suppose so. There's nothing to drink here. You wouldn't be hoping to hook me up with one of your 'brothers'? I've already told you how one in this family is enough." She winked at her sister. "I'm calling the shower first," she shouted, and skedaddled up the stairs.

Syn taunted. "Why shower? Thought you weren't interested in any of TJ's law and order brothers?"

Shevonne poked her head down from the top of the stairs. "I remember how long you took in the bathroom. I'm determined to get some hot water." She wiggled her brows as her sister groaned.

CHAPTER THREE

"Hey, sexy. I knew you hadn't had any home cookin', so I brought some of my famous pot roast." The tapping of her high heels across the concrete announced Brittani's arrival. Jackson paused in his cleanup of the fire engine to stare at the sexy blonde, whose arms were wrapped around a large Crockpot. Her hips swayed with each step she took closer to him. Jackson licked his lips as he recalled Brittani's hips swaying in the sheets. She'd been only one of a long line of girls who'd filled his bed but not his heart.

"Thanks, hon. I appreciate it, but I'm going off the clock in a bit. I'll share the grub with the guys." He took the heavy pot from her hands and set it aside on a table. A pout transformed her face. The mood swings and jumping through hoops to keep the girls happy had become tiresome, but he didn't want to hurt her feelings. "Can't let your good cooking go to waste."

"Aww, baby. You're always welcome to come over for more than home cookin'. It's been a month since I've seen you." Brittani ran a long, talented red fingernail down his chest then leaned in, pressing her 38DD breasts tight against him. The tight pencil skirt and low-cut tank top showed off her assets at their finest.

139

"You're too good for me." He planted a kiss on her cheek. "Sadly, I'm off the market." The lie slipped off his lips, sounding better than the truth. He'd finally reached the end of hooking up without any emotional attachment. Besides, she'd never believe it with his hard member pushing into her stomach. While he didn't want to be with her for meaningless sex, he wasn't dead. Anyone would be rock hard with her hot body rubbing against him.

Her gasp echoed in the garage as she stepped back. "Pooh. If she doesn't treat you right, come visit. I'll take care of you, real fine."

"I'll do that. And thank you for the food. I'll let the guys know who sent it. Would it be a problem if Stevenson returned the pot to you?" Jackson wanted to throw his buddy a bone. Stevenson had recently broken up with his high school girlfriend and needed some TLC. Brittani would keep his mind off his worries. "That poor man has been drooling over you each time we go out. He's a bit shy, though, and wouldn't have had the courage ever to mention it to your face."

"Ooohh. Please do. I'd heard about his recent single status but wouldn't have thought of stepping out on you." He could see the wheels turning in her head by her new dreamy expression. "I'll be waiting for his call. Thank you, sugar. And my offer stands. If she isn't good enough for you..." Brittani turned and sashayed out the door accompanied by the tap, tap, tapping of her heels and her sexy sway.

"Whooeee. Brittani keeps getting sexier and sexier."

"Just the man I'd hoped to see. Brittani brought some home-cooked pot roast." Jackson pointed to the counter. "And I told her you'd bring the Crockpot back when the guys finished it."

"Why me? Why not you? Thought you two were an item."

"Were an item. But mostly in her mind, not mine. I wanted sex, not love. She deserved love." Jackson sat on a bench. "Frankly, I'm over the one-night stands and sex for sex's sake. I'm interested in a relationship, someone to come home to, someone to stand by my side, a partner."

Stevenson slipped a leg over and joined him on the bench. "I understand. I'm in a different spot. Coming off a long-term relationship that imploded, I'm only out for fun. Could it be that Fire Station 35's Sex Machine is out of the game?"

Jackson nodded. "More like hunting for a bear rather than a bunny rabbit."

Stevenson laughed. "Make sure you bag and tag 'em. When you do find one, don't let it get away."

"Will do." He held up his hand, and his buddy high-fived him.

"I'll take the Crockpot in the back and grab a plate. Do you want some?" Stevenson stood.

"No, thanks. I need to get this engine put away before I leave. Enjoy." Jackson got up and headed back over to the shiny red truck, thoughts of the perfect "game" running through his head.

Jackson coiled the hose and returned it to Engine 3. Finally finished with the cleanup, he wiped his arm across his forehead. Getting the tools and truck ready for the next emergency was hard work, but vital to the success of the station. When seconds counted and lives were on the line, faulty or missing equipment wouldn't help anyone. In fact, it'd only endanger victims and the firefighters themselves.

Glad to finally have an evening off after two days on, he planned to grab some food and brews at the VFW hall. With his schedule, he hadn't been grocery shopping, so the likelihood of having food at home was slim to none. Besides, he was sure the pot roast had been inhaled already. Food never went to waste at the firehouse. Too many hungry men.

He wiped his face, pushing his mop of hair off his forehead. Due for a cut, he'd planned to take care of both the groceries and a haircut during his two days off.

Lately, he'd been thinking a great deal about his time working as a cattle hand. He'd never have thought he'd have become a firefighter rather than a rancher. But the accident on the bronc had changed his life's direction. The camaraderie between the ranch hands was not unlike the bond among firefighters. They relied on each other to keep everyone safe and lived like a family, doing kitchen duty and chores around the station.

Summer in Wyoming had been much cooler than in Ohio. The humidity and scorching temps here made fighting fires much more difficult. On a good day, when you added the additional seventy plus pounds of gear then the heat from the blaze…it was hotter than Satan's living room. In this summer heat, hell sounded like a vacation spot.

With everything cleaned and stowed, Jackson headed toward the common bunk room and his gear locker. Grabbing his shaving kit, towel, and clean jeans, he stalked to the showers. Hopefully, the guys had left him some hot water, but he'd settle for lukewarm. Anything to get the grime and sweat off his body. No way was he going to subject anyone to his stink.

He tossed his towel on the hook and turned on the water. Stripping out of his dirty uniform, he folded it before laying it on the bench. With his shoes underneath and everything in place, he checked the water. Warm enough. He stuck his head under the spray. He lathered up his body, and his mind returned to the conversation he'd had with Brittani. He hated lying to her, but living the single life had been getting stale. Too many one-night stands with women he didn't remember the next morning. The guys in the station nicknamed him "Loverboy" and "Stud Muffin." He took the ribbing good-naturedly, but lately he'd wanted something more.

He'd spent some time with TJ Johnson and his fiancée, Syn Wilder. The three had been in high school together and while TJ had dumped her, which broke Syn's heart,

Jackson had been her buddy. He'd always known the two of them were meant to be together, yet it didn't stop him from wishing she'd notice him.

The three of them palled around at the beach or hit the VFW hall for drinks or dancing. Sometimes, they included her father. Not too long ago, nights with the family sounded lame, but spending time with TJ had him jealous. Jackson longed for a woman who'd bring his favorite brownies to work, make sure his uniform was washed, and who would call just to say I love you. Not one who loved what he could do to her. *Yep, the playboy life is tarnished.*

Jackson placed the bar of soap on the ledge and stepped back under the showerhead, rinsing the sweat and soap from his body. Finally, he turned off the water and ran his hands over his arms, abdomen, and legs, brushing the drops off his skin. He grabbed his towel, putting it over his head and rubbing his hair. He had a routine, a precise way of drying off. Always head first then working down the body. Jackson crawled into his jeans, pulling them up over his thighs, adjusting his junk and buttoning the fly. Going commando meant button fly only. *No sense taking a chance with the family jewels.*

Slinging the damp towel over his shoulder, he gathered up his clothes, shoes, and gear then headed back to the bunk room to change. Humming under his breath, he turned the corner too quickly and ran into Travis Jones, one of his fellow firefighters. Jackson's clothes tumbled out of his hands.

"Omph. Sorry, Travis. I didn't see you there." He bent over and picked everything up.

"Hey. Where's the fire?" His buddy reached down and grabbed a shoe, shoving it toward him.

"Always the same joke? You're getting predictable." Jackson rose and shuffled his clothes and shoes into his arms, making sure everything was secure.

"The ladies love it." Travis ran his hand over his buzz cut and down his jawline. "Going out with Brittani tonight? I heard she stopped by."

"Brittani and I parted ways. I'm heading over to the VFW. There's nothing in the fridge at home, and my stomach is a bottomless pit. You wanna come?" He angled his head.

"Sure, but I bet I score before you, Loverboy." He pulled his wallet from his pocket. "Fifty dollars says I go home with a girl tonight. Twenty says I get a kiss before you." He flashed the bills in Jackson's face.

Jackson sighed. This kind of contest wasn't as thrilling as it used to be. Now, he only sought stimulating conversation with someone he wanted to get to know. He shook his head. "Nah. I'm hoping for a quiet dinner and an early night."

"Whoa! Are you okay, Loverboy? I've never seen you pass on a chance to hook up." He paused. "Or are you intimidated by me?" Travis flexed his bicep.

"Nah. Just tired of the game. It's the same every night. Sex with a nameless woman, no love, no meaning." Hanging his head, he couldn't meet Travis's gaze.

"Dude. Meaningless sex is a single guy's dream. No drama, no commitment, no long-term contract."

Jackson chuckled and stared at his friend. "That sounds like a phone plan, not a date."

"Date, skate. I'm not trying to find Miss Right...only Miss Right Now." He stuffed the money back into his wallet. "Maybe we need to change your name to Loser Boy."

His taunts grated on Jackson's nerves. He didn't want to use a woman just to show up Travis, but he couldn't let this slimeball tease him. "I'll take the kissing bet, but I'm passing on the other. After two nights sleeping among you snorers, I'm in need of a good night's sleep."

"Ha-ha. I don't sleep when I have a lady in my bed." Travis elbowed Jackson and winked.

"Hey, if I don't finish dressing, I'm not going to be able to make it before midnight." He glanced at his friend. "Are you ready?"

Travis nodded.

Jackson scrutinized the other man's clothes. Jeans paired with a dark-blue T-shirt with the firefighter image across the front. His blond hair feathered from his face, trapped in the 1980s. Jackson hid a grimace. Clearly, the man felt a need to shout firefighter as if that'd bring the ladies running. Sure, a few would take the bait, but quality dates wanted more than a hero complex. Real women wanted the whole package—a man who cared about them, listened to them, and supported them. Jackson had learned the hard way after his many years of one-night stands. "I'll be ready in about fifteen minutes. Why don't you head over to the VFW, and I'll meet you there?"

"Sounds like a plan. But you're making it easy for me to win the bet. I'll have a head start on charming the ladies." Travis flashed his slick smile.

"I'm cool. Just save me a beer." He turned and strolled over to his storage locker, where he refolded his clothes, laid them into his duffel bag, and hung up his damp towel.

Recalling his talk with Travis, he realized how far apart they'd drifted. They'd often been each other's wingman. Before, they would enjoy those challenges, seeing who'd get the girl first. Now it seemed like a waste of time, a waste of energy. Jackson longed for more. The image of TJ's wife, smiling and laughing at one of the station events tugged at his heart. Worse, he needed to adjust the boner in his pants. It wasn't right thinking about a buddy's wife that way, yet, he couldn't help himself.

Pulling a Jefferson Airplane T-shirt from his duffel, he slipped it over his head then grabbed his brush and it over his locks. "Better get my hair cut tomorrow, or I won't be able to see the fire in front of my eyes," he muttered. As his hair grew longer, it tended to curl, and while the girls liked the boyish style, it reminded him of times better forgotten. Squeezing some product into his hands, he ran them through his hair, taming the curls, giving him a

145

dangerous appearance. He sat on his bed and tugged on his black tactical boots. Finally ready, he grabbed his keys and wallet, slung his bag over his shoulder, and slid down the pole before leaving the station.

"I'm ready for a cold one," Jackson mused as he climbed into his truck and dropped his bag on the passenger seat. "Anything to cool off the hots for my buddy's wife."

CHAPTER FOUR

It was a quick car ride to the VFW hall that used to be an old warehouse. Shevonne recalled the brick building where her older sister had her sweet sixteen party. When the door opened, the sounds of big band music and conversations floated out on the air. As they walked inside, Shevonne felt the heat from the bodies as the crowd pushed against them. She held onto her sister for dear life.

The smell of sweaty bodies, beer, and fried food forced Shevonne to breathe through her nose. The room's lights barely lit the bar. To Shevonne, the darkness had her already-compromised vision, now become nonexistent. She literally couldn't see her hand in front of her face, no matter how hard she squinted.

"Go grab the table by the window, and I'll order us some beers," TJ called out over the voices.

"Let's go, Dad," Syn said and their voices disappeared into the general dull roar. Shevonne's heart pounded. Her breathing sped up, and pain radiated through her abdomen. *Is this a heart attack? Or a panic attack? Does it matter? I'm lost.*

The sounds disoriented her. She couldn't hear her sister's voice anymore, nor could she see where they had gone. Not sure which way to turn or where to go, she stood silently and prayed someone would be back. A strong whiff of cheap aftershave came from behind her.

"Hi there, gorgeous." A deep voice spoke in her ear. "What brings you into the VFW? I haven't seen you before, and I'd remember someone as beautiful as you."

Her face warmed. Shevonne hated attention brought to her. "I'm here with family."

He persisted. "I don't see any family. Are you interested in some action? Maybe with a hero?" He whispered in her ear. "I am a firefighter. I've been trained to give CPR. Can I get you a drink?"

"No, thank you. I've already explained I'm here with someone." Her words were sharp but polite. She didn't know this guy. He could be a friend of TJ or her sister. He'd said he was a firefighter, and offending him wasn't in her plan.

"Come on, pretty lady. Just a drink." The man's tone became forceful causing the hairs on Shevonne's neck to rise. She'd bet he didn't like hearing the word no.

She shook her head. *When will he listen?*

"We can start there. I'd like to get to know you. We can spend the night getting better acquainted." He slid his arm around her shoulder.

Seeing red, Shevonne snatched the man's hand between his thumb and first finger, tightened the pressure then twisted his arm around her body and forced him to his knees. "I said no. Even, no, thank you. And I didn't ask you to touch me." She gritted out her words. The music and sounds stopped. The silence meant all eyes were on her.

"Okay, okay. Just let me up." His voice held a note of pain and fear. "Jeez. All I wanted was to buy you a drink. Talk a bit."

"I said no. No means no. You can't use your persistence to change a woman's mind. She's not going to fold under your constant pestering."

Footsteps approached from the left. Shevonne turned but kept the slimeball down, in case the incoming threat turned out to be someone trying to help him. She doubted he had friends with his sleazy come-on, but she'd learned to evaluate every threat separately and take nothing for granted.

The door of the VFW opened, illuminating the two men who stood in front of her. They towered over her, but she wasn't threatened. A hint of strawberry body wash wafted to her nose, sending a smile across her face. She'd recognized her sister's favorite brand and knew only one man who would wear it.

"Hi, TJ. I hope this isn't a friend of yours." She released the guy who promptly came up swinging.

"Stupid bitch. I'll get you." He took a step toward Shevonne but, before he reached her, the man who'd arrived with TJ grasped him in a bear hug. The bully continued to push against her rescuer. Shevonne wouldn't be able to see the punch coming, so she raised her fists, closed her eyes, and listened for clues. *He may get a hit in, but I'll be damned if he touches me twice. She'd trained for this.* She could do it. Blind.

"Let her be, Travis. I'll buy you a shot of whiskey. I saw Sheila asking about you. You don't want to let her down." Her savior tugged Travis away. The noises of the bar returned to normal. The band played and the conversations resumed.

Shevonne's body stood at attention. Her senses were on high alert. No longer from the potential attack but from desire. The stranger's voice triggered butterflies in her stomach. It caressed her skin, sending shivers down her spine. Heat pooled between her thighs.

Unable to see him clearly, she almost took a step to follow him, to find out who he was, to give him her phone number or ask him to buy her a beer. Instead, she reached out with her other senses. Shevonne sniffed the air, catching the scents of stale beer, strawberry body wash, and a hint of sandalwood.

Squinting, she tried to see him more clearly, however, because of the darkness of the bar, she glimpsed dark hair and broad shoulders walking away from her. A sigh escaped her lips as the man strolled away. She'd never felt this strong about another person. Lust, yes. But it was more. He'd put his body in harm's way to protect her. *I'm sure they are friends so maybe he doesn't think the guy'd hurt him, but no one has ever put me first. I must meet and thank him.* Shevonne continued to stare off into the direction her knight had gone.

"Shevonne, are you okay?" TJ's voice snapped her attention back. "What happened?"

"That guy, Travis, wouldn't take no for an answer. When he put his arm around me, my training kicked in, and I forced him to the floor." She hung her head, hiding the heat of her cheeks. "I'm sorry. I hope I didn't hurt him."

"Only his pride's hurt. He's one of the firefighters I work with."

Shevonne covered her face with her hands. Since losing her sight, she'd dealt with so many changes, fear, and pain. Tears welled in her eyes. "I hope this doesn't cause problems at work." Her voice came out muffled and squeaky.

"He's always been a loudmouth, bragging about his conquests. Don't worry." TJ reached out and rubbed her shoulder.

She peeked through her fingers. "The other guy, who was he? He stepped in and tried to help, diffusing Travis's anger. I hope he didn't get hurt."

Soft footsteps and the strong smell of strawberry body wash approached from the right. Shevonne turned, launching herself into her sister's arms. "I couldn't find you then this guy...I freaked out. I'm sorry. I may have caused problems at TJ's work. Maybe we should go home."

150

TJ closed in behind her and ushered them over to the table. "Really, Shevonne. Don't worry about Travis. I outrank him so he's not going to cause any issues with me. If I'd noticed, I'd have come to your aid. But no need. You took care of yourself."

"Here's the table. Have a seat." Syn helped her sister to a chair next to their father.

"Good job, Shea. No one should touch a woman without permission." The pride in her father's voice took some of the sting of embarrassment away. "Too bad I didn't have my gun. Back when I was dating your mom, we had a chaperone." He shook his head. "Couldn't even hold hands without permission. Your grandpa Riley would've tanned my hide if I'd hurt his little girl."

Shevonne raised her head and wiped the tears with the back of her hand. "I'm fine now." She reached over and squeezed his hand. "Thanks, Dad. I'm sure glad you didn't have your gun. The VFW thanks you, and so do the local police. You're too handsome for jail." She blew him a kiss.

TJ and her sister sat in the remaining seats. Shevonne turned. "Still, TJ, I hope he doesn't make work unbearable." Again, heat flooded her cheeks.

"I'll tell you the truth." He leaned in, over the table. "Travis is always bragging about his score with women. He needed to be taken down a notch, and I'm glad you did. But I am also very thankful you didn't pull a move like that on me the other night when I surprised you." He glanced at his wife. "Please don't teach Syn how to do any of those moves. I don't want my ass kicked." Her sister's laughter lightened the mood.

"I promise. Cross my heart." She made a crisscross motion over her chest. "I over-reacted and should apologize. Getting separated and not being able to find you guys then when the slimeball wouldn't take no for an answer..." She shuddered. "Coming out tonight was a bad idea. I know where things are at home but, out here, I'm lost. All I see are dark shapes in a dark world. Squinting helps but gives me a headache." She rubbed her forehead. "The doctor said using my sight will help it improve, yet it's not without its own pain."

A smooth voice broke through the conversation. "Would you be willing to show me how you brought Travis down?"

The smell of sandalwood whispered to Shevonne. A shiver flew down her spine, sending tingles in her thighs. She crossed her legs, trying to minimize the throbbing in her pussy. His voice sounded like decadent silk caressing her skin. She'd never had such an instantaneous desire for someone else. Could her lack of eyesight cause such a strong reaction?

He set five beers on the table. "TJ, you forgot your beers in all the excitement."

TJ stood. "Sorry, Jackson. Nice of you to bring 'em. Please join us." He held his hand out, indicating the chair next to Shevonne. As he took his seat, his shoulder brushed against Shevonne's back, sending little shocks where he touched.

"I'm Jackson Gambish, a buddy of TJ and Syn's." She finally had a name for her rescuer. She couldn't keep calling him HKISA—her knight in shining armor. It was too long, and no one would know who she was talking about. She squinted, trying to see more of him. Dark hair curled slightly over his brow and strong shoulders but also full lips and a chiseled jawline.

"I'm Shevonne, Syn's sister. Thanks for your help back there. He'd have come after me if you hadn't stepped in."

"You seemed to have it all under control. Are you going to teach me those moves?" His voice held the hint of laughter. Shevonne hoped he wasn't laughing at her expense.

"Sure. Just name the time." "Give as good as you get," a motto from her military days, often kept the guys from teasing the helpless women. Shevonne had been determined to never be helpless, but that was before her accident.

Her father's loud voice piped in. "Jackson Gambish. Was your dad, John Gambish, Amherst's star quarterback of 1969?" Mr. Wilder ran his hand over his chin.

Happy her father took Jackson's scrutiny off her, Shevonne studied the guy who'd gotten her panties in a twist. A fireman, close with her sister and brother-in-law, pretty well-known family in town. She created a list of things she knew about Jackson, hoping to figure out what attracted her to him.

"Yes, sir. He ended up owning a car dealership in Elyria. Did you know him?" Shevonne closed her eyes and laid a hand over her stomach to quiet the butterflies dancing in there. A craving, stronger than chocolate, filled her each time he spoke. She shook her head to clear it.

"We weren't close in school, but I saw him play. Magic hands. John sent balls flying down the field with precision. He won the final game in overtime and sent Amherst to the regional playoffs that year. Nice guy. Too bad we didn't run in the same circles."

He nodded. "He's been gone for twenty years. He'd have been glad to know you remembered seeing him play. His dream of playing for the Browns never panned out. A regular job, marriage, and a family became his reality."

Acutely aware of the man sitting down next to her, Shevonne lowered her gaze to the table and clenched her hands in her lap. Having him so close to her, her heart pounded as if it was dancing the salsa.

She swore he was just as aware of her. She shivered as she felt his gaze on her. While she was instantaneously attracted to this man, she wasn't about to let her heart or her pussy lead her into another messy relationship. She didn't need him studying her, judging her, or finding her lacking like all the other men had. It would take a confident man to see past her walls.

Shevonne hadn't been listening to the conversation, but her ears picked up when her name was mentioned by her brother-in-law.

"Shevonne's recently returned from overseas duty, so we came out to celebrate."

"Congrats. So you are armed and dangerous." He chuckled. "How long were you in the military?"

"I joined right after high school and spent one year in Afghanistan. After my recent discharge, I'm back home again. Hard to believe how much you miss your hometown when you are so far from it." Shevonne tucked her chin into her chest. Warmth filled her face and tears filled her eyes. Being emotional went against every part of her soul, but since the accident, her hormones were all over the map.

His fingertips touched under her chin, gently lifting her face so she could meet his gaze. "Like you, I left Amherst but couldn't get it out of my system. It's a pleasure to meet Syn's baby sister. She's often spoken fondly of you." When Shea rolled her eyes, he continued. "It's true. She's not told me any of your secrets, though. Welcome home, and thank you for your service."

Shea smiled. "I have a vague memory of you visiting our house. But being five years younger than Syn, I didn't pay attention to her friends. None of them were interested in climbing on the wooden bridge or making forts out of leaves."

"Those sound like fun times, but during high school, my focus was on horses and bulls. I worked as a ranch hand and cattle driver for two summers in high school. I'd always thought the West would be where life would take me." His voice held a note of sadness.

"Why didn't you stay?"

His voice softened as he spoke. "My parents died in a car accident right after graduation. They left me the house and everything, so I stayed to keep an eye on my grandfather. Eventually, I found a new love in firefighting and an extended family." He nodded toward Syn and TJ.

"Dad always said, 'You can't have too much family.'

I've enjoyed getting to meet you." She leaned in and kissed Jackson softly on the cheek. "And thank you for keeping the peace with your friend. No one has the right to touch someone without permission."

"I don't think anyone in this bar will try it again." He laughed.

His laugh caused her insides to dance again. While appearances had been important to her in the past, getting to know someone only by her other senses had its own unique turn-ons. Sitting this close to him, small currents of electrical energy zinged between their bodies whenever they accidently brushed each other. Shevonne smirked at him then joined in his merriment. "I suppose not. Maybe I should teach the women of Amherst about self-defense."

TJ chimed in, "Sure, but please, I beg you...not my wife. I need to win at least one argument a year." He groaned and hung his head in his hands.

MELISSA KEIR

CHAPTER FIVE

Travis on his knees before a woman, Jackson would have paid a thousand bucks to see it again. Maybe someone got it on video. He'd have to ask around discreetly because Travis would drop-kick him to the next state if he found out. The man who thought all women loved him had his ass handed to him by a tiny, sexy woman. The whole thing had happened so fast. He'd only just arrived at the VFW and walked in behind TJ and his family. He couldn't help but notice when TJ went to the bar, leaving his wife's sister standing alone, a perfect target for a ladies' man to swoop in.

Shevonne's tinkling laughter had drawn his attention to her. His motivation for bringing over the beers had a hidden meaning. He longed to know more about the woman who moved with a fluid grace in bringing down a man twice her weight yet appeared fearful and lost. This duality pulled at him. Was it the innocence in her gaze? The way her nibbled on her bottom lip? Or her dynamic physical moves? *What is it about her that has my cock bursting against the fly of my jeans?*

Jackson studied the small woman sitting next to him. She appeared a little like her sister but not enough for people to know without indication. Her hair was shorter than Syn's. The milk-chocolate-colored hair grazed her ears and swooped across her forehead. The short cut exposed her neck, drawing his attention. Would the skin be smooth there? Is she ticklish? He longed to lean in and breathe in her scent. He'd not been so suddenly attracted to a woman before. Was it because she was Syn's sister, who he crushed on, or was it something more?

Her teeth tugged on her full bottom lip as if nervous. How could a woman who could bring down a big man like Travis be nervous? Long lashes highlighted her eyes. He wished for more light so he could see exactly what color they were. She wouldn't glance at him but kept her gaze on her hands, now twisting in her lap. How graceful her hands were as they bent over each other, long fingers entwining and releasing. *What would it feel like to have those hands caressing my body?* Her takedown showed the power in those dainty limbs.

Jackson shifted in his seat and adjusted his jeans to accommodate his growing bulge. He scooted his chair closer to the table to hide his erection. He lifted the glass of beer and took a deep swallow then set it down, focusing once more on the conversations at the table.

"Jackson. Jackson…did you hear me?" Syndey snapped her fingers in front of his face.

He reached out and grasped her hand. "Were you saying something? I was mesmerized by your beauty." He smiled, showing off his dimples, which were guaranteed to make women swoon.

She tugged her hand out of his. "Stop your flirting. I asked what your work schedule was. TJ's off tomorrow, and we wanted to have some of the guys from the firehouse over for a fish fry."

"I'm off tomorrow, too. Can I bring anything?"

"Nope. We've got it covered. TJ and Dad went fishing on Lake Erie and got a bunch of perch. Going to be a yummy meal." Syn stood up. "Shea, come with me to the bathroom. We'll leave the guys to talk fishing."

Shevonne scooted her chair out and grabbed hold of her sister's hand.

Jackson leaned over the table. "You're one lucky man, TJ. Syn's a great woman. Not too many wives would put up with all of us for dinner or even an afternoon. You can see how endearing Travis is. Shevonne seems wonderful as well. Man, I wish we had a video of her taking Travis down. He deserved it, for sure." He nodded toward the bar.

TJ raised his beer bottle and tilted it toward his friend. "Syn's a one in a million." A big shit-eating grin broke out on his face. "But, hey, I wanted to tell you, Shevonne received a medical discharge. Her vision is compromised. In places like this, she's running blind. We've done some things around the house to make it better, but I wanted you to know so you could watch out for her, run interference with the guys. And I've noticed your interest in here. She's not one of your one-night stands, Mr. Playboy. Shevonne's my sister, now."

"She doesn't have a mean bone in her body. She's a good kid, always softhearted." Mr. Wilder's gruff voice piped in. "She only lashed out because she felt under attack. I taught my girls to stand up for themselves. We got separated from Shea when we came in, and she was alone and unable to see."

TJ leaned back in his chair. "She's proud, though, so don't treat her like a baby."

Jackson glanced around the bar, searching for the women. "Are you asking me to be her babysitter? 'Cause I'm not interested in babysitting her."

Mr. Wilder slammed his bottle on the table. "TJ's not asking you to. No such thing. We wanted someone else aware of what's going on, in case she needed help in the group situation. Besides, anyone who messes with her will have to answer to me." The old man reached into his pocket then pounded on the table. "Dammit, TJ, where's my gun?"

Jackson's jaw dropped. He hoped he hadn't heard the man right.

TJ reached over and patted the other man's hand. "Now, Mr. Wilder, Tony…we can't bring a gun to the VFW, remember? They got really mad the last time you accidentally shot out a window."

Mr. Wilder slumped in his chair and gulped his beer, grumbling.

Deciding another round sounded like a good excuse to get up, Jackson offered to grab some. He'd heard the stories of "Crazy Old Man Wilder" but he'd not put much stock in small town gossip. Shaking his head, he sauntered to the bar.

***

Shevonne squinted her eyes and stared at her reflection in the bathroom mirror. With the brighter light, she could see her hair and face but not the features. Her eyes that boys wrote poems about in high school were now a shadow in the mirror. She used her memory and sense of touch to apply her makeup and prayed each time she didn't look like a clown. Her natural style was one of necessity, not vanity. Leaning over, she turned on the sink and washed her hands. She reached out and wipes her hands on the cloth to the left of the sink.

"Shevonne, what are you doing?" A shriek echoed in the small bathroom. "You wiped your hands on the back of my shirt."

"I'm sorry. I thought you were the towel." Shevonne ran her hands over her cheeks and down her chin. How was she going to get through a lifetime of blindness if she couldn't survive five minutes in the bathroom? "This is exactly why I can't leave the house. What if I eat something I shouldn't or end up standing in traffic? It's like dealing with a toddler. I have to be watched every second so I don't hurt myself…or someone else."

"Everything's new to you. Once you get acclimated like you have at home, you'll be fine."

"I'll be more comfortable, but outside the house nothing is going to be in the same place when I encounter it. What if some child leaves their tricycle on the sidewalk where I walk? I'll trip over it, possibly hurting myself." She sighed.

"You're right. You can't plan for everything but we can help you get through this."

Shevonne took a deep breath and counted to five before she spoke. Her voice was soft and slow. "I won't be another burden for you. You already have Dad to take care of. Your marriage will suffer with me around taking your time so I don't wear my clothes inside out or swallow bleach. You'll have two children—Dad and me."

Syndey hugged her sister. "Family cares for each other. You aren't burdens. Dad isn't nor will you be. Please let us help you."

Shevonne nodded.

"I noticed you and Jackson chatting. He's a nice guy. Back in high school, he'd wear cowboy boots and Western shirts. I swear he was stuck in the wrong era, or maybe town."

"He seems nice enough. Something about him, though…

"What?"

"His smell is so sexy. It's as if I want to lick him up and down like an ice cream cone."

"Eww. I don't want to hear this." Her sister covered her ears. "I won't ever see him as sexy." Syn's laughter echoed through the bathroom. "He's been such a good friend. A big flirt and a bit of a ladies' man, but he's changed in the last year. Jackson's more serious about life and his future, whereas before, he'd act like Travis— hitting on every skirt. Now he's happiest hanging out with the old married couple." Syn pointed her thumbs at her chest. "It'd do him good to get out and date." Her sister leaned over and brushed her fingers across Shevonne's face. "He'd be good for you, too. Let's get back to those beers. Do you remember how many steps it was from our table to here?"

"I thought you were counting?"

Syn clucked her tongue. "Shea. You were—"

Shevonne laughed and bumped her sister on the shoulder. "Kidding." She looped her arm around Syn's and headed back to their table, more anxious to return to the man who tempted her.

***

Jackson stared as the women returned. Shevonne's eyes were red, even though she had a smile on her face. Something must have happened to upset her while she was in there. He couldn't imagine how challenging it must be to face the world and not be able to see. His vision was vital to his job but, more importantly, it was a piece of him. He longed to take her into his arms and comfort her, but he didn't want to come on too strong. He needed to see what her feelings were. He wasn't going to jump her and end up like Travis.

I'll be her babysitter tomorrow...for Syn and TJ's sake. That's the only reason. I'm not going to take advantage of her nor let anyone like Travis try it either. His vow firm in his mind. Even as his body and heart said something different.

CHAPTER SIX

The smell of cabbage filled the kitchen as Shevonne worked the grinder. Her father had put her to work as soon as she woke up. The perch needed soaking then dipping and coating in his special concoction. She kept her finger just on the edge of the bowl to see when the cabbage came too close to the top. Her arm ached from the repetitive motion of the grinder, and she hadn't even gotten started on the carrots yet. *I'll have one arm like Popeye.* She released the grinder and flexed her muscle. "I'm strong to the finish, 'cause I eats me Spinach. Yick yick yick." It felt good to laugh. Shevonne went back to her grinding and whistled a song.

Soft shuffling alerted her to her father's approach. "I'm glad to hear you laughing, peanut. I've missed you since you left for boot camp. We always spent the spring nights down at Hot Water's tossing a line in the water."

"And I always caught more than you did, Dad." She brushed a kiss on his grizzled cheek. The scrape of his beard against her lips was a reminder of her childhood. She recalled the time he used his stubble to tickle their sensitive bellies and would chase her and her sisters around the house. With a big grin on her face, she drew her dad into a hug. "I'm sorry for running away. I wanted to leave this small town but once I saw a little more of the world, I finally realized just how special life was here. Then it was my pride that kept me away."

He patted her back and held her close. "I'm sorry too, peanut. Syn has always taken after your mom, bless her soul, and while I'm glad your sister's found a wonderful husband, I feel horrible that she's been forced to keep watch over me." He stared at her. "Don't think I don't know what my prognosis is. The Alzheimer's will continue to rob me of my memories. I'll be able to remember when I worked at the mill, but I won't be able to recall your name, or I'll confuse you with my mom, your grandmother, who you always took after. Syn's going to need your steel will to lean on. I've started going through the house, getting rid of things…items I've bought over the years. Now, nobody wants them, and I'm giving them away or tossing them. My life is dwindling."

Shevonne gave him a squeeze then pulled away. "You better let me get back to work, general, or else no one will have coleslaw." She kissed his cheek once again and returned to her grinder. *Maybe I can switch arms. It's worth a try.*

Syn and TJ strolled into the kitchen, hand in hand. They smiled and whispered to each other as couples in love do. Shevonne noticed. "Glad someone got lucky last night. Who wants to take over the coleslaw? I can get started mixing the batter for the perch."

TJ held up his hands. "Can't. I'm heading out for the beers. It appears Syn will have to do coleslaw." TJ hid his laughter behind a cough. "Tony, is Rolling Rock beer okay? The guys won't drink a lot because they need to be fresh for work, but I wanted to have some."

Mr. Wilder nodded. He glanced around the room. When he spotted Syn, he strolled toward her, while tugging at his T-shirt. "Hello, Betty. I didn't know you were coming to visit." He leaned in close. "Where are we?"

His voice weakened. He ran his hands over his face.

Syn took his hand while Shevonne jumped out of the kitchen chair. They helped him sit down while TJ filled a glass. "Here's some water, Tony. Drink it. You'll feel better."

Shevonne hadn't seen one of her father's episodes before. Tears filled her eyes. Tucking her hand in his, she prayed.

"Dad, do you know where you are?" Syn's voice brooked no games yet retained a small wobble as if she kept her fear in check by the skin of her teeth.

Her father peered around the room. "Of course, I know where I am. I'm at home." Anger tinged his voice.

"Dad, did you take your meds this morning?" Syn nodded her head toward her husband, sending him running up to the bathroom. TJ's feet pounded up the stairs.

Shevonne's tears slipped quietly down her face onto her and her father's entwined hands. She kept her face lowered as she recited a Hail Mary.

"Syn, why are you bossing me around? We've got a lot to do before the fire department comes over. We're wasting time." Mr. Wilder tried to stand but, as he tugged on his hand, he stared at his youngest daughter. "Peanut? Why are you crying? Syn. Tell it to me straight. What's going on?" His voice lost its anger and became as weak as a kitten's.

Syn took her father's other hand. "Dad, you had an episode. You thought I was Betty and didn't know where you were. Do you remember any of it?"

He shook his head then, using his free hand, wiped the tears from Shevonne's cheeks. "I'm sorry, peanut. I know it scared you but, as I said before, these episodes are a product of my disease."

TJ returned, breathless, with her father's pill case in his hands. "He took them, honey. See?" He shoved the case at his wife. She studied it then sighed.

"We need to make an appointment with Dr. Allsop to see about adjusting the meds. Until then…" She turned her head, making a point to pin everyone with her eyes. "We all need to be diligent and not leave Dad alone. We don't want him to get upset or frightened if he doesn't recognize where he is."

TJ and Shevonne nodded. Tony's chin lay on his chest. Shevonne released her father's hand and then tipped his face up. She met his gaze. "I'm sorry I freaked out. Now I know being prepared is the rule for the military. You said I have steel will…well, I'll use it to keep you safe." She brushed his wild, white hair off his face and smiled. "I thought you said we had perch to make. Better get crackin'."

Tony ambled to the fridge and removed a large bowl filled with perch and milk. He set it on the counter then returned to the fridge for the eggs, the gallon of milk, and a beer, which he also put on the shelf.

As he worked, Syn pointed to the hall. TJ and Shevonne followed her. As they stood in the front hall, surrounded by photos of their ancestors, the family held a powwow.

"It must be the dosage of the pills. They had kept him focused in the here and now, but now they don't seem to work." TJ grabbed the pill case back from his wife. "I'll return this to the bathroom. I've still got to get the beer, but is there anything else you want me to pick up?"

"No, thanks." Syn reached out and pulled him into her arms. "Thanks for doing it. We'll keep him busy with the fish until you get back. No worries." She forced a smile on her face but it didn't convince anyone.

When TJ headed back upstairs, Shevonne demanded answers. "How many times has he forgotten his meds?"

"A few in the beginning, but once he saw the way they helped, he got on a routine and everything was going well. I almost wish this had been just missing a pill."

"Why do you say that?"

"Because it means his disease is progressing. He's getting worse. I'd hoped we had found a way to keep it at bay." She sighed and rolled her shoulders back and forth, releasing tension.

Shevonne's soft voice held a note of despair. "Is this because I'm here?"

"What?" Her sister grabbed her arm and pulled her out the front door. "This has nothing to do with you. How can you think it?"

"You said he had a routine. My being here has upset it. I've added to the stress around the house, making noise and creating problems for all of you."

Syn ran her palm over her forehead and took a deep breath. "You're right about changes and stress. Those things can cause problems but your being here has been wonderful. Dad's happier than I've seen him in a while. I know he said prayers for you each night you were in Afghanistan. Knowing you are safe at home is a relief and a blessing."

"Are you telling me the truth? You wouldn't lie to spare my feelings?"

"I'd lie about Santa Claus or where the Easter Bunny hid your basket but only after I saw what you got and switched with my own." Syn reached out and tucked a strand of hair behind Shevonne's ear. "But for this...I wouldn't lie. We better get back inside so TJ can leave. And since you stuck me with the coleslaw, you're going to have to clean the bathroom. Just think of it as latrine duty, private." She snickered.

Shevonne sneered at her sister. "Paybacks, baby...paybacks." Shevonne took hold of her sister's arm. They both chuckled as they returned to the kitchen.

CHAPTER SEVEN

Somehow everyone got the food made, the beer picked up, and the house cleaned in time for TJ's firefighter brothers to arrive, although Shevonne wasn't sure how it happened, especially without one of them going ballistic on each other. Events like this always stressed her out, but having strangers in her space when she wasn't at her best...it set her nerves on edge.

While the house still reeked of cabbage, the aroma of the brownies Syn had cooking in the oven was overpowering the coleslaw odor. The hot August humidity decided to head south, so the temperature outside felt more like early fall than sweaty summer with chairs spread out over the deck and lawn. TJ strung up old Christmas lights around the deck, giving it a festive feel. Tony took the deep fryer out in the garage along with a picnic table. It would become the cooking zone.

Shevonne stuck her head out into the garage. The scent of peanut oil and wet potatoes wafted to her nose. "Dad, did TJ put all the beer in the garage fridge?"

"He put a case of beer in there, along with water and soda."

"How will I know what is which?"

"I had him put a couple in the main fridge just for you. They're in your assigned spots so you can decide what you'd like to drink. Just do it responsibly!"

She ran over and gave him a hug. "I'll be good." She wiggled her brows at him and laughed.

"Careful, missy. This oil's boiling hot."

She stepped back and squinted at her father. "Do you think it's safe for you to be doing it?"

He growled. "The day I can't fry up some food for my family and friends is the day you'll have to put me in the ground." He reached over and squeezed her hand. "Sorry, peanut. I know today frightened you. But I'm fine."

Shevonne moved to the picnic table and sat down. "It did, Dad. I can't help but worry you'll have another episode and I won't be able to help you. I won't see it or will be more of a burden because of my vision problems."

"You're coming to grips with so many changes. The loss of your eyes is huge. We rely on them so much and, without them, you stumble in the darkness. But if the time comes and I need help, I know you'll be there. Your heart's big enough to take on any challenge and your strong will gives you the courage to face your fears." He lifted the basket out of the oil and checked the color of the fries then dropped them carefully back into the fryer. "You remind me a lot of your momma. She had your determination."

"Everyone talks about how Syn looks like her. I always thought I wasn't like Mom at all."

"Yep, Syn's her spitting image but she doesn't have her personality. When your momma decided something, she went all out. I remember when we married. She was determined to keep working until you girls came along. However, since we both worked in the same department, it was frowned upon. They didn't want anyone getting preferential treatment, I suppose. But rather than leave the company, she updated her resume and set out to land a job in a different division, far enough away from my job no one would even hint at any fraternization."

"Really? I've never heard that story." Shevonne strolled over and grabbed the cookie sheet off the counter. She laid out two layers of paper towels on top of the pan then handed it to her father.

"Thanks." Tony raised the basket and dumped the fries onto the tray then picked up a handful of fresh-cut potatoes and dropped them into the basket before lowering them into the oil. "I guess, after your mom passed away, I didn't have the heart to talk about her. I missed her so much. Do you remember the time Sherri got in trouble in school and had to write sentences?"

"Sort of. Didn't Mom cause a stink at school?" Shevonne snatched a French fry off the tray and slipped it into her mouth. The salty flavor had her reaching for another.

Her father playfully slapped the back of her hand. "Save some for the guests. Where was I? Your sister was supposed to write 'I will not talk in class' one hundred times in cursive as a punishment. And while your momma felt she deserved a punishment, she didn't agree with writing as one. So she had Sherri write her sentences twenty times and then finished the rest herself." Tony checked on the fries again.

"I don't understand how she showed her determination."

"Of course, Mrs. Norris knew the handwriting was different but to make sure everyone understood her reasons, your mom attached a note to the homework about what punishment she gave Sherri and warned the teacher about any future punishment writing assignments."

"Must have worked. I never had one single sentence to write."

"Your momma was a fierce tiger protecting her girls." He held out the tray now filled with two batches of fries. "Put these in the oven at 250° to keep warm and bring me the perch. I might as well start some of those." A car door

171

slammed. "Hey, our company is arriving. Get moving."

She leaned in and kissed her dad on the cheek. "Thanks for the stories. I'm proud I'm like Mom. I'll be back in a minute."

Shevonne handed the tray to Syn who'd just removed the brownies from the oven and set them on the stovetop to cool. "Dad said to keep these warm while he starts the perch."

Syn turned down the oven and slid the cookie sheet in. "The perch's in the fridge. It's a lot of work to batter and bread those buggers, but they are yummy."

"I seriously had dreams about Dad's perch while in Afghanistan. I even tried to see how much it'd be to order fresh perch and have it shipped, but the cost was outrageous."

"I hear you. I'd order it now and again in Chicago, but it wasn't the same. Dad's three-step breading process is the key."

TJ stomped through the kitchen. "A couple of the guys arrived a few minutes ago. We'll probably throw some horseshoes or play a game of bocce if you want to join us?"

Syn shook her head. "No thanks. I'll leave you and your guys to the games. I'll see if Dad needs any help." She slapped her husband's ass on her way by.

Waving her hand in front of her face, Shevonne shot him a glare. "Hello, almost blind here. You'd win in a heartbeat."

"Actually, with horseshoes, you can hear the sound of the pin if someone taps it and throw toward the sound."

"Then sign me up!" She opened the fridge and pulled out a beer. "When do we start?"

"Meet me on the deck. I'll grab the shoes."

Shevonne slid open the back door and strolled out onto the deck. Voices filled the air. Men conversing about a recent fire run, talking about the upcoming football season, and laughter. The smell of sandalwood and clomping of boots on her left indicated Jackson's arrival.

"Hello, Shevonne. Thank you for having all of us out." His fingers lightly touched her elbow.

She turned and squinted at the handsome man standing next to her. "Good afternoon, Jackson. Dad always puts on the best picnics. I'm glad everyone could come."

"Are you out here to play shoes?" The heat from his body warmed her skin, as she stood near him. She inhaled his scent and tramped down her wayward thoughts of his unclothed body. Unable to see him with her eyes, she could still "see" him with her fingers. She licked her lips as a trickle of sweat slid down her back. Was it hot today or just him? Using her free hand, she fanned her face.

She nodded and allowed Jackson to lead her down the deck steps into the yard. "TJ convinced me I could play even if I can't see the pole. I'm hoping I won't kill anyone with a wild toss." She giggled. "But if it should happen, I'm running and blaming TJ. Just be forewarned. Besides, Dad doesn't need me over his shoulder while he's cooking."

"I'm glad you agreed to play. However, I'll stand next to you when you throw, for my own safety, of course." She nudged him with her hip, stumbling and losing her balance. He tightened his arms around her, keeping her upright. Pressed tight against his body, she felt the evidence of his desire for her. With their lips so close, Shevonne inhaled his exhaled air. *Will he kiss me?* What would his mouth taste like? Time appeared to stand still as she focused on his face. This close, she could see the dimples in his cheeks as well as the dark blue of his eyes. Slowly, the sounds from the backyard returned to her focus. The clank of the horseshoes and the laughter of the men. Shevonne pulled away as she righted herself. Her cheeks burned. She hoped no one had seen how close she and Jackson had been.

"I'm sorry. Such a klutz. I promise not to fall into you anymore." She ran her hands down her jeans and tugged at the hem of her shirt, straightening it.

"No worries. I didn't want to risk you getting hurt." Jackson leaned in and brushed a strand of hair off her face, sliding it behind her ear. "I'd really like to get to know you better."

"Okay..." She was confused. What did he mean? Was he coming on to her? Could he be as tempted by her as she was by him?

"You're adorable with your forehead all wrinkled up. I've probably surprised you. Yet, I'm hoping I'm reading the signs right."

Shevonne rubbed above her eyebrows, trying to erase her creases. Awkward with romance, she didn't believe him about being cute.

He tugged her hand away from her face then leaned over and kissed her cheek. "Can I take you on a date? Spend time with you? Show you I'm serious and not like the guys you've known?"

Shevonne stood in a state of shock. She pinched her arm to see if she'd fallen asleep and was dreaming. Hadn't she been fantasizing about Jackson?

Shevonne nodded then smiled. "I'd like it."

"Good." Jackson folded her smaller hand into his larger one as they walked toward TJ and the other guys. Shevonne saw TJ tilt his head toward her and Jackson, so she smiled at him, giving him her biggest grin.

CHAPTER EIGHT

"Let's get this game started. I call team captain. Jackson, you can be the other captain." TJ bent over and picked up the two silver shoes and banged them together. Jackson grabbed the copper-colored ones, setting them aside on the grass. "Shevonne's on my team. Jackson, you pick a partner."

Jackson glanced around the yard. Some of the guys were stepping away from the game. Two headed into the house. Only Travis appeared interested. Jackson swore if he didn't pick him soon, the man would be jumping up and down screaming "pick me." "Travis, you're with me."

"Are you sure he's going to be okay today?" Shevonne whispered to Jackson.

"He's never been one to hold a grudge. I'll keep an eye on him, though, if it makes you feel better." He ran a finger over her temple and down her cheek. Her voice tight, she could only nod.

TJ used white spray paint to mark the tossing lines and checked on the boxes with sand and poles. He peered at the other players. "We'll let you guys throw first, Jackson. The first team to forty wins."

Jackson tossed his two shoes then Shevonne picked

hers up. TJ used a metal rake to bang on the pole, alerting her to where the pin was. Jackson placed his hands on her hips and helped to make sure she was facing in the right direction. "I don't want to get hit. Remember to listen for the pinging."

Shevonne swung her arm back and let the shoe fly. It hit the pole but rolled away.

Jackson rubbed her shoulder. "Good shot. You were close."

TJ and Travis tallied the points. Then they picked up the shoes for their round.

Jackson grabbed her hand and pulled her off to the side, away from the flying metal, and wrapped his arms around her. She leaned back into his embrace while he whispered the locations of the shoes. After the horseshoes settled, he walked over to count the points. "We're ahead nine to four."

The game continued with Jackson taking every opportunity to touch Shevonne. Her laughter and smiles brightened his day. He enjoyed spending time with her, without trying to score or get her in bed. Eventually, TJ and Shevonne won.

Her laughter echoed through him. "Yes! We won!" Her silly victory dance had other parts of him standing at attention. "And no one got hurt. I'd call this a win-win situation." She jogged toward her brother-in-law and raised her hand for a high five but pulled it out of the way before he could hit it. "Too slow. Who's the blind person now?"

Travis strolled over toward Jackson. A sneer crossed his face as he glanced from Shevonne to her brother. Pulling his wallet from his back pocket, he withdrew a fifty-dollar bill. He waved the money in Jackson's face. "Here. You obviously won it. You got the first kiss and brought her home. Don't know why you picked this one, though." He examined her from her toes to the tip-top of her head. His expression appeared like he'd eaten a rotten peach. "She's too butch for my taste."

"Grrrr…" Jackson gritted his teeth. He pushed the money back at Travis. "You shouldn't have said anything about her. First"—Jackson took two steps toward him. When Travis's eyes widened, he knew he'd made his point but he couldn't stop—"no one talks to a beautiful woman that way." He pushed a finger into Travis's chest, forcing him to take a step back. "And, second, she's the woman who took down your scrawny ass. She doesn't need me to fight her battles. She can kick your butt with one hand behind her back."

Out of the corner of his eye, Jackson saw TJ stomping his way toward them. Shevonne held on to his arm, trying to keep him from exploding on Travis. "Why you son of a bitch…" TJ reached out with his free arm, trying to grab Travis, but Jackson stepped in front of him.

"I've got this. No need for you to kick his butt, too." Jackson tried to soothe TJ's anger. However, when he saw the pain on Shevonne's face, he stepped aside. "On second thought, he's all yours. I've got someone more important to worry about."

Jackson pulled Shevonne into his arms. "I'm sorry about what he said. You have to know it's not true…not to me." He wished she could see herself through his eyes. "One of the things I admire most about you is how you've stood on your own feet, first fighting in Afghanistan, among a primarily male group of soldiers, and secondly, here with your family. You've not let your vision problems get in the way of remaining independent. Finally, I've enjoyed the time we spent together, and I know we haven't known each other very long, but I'd love to spend more time with you if you'll let me." He leaned over, cupped her face in his palms, and kissed her passionately.

Her hands slid under his T-shirt and over his back, alternating gentle caresses with tight grips. His tongue pushed against her lips, demanding entrance, but the loud sounds of skin hitting skin had Jackson pulling away. He brushed his thumb over her now-swollen lips. "Sorry, darling. I've got to stop this before it gets out of hand." He loved the sensual daze that filled her eyes. He longed to lift her into his arms and sneak away where they could be alone and he could prove to her how sexy she was. But since Travis had started this by being a certified asshole and the party was at TJ's house, Jackson didn't want the whole thing ruined.

He trudged over to the fight. TJ landed his fair share of punches on Travis, even though the younger man was stockier. Many of the other firefighters had gathered around and were shouting, egging them on. Suddenly, gunfire filled the air causing everyone to jump and TJ and Travis to break apart.

Mr. Wilder stood on the deck, his twelve-gauge in his hand. Syn stood next to him, holding onto his belt loop. For her support or his, Jackson wasn't sure. Syn ran to her husband the minute he stepped away from Travis. TJ rubbed his chin as if it hurt but seemed no worse for wear. Travis's eye had begun to swell and his bottom lip bled.

Heat flooded Jackson's face. "Thank you, Mr. Wilder. I'm sorry this happened at your party. You were kind to invite all of us here to enjoy your perch, ones you caught along with TJ." He pointed to his best friend. "And we take advantage of your hospitality by starting a fight. I'm sorry, sir, for disrespecting your home."

TJ held onto Syn's hand as they wandered over to Mr. Wilder. Jackson hadn't meant to cause trouble, nor did he want to upset Mr. Wilder or leave Shevonne. He desired to get to know her and convince her he truly had fallen for her. He scanned the yard for her, only to find her leaning on the back wall of the garage, not far from where he left her. Jackson ached to go to her side, but he didn't dare move until things were settled. For all he knew, he would be asked to leave and never return. Moving from one foot to his other, he anxiously awaited their next move.

TJ whispered to his father-in-law while everyone waited for the verdict. Finally, he stepped forward. His voice carried across the backyard. "The perch is ready. Let's forget this and enjoy some local treats. Tony and Syn have everything set up in the garage. Come fix a plate and feed yourselves." Carefully, TJ pried Mr. Wilder's fingers off his gun, checked to make sure it no longer had any shells inside, flipped on the safety then slipped his arm around his wife before leading the group to the garage.

Travis pulled his keys from his pocket. "Steve. You'll have to catch another ride home. I'm not staying here." Not even waiting for his friend's answer, Travis stormed to his car and drove off.

***

Shevonne had seen red once again because of Travis. Was he a sore loser? Or did he have a grudge against Jackson? He certainly set out to cause problems. She'd be more than happy if he never returned, but she knew this incident, combined with the one at the bar, had caused a rift in the fire department. She hoped they wouldn't be asked to take sides.

She lifted her finger to her lips and softly rubbed it over them as she thought about Jackson's kiss. Closing her eyes, she recalled how demanding he was, devouring her mouth. Shevonne tugged at her jeans, pulling them away from her core where her now-wet panties clung.

Had this really happened? What about my decision not to get involved? Are we involved? Questions flew through her mind so fast she needed speed limit signs to figure them out. Had this only begun yesterday? Was she rushing into disaster? When Jackson touched her, even just a brush of his body against hers, she couldn't think. Certainly, her body responded to him, but had her heart? She pondered these questions, not listening to her father's and TJ's speeches. The smell of sandalwood alerted her to Jackson's presence. She turned and squinted at him. What was it about him that made her melt?

"I'm an ass for letting Travis start the fight." He dropped down onto the grass and leaned his back against the side of the garage.

She glanced over at him. He appeared forlorn and genuinely upset. His eyes were focused on his hands twisting in his lap. Shevonne scooted down and sat next to him. She gently placed her hand on top of his, stopping his motion. "It wasn't your fault. From what I've seen of Travis, he's an arrogant toad. He pushes people's buttons when he can't get what he wants. It's like a spoiled two-year-old."

"How did you get so smart?" He brushed a strand of hair off her face and behind her ear.

"Met a lot of arrogant jerks in the military. Many of the privates had chips on their shoulders, trying to prove something, especially to the women. They picked fights with us, name-called, hit on us, and lied about things we did or didn't do." She raised her chin and stared up at the sky. "It wasn't all of them, but enough. Usually, the ones who treated us like slaves or whores were the ones who came at us in the other ways once they noticed we weren't giving in."

"It sounds like your days were constant battles."

"Only in the beginning. Once we established how we wanted to be treated, they left us alone."

"How did you do it?"

"Sometimes, taking them down a peg like I did with Travis. Other times, it was reminding them of my rank or skill set."

"You are so very talented." He leaned in for a kiss but Shevonne raised her hand.

"We need to talk."

He pulled away and relaxed against the building. "The final words of all relationships, dreaded by couples everywhere."

She tugged his hand into hers, entwining their fingers. It felt good to sit and simply talk, get to know each other and connect on a non-physical level. "We've known each other for two days. I want to explore what's going on. I've seen the men in uniform come on strong but I didn't have any feelings for them. I only want to know where I stand and what's going on in your mind."

He smiled. "I'd hoped I was clear. I want to spend time with you. You turn me on...both my body and my mind."

Shevonne tilted her head and thought about his words. "I thought you were a playboy. TJ warned me before the party to be careful. He noticed your attention last night." Carefully she selected what she said. "What's changed? What makes me different?"

"Seriously, I was jealous of TJ for finding such a wonderful woman to spend his life with. But you're ten times better than Syn." He placed his hands on her face, leaned in for a quick kiss then returned to holding hers. "Don't get me wrong. She's great. But you can hold your own. We're equals, not me taking care of you."

"So your playboy status was a result of the women being weak?" Still struggling to get at the heart of what he'd said, she pressed the issue.

Jackson kissed her fingers then squeezed her hand. "In high school, I didn't belong in the cool crowd. When they wore their designer clothes, I wore Western shirts. TJ and your sister were the exceptions to the rule. They welcomed me for me. Returning to Amherst and becoming a firefighter wasn't my dream in school, but it became a dream come true after my folks died. Since I'd never sowed my wild oats when I was younger, when the girls noticed I was a fireman, they jumped on me. It messed with my head."

Shevonne nodded. "I understand..."

"It didn't take long for me to gain a reputation as a ladies' man, and once you have a rep...it's easy to keep it. I haven't been with any woman in the last year. The single life had soured and I wanted a real relationship, one like my parents had. I longed for a companion in the truest sense of the word…a partner." Jackson hung his head and didn't glance at her.

"How long have your parents been gone?" She ran a finger over the back of his hand.

"They've been dead for four years. This might sound strange, but I'm glad they went together. They wouldn't have been happy apart." He surveyed the sky. "In my lifetime, they never spent more than a few hours away from each other."

Shevonne stood and tugged on Jackson's hand, helping him rise. "I'd love to have a relationship like theirs someday. And I'm willing to give you a chance." She leaned in and kissed him on the cheek. "But, right now, I'm hungry. It's been too long since I've had some of Dad's Lake Erie Perch."

She jogged around the garage, pulling Jackson along behind her. As they rounded the front corner, she heard the sizzle of the fryer and smelled the fish cooking. "Dad…" she called out. "Please, tell me you have some perch left."

She stopped. Her mouth hung open. "Dad?" The garage was empty. Walking into the garage, she examined the fryer. The basket held floating fish, cooking in the oil. "He can't have gone far. Can you go into the house and see if he's in there?"

Jackson ran through the back door while Shevonne pulled the overcooked fish from the fryer. She unplugged the oil and strolled around the outside, searching for her father.

As she returned to the garage, Jackson, TJ, and Syn were waiting. Her sister ran toward her. "Did you see Dad?"

She shook her head. "I walked around the house but no sign. I even asked the guys out back playing cornhole if they'd seen him. But nothing. Wasn't he in the house?"

"TJ, Jackson, and I searched the upstairs, the bathrooms, his bedroom, the basement, even the closets.

He wasn't anywhere. It's like he disappeared."

TJ came over and stood at his wife's back, placing his hands on her shoulders.

"Has this ever happened before?" Shevonne twisted her hands as she stood outside the garage. She hoped her father would materialize from behind the tree and shout "surprise" as he often did when they were kids.

"No. But, Shea...I'm worried. With the episode he had today, we know the meds aren't working as well. What if he wandered off?" She turned into her husband's embrace.

Shevonne glanced at Jackson. "You don't think Travis would have done anything to Dad, do you?"

"He'd be stupid to do it. But we have to check out every situation. I'm going to get the guys from the backyard and organize a search." He sprinted over and kissed Shevonne's cheek before heading around back.

Shevonne darted over to where TJ and her sister stood then patted Syn on the back. "Don't worry. We'll find him."

MELISSA KEIR

CHAPTER NINE

TJ set up a command center in the home with the firefighters fanning out in the neighborhood to search for Mr. Wilder.

TJ stated, "None of the cars were missing, so he had to be on foot." Unless...Jackson didn't want to consider if Travis had a part in Shevonne's missing father.

Syn, as the voice of reason, jumped in. "You guys are wonderful, but if we don't find him within five hours, we'll contact the police. They have more resources than you do."

"Agreed." TJ's voice held a touch of anger.

"The fish were only slightly burnt, so your father can't have been gone long." Jackson wrapped his arm around her, offering hope. "I'll bring him home." His feelings for Shevonne surprised him, but his father had been the same way with his mother. Love at first glance, he used to say.

"He's going to be found." She lifted her chin and stood taller.

He stiffened with her announcement then nodded.

"But I'm going to search, too."

Jackson didn't want to leave her out. Her lack of sight could hinder her, even with her knowledge of her father.

He'd rather she stay behind, but it appeared as if she was ready for a fight. "Sure. Come with me. I could use the help. TJ's staying here with your sister. He's pulled up a map of the neighborhood on his computer and has sent teams to each quadrant."

"Where's he sending us?" She grabbed a jacket out of the front closet along with a flashlight and tied a large gray sweatshirt around her waist.

Jackson examined her getup, a big grin on his face. She appeared adorable, but he'd risk an ass kicking if he told her so. "What are you doing?"

"Being prepared. The sweatshirt is for Dad, when we find him. I can use it for a variety of needs from bandages to warming him. The flashlight's handy for garages or as evening falls. I'm not coming home without him, even if it takes all night."

Her determination filled him with pride. Wasn't being prepared a part of military training? It was obvious she thought things through, better than any of the other groups did. None of them brought anything with them other than their cell phones. "Let's grab a bottle of water and some extra batteries. You're right about being prepared." He pulled on a jacket and stuffed the batteries and water into the pockets. "We are heading west to the VFW Hall and surrounding area. Are you ready to roll?"

"Let's go."

Since Mr. Wilder had been on foot, Jackson and Shevonne walked along Lake Street. "Dad," Shevonne called out every other minute.

They examined each driveway and backyard, inspecting under decks and listening for noises. But nothing. With each step farther away from Shevonne's home, Jackson's worry grew. It would be dark in an hour. The temperature would drop. He recalled how cold it'd been in Wyoming those summers. He needed to break the tension building from the unsuccessful search. "We need a break. Let's sit for a minute. Did I ever tell you how I almost stayed out

West and ran a ranch?"

Shevonne plopped down on the grassy area off the road. "You mentioned how you came home after your parents' deaths but not much else about your summers as a cowboy." Shevonne hugged her legs, laying her chin on her knees.

"I met a girl."

She giggled. "Doesn't every story begin with I met a girl?"

"Probably. In this case, Jenna, the ranch owner's daughter, and I dated. We were both young and thought we knew what love was. While her dad didn't mind the idea of our dating, Jenna took exception with my bronc riding."

Shevonne's eyes widened. "I've seen people get killed riding those horses."

"That's almost what happened. Bucked off and stomped on, I broke more bones than I'd like to recall. The doctors didn't want to let me back on and neither did Jenna. That didn't deter me from doing it again and again. Jenna couldn't handle seeing me in danger and gave me the ultimatum to stop or she'd dump me. Being stupid, I rode one last time then walked away, headed back to Amherst, and enrolled in firefighter training. All in all, while I lost her, it turned out for the best. I got to spend time with my folks before they died."

She leaned over and laid her head on his shoulder. "Each time we seek to escape our small town life, it draws us back."

"True. If it hadn't, we wouldn't have met." He brushed his lips across her forehead. "We've rested enough. We'd better get back to searching." Jackson stood and held out his hand to Shevonne. She placed hers in his and he tugged her up, pulling her into his arms. His body molded against hers. His hardness to her soft curves. He watched as she licked her lips and knew she wasn't immune to this desire coursing between them. Jackson tipped his head down and captured her lips with his. A gentle kiss, promising more later. As he pulled away, she sighed. The sound almost brought him to his knees. What began as passion had deepened into more.

"We should check in with TJ and see if anything's come up." Shevonne shivered and pulled her jacket tighter around her body.

Jackson pulled his cell phone out of his pocket and called. "TJ, any word?"

"Most of the other guys have returned. One group found a jacket on the ground and thought it might have been Tony's, but nothing. Turned out to be a woman's coat. Syn's cleaning the house. It's her way of coping with stress. How is Shevonne holding up? Any luck on your end?"

"No sight, yet. We're about two blocks away from the VFW. Just rested for a bit. We're going to keep searching. Shevonne is determined to not give up."

"I don't know what those girls will do if something happens to him. Take care of her for us. Check back in when you reach the VFW."

"Will do." Jackson ended the conversation and slipped his phone back into his pocket. "No word yet. A few teams are still out. Let's keep going."

***

Shevonne's body zinged like a live wire. She ached to pursue her passion with Jackson. However, her heart needed to find her father, alive and well. Conflicted didn't express her feelings strongly enough. She beat herself up inside for even considering falling in love when her father was missing or perhaps hurt. The names she called herself each time she "forgot" about her father for a second, the anger at allowing herself to be happy...hateful messages played over and over in her mind.

As they continued down Lake Street, Shevonne

shouted her father's name. With the darkness, she swung the flashlight back and forth along the yards and houses. While she couldn't see anything besides shapes, she counted on Jackson to search the shadows for her dad. At each house, they paused to listen for sounds. She'd begun to lose hope.

At the corner of Jackson and Lake Streets, a small city park sat waiting for the sunshine and school kids. A lone swing squeaked as the wind blew it back and forth.

"Dad. Are you here? Answer me?" Shevonne hollered.

As she turned away from the playground, a sound whispered across the distance.

"Pea?"

Unsure if she'd heard it, Shevonne paused and held up her hand to Jackson. "Wait. I thought I heard something," she whispered. *Please, please, please be him.*

They stood frozen, waiting. Squeak. The swing moved again.

"Help." The voice came again, soft and from off to the side, near the play structure.

Shevonne pointed. "I hear something coming from over there."

"Are you sure? I didn't hear anything?" Shevonne nodded. "Let's go check it out."

They marched toward the large wooden structure standing sentinel in the dark playground. The sound of their feet crunching over fall leaves covered any other noises. But they'd stopped listening in an effort to reach the area. Shevonne silently said a prayer, hoping they'd finally found him.

Shevonne shone the flashlight on the playscape. The glint of eyes near the ground flashed.

"Here. Let me have the flashlight." Jackson reached over and scooped it out of her hands. "I thought I saw something." He shone the light again on the ground under the two-story platform.

The sickly sweet odor of skunk floated on the air.

Shevonne moved from one foot to the other, hoping her father had been found.

"What did you see? Was it Dad?" Shevonne tugged on Jackson's sleeve.

"Not unless your dad can become a skunk. This one seems angry, too."

She sighed. Shevonne swore she'd heard him call out her nickname. Could she have let her wishes drive what she heard? "I smell Mr. Skunk when the wind blows this way. I hope he didn't get anyone's dog. Poor thing would be miserable."

Jackson turned away from the wooden structure and shone the flashlight beam over the rest of the playground. "We should keep going, head to the VFW."

Shevonne dropped her shoulders. Defeat filled her heart. "I suppose. But I know I heard something."

"Probably the skunk in the leaves. Or maybe the dog he blasted." He patted her on the shoulder. "We will find him. I promise."

"Doooooonnnnnt..." the voice whispered across the breeze. Shevonne startled and turned back toward the structure. "I heard it again. Shine the light higher on the structure."

Jackson splayed the light across the second story of the structure. The slats protecting children from falling filled in the shadows, but the light revealed what had been hidden. "Oh my gosh."

"What?" Shevonne's heart beat so loudly, she was sure the skunk could hear it. "What do you see?"

"Your dad."

CHAPTER TEN

Jackson couldn't believe his eyes. Mr. Wilder rested against the side of the railing on the second story of the playscape. "Hold on, Tony. We're coming."

Shevonne hopped up and down as if she might take off at any minute. He couldn't have her climbing blind in the dark. He shoved the flashlight at her. "Hold this on him so I can get him down."

First things first. He needed to get rid of the skunk. Jackson studied the ground around him and found a few rocks and a stick. He certainly didn't want to end up smelling. First, he tossed a rock at the animal, hoping it would take the hint and run off. But it didn't move. Another rock went sailing. This one hit the skunk on the nose, eliciting a screech from it.

"Be careful. But hurry." Jackson heard the worry in her voice but also knew she was anxious to see her father.

However, still no movement by the bloody beast. *At least, it's not coming at me.* Jackson needed to get Mr. Wilder down. He couldn't assess him from the ground. Growling like a bear and swinging his arms, Jackson advanced on the animal. He would use the stick as a last-ditch effort if it didn't move. Luckily, acting like a large ferocious animal

191

worked. The skunk took off away from the playground, through the tree line.

With his impediment removed, Jackson climbed up the side and over the railing. Finally, he could see Mr. Wilder. "Shevonne, can you move to the left and shine the flashlight up higher? I need the light up here. But keep your ears on the woods. If the skunk comes back, let me know."

"All right. But how is Dad?" Her voice held frustration. He knew she'd scamper up here after him in a second, just to see her father and hold him tight.

Jackson ran his hands over the man's limbs. "Mr. Wilder. It's Jackson Gambish. I'm here with your daughter, Shevonne. She's down below. Are you okay? Do you hurt anywhere? Any injuries?"

Other than the dampness of his clothes and the reek of skunk, Jackson couldn't find anything wrong. As the light shifted, he saw how incorrect he was. Mr. Wilder's eyes were red and swollen. His face appeared sunburnt, although his skin was chilled, and some scratches marred his hands. "What happened?"

"Skkkuuunnnkkk." Tears slid down Tony's face.

Jackson hollered down to Shevonne. "Your dad got into an altercation with the skunk. He reeks and his face is swollen, but he's okay. I'm going to bring him down."

The flashlight's beam danced with Shevonne's excitement.

"Mr. Wilder. We're going to get you home, but we need to get down. I think the slide is the best. Can you move over to it?"

"Skkkkkuuunnkkkk." His body started shaking.

"The skunk left. Shevonne's waiting and Syn's at home cleaning the house. Scoot over to the slide. We'll go down just like I did in school, you in front and my body holding yours." Jackson helped the older gentleman to the slide. His shaking stopped when Jackson pulled him into his arms. He laid his legs on the outside of Mr. Wilder's then wrapped his arms around Tony's stomach. Once secure, they slid down the slide.

Shevonne ran over and tugged her father into her arms, squeezing him tight, despite the horrible odor coming off his body. Tears slid down her cheeks. Was it from the smell or happiness? Did it matter? Jackson led Mr. Wilder over to the nearest bench. He tugged the sweatshirt off Shevonne's waist and wrapped it around his shoulders. Shevonne slid on the bench next to her father.

"Can you hand me the water?" Jackson held his hand out toward her. He tore a small piece of the bottom of his T-shirt off, poured the water over it, and gently wiped Tony's eyes and face. "This is only a temporary cleaning. When we get you back to the house, we'll get you all cleaned up."

Jackson pulled the cell out of his pocket and held it out for Shevonne. "Can you call TJ and your sister? We also should get a car to pick us up. I don't want Tony walking back."

Shevonne jumped off the bench and dialed the number.

"TJ. We found Dad..." She spoke with her brother-in-law and set up the pickup.

Jackson cupped Tony's cheeks and forced him to meet his gaze. "Are you okay? I need to know. Your daughters have been frantic with worry."

"Ffffiiinneee. Eyyyyyeesss bbbbuuurrrnnn. Sooooo Goddddd Dammnnn Ccccooolllddd."

Mr. Wilder continued to stutter, which worried Jackson. He didn't like how fragile the older man looked either. It seemed as if he'd been gone a year even though it'd been less than three hours. He tore another strip off his shirt and cleaned the scratches on his hands before handing the water bottle over to him.

"You better drink some. Frankly, sir, I'm not sure I'd have wanted to go toe-to-toe with that beast. You'll have a story to share when we get you home, safe and sound."

Shevonne put her hand on her father's shoulder. "TJ's on his way with a change of clothes. I heard Syn screaming in the background." She bent over and brushed a kiss over her father's whiskered cheek. "I'm so glad we found you." She shook her finger at him. "We were worried sick." Suddenly, she broke into tears.

"Ppppeeeaaannnuuuttt." Mr. Wilder reached out a hand as Shevonne crumpled to the leafy carpet.

Jackson scooped her up in his arms and sat on the bench, cradling her in his arms. Large sobs and gasps for breath echoed throughout the park. "Shhh…honey." Jackson kissed her forehead. "Your dad's safe and going home. No more tears."

***

As a vehicle drove into the park, the crunch of tires on the rock driveway calmed Shevonne. Her face heated over her breakdown. She'd always been so strong, but she couldn't maintain this time. Imagining losing her father, she'd knotted up her stomach and blockaded her feelings. When she knew he was safe, the dam broke, sending her into a mess of tears. She hadn't broken down like this since her mother's funeral. She hadn't shed one single tear over her own vision loss, but the fear of losing her father turned her into a bawling baby.

Now composed, she sat up, wiped away the water on her face, kissed Jackson on the cheek, and slowly got to her feet. She took a deep breath before meeting the gazes of the two men she cared about. "I'm fine, now. I guess I held everything in too tight and it collapsed on me."

"You've been brave for so long. We understand, right Mr. W?" Jackson patted her father on the back. "Sounds like your ride is here. Let's get you home."

TJ and Syn jumped out of the car as soon as it was parked. They sprinted over and took turns grabbing and hugging everyone. Shevonne smiled at the tears on Syn's face. She didn't feel so awkward about her own meltdown anymore.

"Dad, you need a bath. We brought some warmed-up tomato juice to use to cut the smell, a bag for your clothes, and even a heated jug of water for a quick shower. You will be back to your old self in no time." Syn waved her hand at TJ, which sent him running back toward the car. She put her arm around her dad and assisted him. Just like her sister to come in and take charge. *I suppose it comes with being the oldest. Syn always likes things her way. Better not to argue.*

Shevonne hung back and stared at the play structure. Still so many unanswered questions. The crunch of the leaves heralded Jackson's arrival. He wrapped his arms around her from behind, pulling her body back against his. She laid her head on his chest and sighed. "Thank you."

"For what?" His breath brushed over her ear, warming her cheek.

"Everything." Shevonne struggled to put into words all he'd done, not only the finding of her father and bringing him down safely but the strength he gave her during her meltdown.

"I haven't solved the world peace problem, yet. But I'm working on it." His voice held a note of teasing, and she couldn't help but smile.

Shevonne turned in his arms and gazed up at his face. She ran her hands over his face, hoping to memorize with her fingers what she knew with her vision. The scruffy whiskers that graced his chiseled chin. The strong brow framing his light-blue eyes. The full lips prone to smiles more than frowns. Had it only been two days? How could she have fallen in love so quickly? While she'd not been able to see his features clearly with her eyes, she knew him deeply within her heart. "I'm sure we reek as well as Dad. What are the odds Syn thought of it and brought things for us, too?"

"With your sister, anything is possible." Jackson leaned in and placed a kiss on her nose then stepped back. He curled her hand in his own, giving it a squeeze. "Let's see how your dad is doing and find out about the clothes."

The crisp fall air blew Shevonne's hair around her face as they strolled toward the parking lot. Occasional shouts and swear words punctuated the silence. Even with warmed water, Shevonne was convinced bathing outside would be miserable. Hearing her father's screams, she smiled. The hollering was a blessing since it meant he was safe and alive.

When she reached the lot, she paused for a moment to take in the sight.

Her father stood in a large metal washtub, wearing only his boxers. Tomato juice pooled around his feet. He scrubbed his skin and hair with soap. TJ held a pitcher of water which he poured over Mr. Wilder's head about every other minute. The dowsing was what caused the fiery outbursts.

"Hey, Dad, I didn't know you had such a colorful vocabulary. Your words would beat the guys in camp. I vow, sometimes they made up new swear words so they could outdo each other." She hid her smile behind her hand.

"It's okay, Mr. Wilder. The firefighters have a pretty spectacular vocabulary, too," TJ explained. "Hold your breath. Another dousing." He poured the water over his head.

This time, he held his language in check.

"The ranch hands have all of you beat. Those men swore a country mile. They liked to chew as well." Jackson added his two cents.

"Glad you never took it up." Shevonne leaned in and kissed him on the cheek.

"All right. I think Dad's had enough." Syn handed her father a large bath sheet and helped wrap him up. TJ opened the back door of the car and waved Mr. Wilder in. "There's clean clothes on the seat. Put them on and we'll go home."

Shevonne motioned TJ over while her father dressed, determined to get answers. "Did he say what happened?"

"He mentioned a battle with the skunk but not how he got there." He shrugged.

"Do you think it was an episode? You've seen them before." She bit her lip.

"Quite possibly. He doesn't seem to remember, which isn't a good sign. Then there was the issue earlier today. He needs to see the doctor right away." He reached over and squeezed her hand. "We'll call in the morning."

A gruff voice boomed. "I'm dressed. Can we go home now? I've had enough adventure for one night."

CHAPTER ELEVEN

"The dementia's getting worse," Dr. Allsop explained. "However, in moderate stages, there's a new medication that has shown some promise. With your approval, I'd like to add Namenda to his other medications."

Shevonne sat holding her father's larger hand in her own. His memory losses had become scary when they led to him going missing or accidentally setting the house on fire. While she wasn't convinced medications were the way to go, Shevonne would do anything to get her dad back to normal.

"What side effects can we expect?" Syn piped in. She'd been his caregiver for the last six months. It was only right she get her say.

"Headaches, constipation, confusion, and dizziness...but these vary in each individual." The doctor tapped his pen on the desk. He reached for a package of pills and handed them across to Syn. "Here's a sample pack. Tony, you can begin it right away, while I also give you a prescription."

Shevonne abruptly stood. "Confusion? He's already confused. This med's going to make it worse?" She paced behind her father's chair, her hands clenched in fists.

Syn reached out and stopped her. "Shea. We have to do something. We are losing Dad." Shea watched the grimace cross her father's face. It broke her heart to see him having to make these decisions.

Syn's pleading continued. "Neither of us wants to make things worse, but we have to do something. He could've been really hurt last night. Again, his guardian angel kept him safe."

"I was there. I found him."

"Well, I helped wash the skunk off and took care of him while you were off overseas."

"Girls. No fighting. I'll take the meds. It's my call and what I say goes." Tony's gruff voice sounded less forceful than it had only the day before. *Did I hear it wobble? See, even Dad's not convinced he should take the medicine.*

Shevonne paused, squinted, and studied her father. Never had he appeared so worn down, old. The events of last night had only made it worse. She turned to the doctor. "What happens if this doesn't work? Are there any other treatments? Things we can do at home? I've heard about using brain-type activities such as word searches and such can help." She hated how needy she sounded. But if she needed to beg or make a pact with God, she'd do it.

At this point, Shevonne hated the entire world. She didn't understand why so many people in her family faced challenges. Her brother-in-law Adam had almost died this past Christmas, her father's disease, the loss of her mother all those years ago as well as her own vision issues. Only Syn had escaped the bad karma. Shevonne hoped things would turn around soon, especially now that she'd found love.

"The studies have shown doing those things help slow early onset. Your father is past the early stage. While maintaining a healthy lifestyle, low-fat food, exercise, and no smoking, everyone will live longer. Those would help your father, even in his condition. However, we need to be more aggressive with the medications. If this one doesn't work, we do have a different one we can use, but I'd rather try this one since the side effects aren't as strong."

Shevonne plopped back down in her chair, a big sigh escaping her lips.

"I understand your frustration." Dr. Allsop stood and strolled around his desk, perching on the front and leaning over to talk with Syn and Shevonne. "Did you know most Alzheimer's patients can live twenty years with this disease? That's providing other things don't kill them in the meantime." *Get on with it.* Shevonne wanted…needed, so strong it felt like tightness in her chest.

The good doctor continued, "Your father has many wonderful years left. The medication will slow down the memory loss."

And, just like that, the tightness lifted. Shevonne jumped out of her chair. Unable to contain her emotions, she paced once again.

Her dad would be with them for years yet. While she understood the words from the doctor weren't promises, they were a gift. Healing and hope. Shevonne released the deep breath she'd been holding and smiled at the doctor. "As long as the meds give him time." She nodded, indicating the other people in the room. "Dad's got to live to see the second generation grow up. Mom missed out on too much. I'm"—her voice cracked—"not ready to lose him, too."

She leaned over her father, wrapped her arms around his shoulders, and squeezed. "Did you hear what the doctor said, old man? You have to take your meds, eat healthy, and exercise. I'm going out later today and signing you up for the gym."

Syn shook the doctor's hand. "Thank you. Can your nurse phone the script into the pharmacy? I'll have my sister get it when she gets back from the gym." The happiness in her sister's voice had Shevonne laughing inside.

"I can get a family discount," she teased. "We can all

go." Shevonne looped her arm in her father's, while she grabbed onto her sister with her other arm. "Let's leave the good doctor. Poor man must have some sick patients around here. Not the Wilders though. We can stop at the Quarry Café for lunch. My treat."

After lunch, they returned home. Shevonne couldn't sit still. She paced the floor, her boots clomping on the carpet. "Syn, I need to get out. I'm walking uptown. I'll stop at the pharmacy and grab Dad's script."

"Thanks. Can you drop the leftover fish to the station? I'm sure the guys would appreciate the treats, especially the guys who missed yesterday's feast. But don't worry. I left enough for us to have some for dinner tonight."

"Will do." Shevonne ran upstairs and grabbed her backpack then stomped back down to the kitchen. "You got the to-go package ready?"

Syn handed over the fish wrapped in foil. "Here you go." Pulling a card off the fridge, Syn held it out to her sister. "Here's Dad's insurance card. Call if you have any problems."

Pocketing the card and stuffing the leftovers in her backpack, Shevonne slung it over her shoulder. She waved and skipped out the front door.

A light breeze blew through her hair as the sun warmed her skin. Shevonne pulled her earbuds out of her pocket and turned on her jams. Wearing only one of the buds, she set her pace to the beat of classic rock. With the bright sunshine, she could see the houses and trees as shadows, although she'd walked these streets so often as a teenager, she knew them by heart. One block, two blocks, three…she headed toward the downtown business district.

The rumble of the train on the track bridge above her pounded on the pavement. She pulled her earbud from her ears and paused to watch the rail cars loaded with automobiles go by. Finally, when she saw the last car pass, she stuffed the left earbud back in and continued on her way.

Two more blocks and Shevonne stood in front of the pharmacy. The large glass doors opened with a whoosh. The smell of perfume hit her nostrils as soon as she entered. Some child must have been playing among the aisles. She recalled the many times she and her sisters had come home drenched in Chanel. How Mom tolerated being in the same car, she'd never know.

Elevator music floated through the store, along with coughs and cries of sick children. As she approached the pharmacy counter, she noticed a familiar scent— sandalwood.

Craning her neck to try to find him, Shevonne jumped when a hand touched her shoulder. "What?"

"I'm sorry. Are you one of the Wilder girls?" a soft voice asked. Disappointment coursed through her veins. She'd hoped Jackson had stopped her.

Shevonne squinted to make out who spoke. An older lady stood next to her. Light-silver hair was piled high on her head, adding three inches to the very petite woman. "Yes. I'm Shevonne, the youngest. And you are…?"

"I'm Betty Carson. I belong to your father's church. We haven't seen him in a while, and I wanted to ask about his health." The lady leaned in. "We miss having him sing at Sunday service."

Shevonne's eyes widened. Her dad, singing? She'd enjoy seeing it. "I'm sorry, Mrs. Carson. Dad's been dealing with a health crisis, but since you asked, I'll be sure to mention it to him."

The woman put her hand on Shevonne's arm. "I'll say extra prayers for him. And once I let the rest of the girls know, I'm sure he'll receive many more. Would it be possible for him to have visitors?"

Shevonne couldn't say no, especially after the hopeful note in the woman's voice. "I'm sure he'd be happy to see a friendly face. I'll also make it my duty to see he gets back to church on Sundays."

Betty patted Shevonne's arm. "Thank you. You're such a dear. He spoke about you."

"Really?" She hoped she didn't sound too needy.

"He's very proud of all his daughters. Shows off his pictures every chance he gets, but he's extra proud of you and your service. According to him, you singlehandedly prevented many world crises." She giggled.

Shevonne placed her hand on Betty's. "Thank you for sharing. Please feel free to stop by. A friendly face will do Dad a world of good. I'm sorry to leave you, but I have to pick up Dad's script. I'm sure we'll see each other soon."

As she turned away, she bumped into a brick wall that smelled of sandalwood. "Omph." She glanced up and squinted. Her heart beat extra hard in her chest.

"Hello, there." His deep voice resonated through her.

"I'd hoped to run into you, but not like this."

"How did you know I was here?" He stabilized her then took a step back.

"Your cologne. It's distinctive, and I smelled it when I walked back here." Shevonne gripped the straps of her backpack. She longed to touch him but didn't know if she should. The rules of dating confused her.

"Do you like the way I smell?" His voice held a hint of teasing.

She wasn't sure if he was laughing at her or flirting. *Damn. It's appears so much easier in romance novels.* Fear settled in her stomach. She'd remembered being the butt of jokes at school when she told Frank how much she liked him. Her straightforward style sent the boys running in the other direction. "Yes. The cologne's pleasant. I've got to grab Dad's script and drop off the fish at the station. I'd better get going." Shevonne sped away toward the pharmacy register.

CHAPTER TWELVE

Jackson watched her go. *Are the meds urgent? Did something happen to Mr. Wilder?* He was confused. One minute they'd been flirting, and the next, Shevonne buzzed away like her butt was on fire.

Whenever he was around her, he became tongue-tied and unsure of himself. He couldn't gauge her reaction either. It was hot and cold. He mulled things over as he wandered the store. He'd forgotten what he'd come in for. His mind played with the puzzle that was Shevonne.

Frustration set in. Jackson had spent last night tossing and turning in bed. He'd spoken to TJ when they got Mr. Wilder home and settled. Jackson didn't want his feelings for Shevonne to be a problem with her family. After receiving TJ's blessing, he thought things would be fine, but after this latest meeting, he wasn't convinced. He needed to come right out and ask her.

He paced around the pharmacy, hoping to find her, but she'd likely left. She'd said she needed to drop off food at the station. *I'll catch her there.*

Jackson hiked over the two blocks to the station house. The garage doors were open and a few of the guys were sitting out front in lawn chairs with plates of fish in their hands. "Hi, Moore. Howdy, Reynolds. Is Shevonne still here?"

"Was she the angel who brought the fish?" Reynolds spoke around the food in his mouth.

"Yes. She's TJ's sister-in-law." He watched Moore continue to stuff fish in his face. The man didn't stop to breathe. *He'd be a shoo-in at the hot dog eating contest at the church fundraiser.*

"She left about five minutes ago." Reynolds pointed toward the road. "She was on foot. You'll probably catch her."

"Thanks!" He started to leave but paused. "Hey, Moore. Be careful and watch out for bones. I know the fish was filleted but you know how those small bones can get by. I don't want Reynolds here having to do CPR on you." Jackson waved to his friends and jogged up Main Street, his gaze searching for Shevonne. *Where are you?* Jackson Street—no sign. He sprinted under the train bridge, his breath escaping in pants. His heart beating against the sides of his chest. It'd been a long time since he'd run this quickly.

"Where's the fire?"

Her voice stopped him dead in his tracks. Turning, he saw Shevonne lounging along the side of the hill. He paused with his hands on his knees, bent over. "Someone call for a fireman?" When he caught his breath, he trotted over to her and plopped down on the hillside.

"Were you following me?" Shevonne's head remained down while she spoke. Her body language seemed closed off and hesitant with her hands clasped in her lap, gripping her earbuds.

Jackson took a deep breath. "Do you like me? No, don't answer. I'm not asking like a third grader asks the third grade girl who sits beside him." He cleared his throat. "This is hard." He needed to see her expressive face. He placed his fingers under her chin and lifted it. "Please look at me."

She ran her tongue over her lips.

"Women have always been easy for me. They flocked to my side, enjoying the flirty banter and charm."

She raised her brows and opened her mouth to speak.

Jackson put a finger to her lips to silence her. "Let me finish."

She nodded.

"After I returned from out West, I never had to work at getting a date. A smile, a little small talk, a couple of drinks, and I had company for the night. But it got old, emotionally draining. Seeing TJ and Syn so happy, I was jealous. I wanted what they'd found. I despaired at ever finding it. Then you came along and turned my world upside down." He laughed. "More like flipped Travis on his ass...but you get what I'm saying."

"Can I talk yet?"

"No. I'm not done." Jackson glared at her as she giggled behind her hand. "You're not like other women. You aren't fawning over me, hitting on me, or trying to steal kisses. Not that I'm complaining about how you are..." His voice dropped. "I don't know how you feel. I thought we connected when we were out searching for your father. But, then, at the pharmacy, you were more reserved. So I second-guessed myself. Was I reading too much into us? Is there even an us?" He broke eye contact and stared at the trees in the distance.

"I'm not going to ask this time. It's my turn." Shevonne reached over and laced her fingers through his. "You know about my vision issues, so I believe some of the miscues come from me not seeing what others do. But I know most of this is we are only getting to know each other. I'm not a flirty girl. Never have been. I state it like it is and damn to anyone who gets in the way of my somewhat harsh tongue. Just ask my sisters."

"You didn't..."

Shevonne put a finger over his lips. "My turn." While her tone sounded firm, a smile filled her face, and gave him hope.

"In school, when I said I liked someone, the bullies used it against me. Knowing I wouldn't back down, they'd taunt me and invariably the poor guy as well, thereby ending any relationship. The teasing was the reason I left after graduation. I figured getting some military training would keep me from ever being bullied again." She glanced up at the sky then returned her gaze to his face. "Your voice sends warmth pooling low in my belly. The scent of your cologne makes my mouth water but not for food…for you. I've fantasized about your kisses and caresses. I've done three hundred pushups over the last few days, trying to temper my body's reaction to you."

Her words had his cock pushing against the fly of his jeans. But he wanted more than sex. He wanted it all. *I have to know, better ask the tough question.* "Is it only lust you're feeling?"

"No. I think I fell in love with you when you fought off the skunk. You did it to protect me and rescue my dad. My previous boyfriend didn't find my independence endearing, while you do. However, it's not an 'all or nothing' with us. We each take care of the other without being bossy or demanding."

"It's a partnership." Jackson pulled a chain from inside his shirt, lifted it off his head, and held it out in front of him. "This ring was my mother's engagement ring. I'm not proposing, but I'm giving it to you as a promise of my commitment to you and this relationship."

Tears filled her eyes. "I can't accept this family heirloom."

Jackson slipped the chain around her neck and slid it down under her T-shirt. "Please wear it close to your heart. My parents would have loved you." He gently brushed the tears from her cheeks. "The ring is my promise to you to always love and respect you, your opinion and support you."

Shevonne wrapped her arms around his neck, tugged

him closer, and kissed him.

Unable to hold back his passion, Jackson deepened their kiss, while his tongue teased hers, twisting and touching. He softly ended the kiss. It delighted him to see her lips red and full, as well as the glassy-eyed expression.

Shevonne slowly smiled. "I'm going to enjoy getting to know your desires better. Will you walk me home and stay for dinner?"

Jackson stood up and held out his hand. "I'd be delighted to."

Holiday Homecoming

A Wilder Sisters Novella

DEDICATION

To my family who puts up with juggling the holidays between families. You are the best part of the holidays.

To my own hero…you are the reason for my happiness!

CHAPTER ONE

Darkness had been her constant companion for the last three hours. The headlights of other cars were the only illumination, brightening up the car's interior. Even while she couldn't see the landscape, she knew its small rolling hills and rich farmland like the back of her hand. She glanced in her rearview mirror at the bundle in the backseat. Sheryl had memorized every feature of her daughter, from the tip of her pert turned-up nose to her chubby little toes. Unable to see her, she felt comforted by her presence. An illuminated sign in the distance announced her exit. Sheryl clicked her signal and turned her car toward home.

The bright lights at the gas stations and shopping centers blinded her for a moment. She blinked. *So much has changed in the last five years.* What once had been mostly farmlands and homes, now sported Wal-Marts and Costcos. Out of habit, she peeked over her shoulder, checking again on her angel. *Still sleeping.* Mattie had been a great traveler—quiet, happy, and easily entertained. She supposed nighttime travel played a big part, but her daughter wasn't a fussy baby.

Sheryl hadn't planned her flight, but when opportunity

occurred, she jumped at it. Away and free. She prayed he wouldn't look for her in Ohio. She prayed he'd think she'd run somewhere else since she hadn't spoken to her family in five years. He'd been traveling through and swept her off her feet. Their whirlwind romance had upset her parents who forbade her to see him. With a show of independence or was it carelessness, she left town with him on her eighteenth birthday, thinking he'd marry her but finding out a week later he'd already had a wife back in Texas.

At least, if he did come to Amherst, this was her home turf. She'd grown up here even if she hadn't bothered with a goodbye to anyone all those years ago. Unable to put her family in risk, Sheryl was determined to hide out and go it on her own. If she ran into her father, would he even recognize her? Could she face him and eat crow? Would he allow her back into his life?

Sheryl regretted running away with James against her father's orders, but she'd always needed to learn the hard way. She rubbed her thumb over her brow, brushing the scar she'd gotten for disobeying James when he'd refused to allow her to go to the store. Defying him by escaping, she'd face more than a beating if he caught up to her, but she had a good reason. Holding the steering wheel tight, she glimpsed her daughter in the rearview mirror.

Unwilling to ask her father to put her up, she pulled into the only hotel in town. The Towne Motel, a small rundown building, stood behind a gas station and fast-food joint and backed up to the freeway. Notorious for hosting illicit affairs between local businessmen and their secretaries, the two-story building reminded her of an old movie motel with metal railings and concrete stairs on the ends. She parked the car by the office then unbuckled Mattie, not wanting to leave her in the car. She'd hoped her daughter would keep sleeping, but from the small cries, she guessed her luck had run out. She slid a pacifier into the baby's mouth, and Mattie quieted.

A bell jingling on the door as she pushed it brought the clerk to attention. Sheryl squinted at the bright fluorescent lights in the hotel office and tugged a blanket over her daughter's face. The sterile office reminded her of a hospital. One uncomfortable-looking chair sat along the left wall. Boxes selling chocolate, peanuts, and other snack items for sale filled the small coffee table in front of the chair. Along the other wall, a display stand filled with coupons to Cedar Point and other local attractions and maps. A tall, smiling gray-haired woman stood behind the desk. Her face was lined with creases, yet her eyes appeared warm and friendly.

Sheryl offered a small smile in return. "Hello. Do you have a room?"

"Let me check." The clicks of the computer keys sounded like rain in the silent office. "How long are you staying?"

"A week. After that, I'm moving into my place." The glib lie fell from her lips. Falsehoods had become a necessary part of her life—for safety.

"We have a room with two double beds on the second floor around the back side of the building. It overlooks the parking lot, not the pool, though." She met Sheryl's gaze. "The charge is forty-five dollars a night plus tax."

Sheryl swallowed the bile that slid up as she did the math in her head. The cash she'd hidden away wouldn't last long. She'd need a job and a better place to stay quickly. Not willing to let the woman see her fears, Sheryl nodded. "That's perfect. Do you have a crib I could use for my son?" Another lie, but if anyone was looking for a woman and little girl, the clerk wouldn't be able to say yes.

More tapping of the keys. "Yes, I will have it brought to your room and set up while we sign the paperwork and get you the keys." The clerk picked up a two-way radio and instructed someone to put the crib in 205.

Sheryl rocked her daughter while she waited. At least they'd be safe for the night. She'd worry about the money later. Going begging to her father wasn't an option.

The clerk laid the rental agreement on the counter along with the plastic keycard. "The total is $341.77. Will you be putting this on your credit card? If so, I'll need your driver's license."

Her heart jumped. Thankfully, she was using cash. Just like all those who checked in for an afternoon quickie, she didn't care to give her real name. She didn't need another clue for James to follow in his quest to bring her back. Sliding her purse off her other shoulder, Sheryl set it on the counter and tugged out the cash. She placed each twenty-dollar bill on the counter as the clerk counted along. When she reached three hundred and forty, she reached into a different pocket and pulled out a five-dollar bill. "Three hundred forty-five, even."

"Let me get your change." The clerk pushed a button and a drawer opened. She placed the cash into the drawer and counted out the change, laying it on the counter. "Now, if you will sign the agreement, we are all set." She held out a pen.

Sheryl signed her mother's name on the paper and slid the keycard in the back pocket of her jeans. "Thank you."

The woman collected the papers then waved. "Your room is near the middle stairs around back. Thank you for choosing The Towne Motel and let me know if you need anything further."

Back outside the door, Sheryl slipped her daughter back into the car seat. "You were such a good girl. We're almost done traveling. Just a little farther, and we can change your diaper and get you fed." The whizzing of the freeway echoed across the parking lot. As she slid into the driver's seat, she let the fear seep out. Would they ever be safe? Her body slumped over the steering wheel, exhaustion hitting her hard. Since the birth of Mattie, she'd prayed for a miracle. The daily stress and emotional abuse had taken its toll on her, and she didn't want her daughter growing up in that household. Recently, the abuse had amped up. Fearful for not only her own life but her baby daughter's, she'd begun thinking about escape. She pulled out the small cross she wore on a chain around her neck and gave it a kiss. Sheryl had thought her mother's necklace long gone, but when it turned up in the bottom of an old purse she'd found in her closet, on a night when escape seemed out of reach, she took it as a sign and began hiding money.

With a silent prayer to her mother in heaven to keep them safe, Sheryl put the car in park and headed over to their new home and hopefully her first good night's sleep in ages.

CHAPTER TWO

Tanner Watts plopped down in his recliner, pain his constant companion. His feet hurt, his back hurt. Even his hair hurt. But the opening of Brew Spot would be in two weeks. Everything had started coming together nicely. Yesterday, the contractors had laid the dark hardwood floors as the painters completed their work on the walls. It might actually open on time. He rapped his knuckles on the table next to him to avoid jinxing himself.

"Dad, can you help me with this math problem?"

He glanced over at his beautiful daughter. Each day, he saw more and more of her mother in her features. A burn hit him in the chest. *Jessie, I wish you were here to help. She's everything we dreamed of and more.*

"Sure, Allie bug. Just bring it over here. I don't think I can climb out of this chair to save myself." He pushed the footrest down and patted the arm of the chair.

Allie perched on the armrest and laid the math book on her lap. "What is the dividend again? I can't remember if it's the number in front of the division problem or the one inside the house."

Tanner inhaled his daughter's fresh scent and recalled the first time he held her in his arms nine years ago. She'd been so tiny but such a strong fighter. Her loud wails had echoed through the delivery room. Allie gave him a reason to keep living, even after Jessie, his wife had passed after her battle with cancer. Each day, he wished she'd have been able to see their daughter—to hold Allie in her arms, once more. He shook his head, dispelling his memories.

"Does the book have a glossary in the back? We can look there." He tugged it off her lap and flipped through the pages. "Yep. Here it is." He pointed to the definition. "A dividend is the one in the little square. The one outside is the divisor."

"Thanks, Dad. You'd think they would have called them something different. Divisor, dividend, divide. They are so confusing, too alike." Her stomach growled.

"Go tackle the rest of the math problems. I'll figure out something for dinner." He nudged her with his shoulder then stood and strolled off to the kitchen. As he examined the contents of his fridge, Tanner tried to shake off his anxiety. He'd moved his family to Amherst in the hope a small-town life would mean a close-knit community to raise his daughter in. The big city wasn't a good place to raise children these days. But leaving New York meant selling his restaurant and walking away from his friends and family, the very people who'd helped raise Allie.

Tanner removed mushrooms and a small yellow squash then closed the refrigerator. "How does pasta ala Dad, sound?" His voice boomed in the small home.

"Sounds good. Do you need help? I'm happy to put this homework aside and help." His daughter's teasing voice always made him smile. Nothing in life seemed to get her down. *How'd I get so lucky?*

"I've got it. You'd better stay with the homework. I might need you to support me in the future if this restaurant idea doesn't go well." While he tried to keep his tone light, the fear of failure rang in his mind.

Tanner chopped the squash and dropped it into a frying pan with the mushrooms and a little butter. Turning on the stove, he set about gathering a pot and egg noodles. This recipe was simple, however, it tasted different each time he made it. Sometimes, he'd toss in cherry tomatoes or a little garlic while sautéing but, other times, the plainness of the noodles and squash was enough. The soft scent of melted butter and squash filled the kitchen and made his stomach growl. Setting the water on to boil, he grabbed a wooden spoon and stirred the mushrooms and squash. The trick was to not overcook the fresh vegetables. He liked them to still have a little crunch with the softer noodles.

From his pocket, his cell phone buzzed. Tugging it free, he glanced at the screen and answered. "Hello, Julia. How is the corporate world of international shipping?" Even after all these years, he enjoyed teasing his older sister. She might be more successful than he was, but she'd drop everything if he needed her—in fact she had.

"You know… ships come and ships go. Or, in this case, mostly airplanes. Have you taken any time for yourself this week? I think if I didn't poke at you about it, you'd forget to eat and sleep." Tanner felt homesick hearing his sister's kids laughing and joking in the background. Then he glanced at his daughter on the floor in the living room, working on her assignment. He wanted her to be the one joking with a friend. It was why he'd moved here, Jesse's hometown. Allie had been so lonely in NY. No close friends, only him. With her private school in NY and his late hours, it'd been hard to schedule playdates with other girls. While they were doing things after school, Allie was at her grandparents or the restaurant.

He tried to keep the sorrow from his voice. "In fact, you caught me cooking dinner. Allie's working on some math, and I'm making my famous throw-in-what-you-have pasta."

The background noise on his sister's end quieted. "I'm glad to hear you are home and cooking at a decent hour. I'm not trying to be nosy or picky, but when you lived here in New York, we could help out. You sound tired, and I'm sure you are working yourself to death, trying to get the new business up and running. I remember those days."

He rolled his eyes toward the ceiling, entreating his wife to help him out. How do you tell your family that your child spent more time with Grandma and Grandpa than with her own dad? How do you explain your need to be the dad and have a quality relationship with the one person who means more to you than yourself? And how do you say it over and over when no one is listening?

"So, Sis, got any big ideas or just a call to check in?" Tanner tried to keep the irritation from his voice and hoped he'd not upset his sister. Her heart was in the right place. Tanner dropped the noodles into the boiling water and turned off the vegetables so they wouldn't overcook.

"Actually, I do have an ide—"

"Better not be 'Move back to New York.'"

"No. I realized maybe you could hire someone to help around the house."

"Like a maid?"

"No, more like a nanny."

"But Allie's too old for a nanny." *Doesn't my sister realize my daughter is ten years old? Has she lost her mind?*

"Not really. You need someone to help with managing Allie's schedule from after-school activities to starting dinner…all those things wives do."

Lowering his voice so it wouldn't carry into the other room, he bit out, "Look. I know you mean well. I had a wife. I don't need another. I see what you are getting at about a nanny. But I don't need any help with my daughter." Great, he sounded defensive. Maybe he'd be better off, ending this conversation now.

"All right. I tried. I love you, Tanner, and if you or Allie need anything, anything at all, call me. I'll be on the next plane. Ohio isn't that far from New York. Just think about my suggestion. Please, for Allie's sake."

Tanner removed a colander from the cabinet and

dumped the noodles into it. "Thanks for always being there, Julia. I don't say it enough, but you're a great big sister. Now, I'd better go feed my hungry kid. Take care and give my love to the rest of the family."

He laid his phone on the counter and brushed his hair off his forehead. *Families are a challenge, even when they mean well. I hope I never get caught back up in a big family again. Too many bossy, take-charge people.*

Dumping the noodles back into the pan, he poured the sautéed vegetable mixture on top and stirred it. Buttering four slices of thick Italian bread, he sprinkled some garlic powder on them and slid them into the toaster oven. As soon as they started browning, he pulled them and set them on the two plates he'd gotten out for dinner. Spooning the pasta onto each plate, he hollered into the living room. "Allie, dinner's ready. Bring your homework in here so you can finish it."

"Fine, Dad. But then you have to clean up since I'm still doing my work."

Tanner smiled. *The joys of parenting.*

CHAPTER THREE

While not a home, the cheap motel was a blessing for Sheryl. A warm bed, two locks on the door, hot and cold running water. Now, she needed food. With only a small fridge and microwave, she wasn't going to be making big dinners, even if she could afford them. But Mattie needed formula and baby food, and Sheryl needed something other than junk or fast food. Surviving on coffee and potato chips didn't help with stress. A trip to a grocery store was in order.

Sheryl bundled Mattie up in her snowsuit then laid her into the car seat carrier. Adding a blanket to protect her face from the cold, Sheryl hoped she'd be warm enough in her crappy car. Sliding her arms into a threadbare wool jacket, she slung her purse over her one shoulder and then grabbed the carrier with her other arm. As she reached the door, she whispered a silent prayer no one would recognize her. Sheryl wasn't ready to face her family. How could she explain to them why she was hiding in Amherst? What would she say when they asked about James? Too embarrassed about the lies he told and the mistakes she made, she'd never explained the truth to her father. Nor had she been home for her mother's funeral. A familiar twinge of pain flooded her limbs as she recalled asking James for the money to return home to say goodbye to her mother. She closed her eyes momentarily, took a deep breath then let it go. She touched the silver cross necklace around her neck and then opened the door, before finally starting down the stairs.

A blast of cold air and snow hit her in the face, forcing her to gasp. She'd forgotten how cold late autumn was in Northern Ohio, even if it was only early November. The jet stream blew across Lake Erie, sending lake-effect snow barreling down and coating the small town in white. The world had changed since she'd gone to sleep last night. It appeared winter had hit.

Trying to juggle the baby carrier down the snowy steps, Sheryl took her time. Finally, she made it to her car. Studying the covered vehicle, she felt a sigh of relief. With the snow, she could see that no one had been near her car since last night. Not a single footstep marred the pristine whiteness. *Will I always look over my shoulder and fear for my life?* She couldn't let the fear paralyze her, but not being cautious could get her killed.

"Stupid bitch. I told you to get me a beer. Not this swill." The bottle of Pabst flew past her head and shattered on the kitchen wall. Pain radiated through her shoulder. Not from this bottle but from his need to exact punishment for some unknown crime. He hadn't let her do the shopping, so if he wanted different beer, why didn't he buy it? Usually Pabst was fine, and the cheaper price meant he could buy more, but tonight she prayed a different brand remained in the fridge.

Mattie's cries escalated from the shouting. Instead of grabbing that beer, Sheryl detoured to pick up and calm her fearful child. If she didn't, she worried James would harm their daughter. If someone had told Sheryl years ago about the abuse she lived with, she wouldn't have believed them. Now, she not only feared for her life but her daughter's, too.

Shaking her head to free herself from her memories,

228

Sheryl opened the car door and placed the carrier into the base, securing it. She tugged the blanket off her daughter's face and kissed her pink forehead. A smile flitted across her lips. Mattie was the one person who got her through all that pain. She was worth any beating.

Quickly brushing the snow off, Sheryl jumped into the front seat and blew on her bright-red, freezing hands. With the turn of the key, the car started. She cranked up the heat and sat for a moment, waiting and hoping for the pile of rust to heat up.

Glancing in the mirror, she smiled at Mattie. "It's been a while since I've been shopping. I saw a Giant Eagle in the shopping mall across the street, or we can head to the smaller grocery store out by my father's place." The baby cooed. "You're right. I just want to drive by Dad's house to see if anything has changed. The grocery store was an excuse. Let's go to Giant Eagle and save the gas." With the heat filling the car, she put it in reverse, and they were on their way.

***

"Another perfect checkup. I'm so proud of you, Allie-bug." Tanner hugged his daughter then ruffled her hair. "This deserves a treat."

Her eyes widened. "A case of soda?"

He shook his head. "You ask for that right after seeing the dentist? It'll ruin all the hard work you do on your teeth. So many kids your age have a dozen fillings from the soda and candy they consume on a daily basis."

Allie pouted and looked at her feet. "Fine. Ice cream."

At the swish of the doors opening, Tanner glanced at his daughter. "Good compromise. Still sugar, but the milk will help with your teeth. Maybe I'll pick up a second half gallon, and we can have two different flavors." He picked up a shopping basket and headed into the large grocery store. "I'm going to grab a few things for dinner tonight.

I'll make homemade pizza to celebrate. Mushrooms, okay?"

"Sure. While you're getting the stuff, I want to check out the books. Just come find me before you head to the frozen section."

He waved as she headed away from him. Tanner hated the idea of letting his daughter off alone in such a big store, but he reminded himself this was Amherst, not New York. He knew she'd stay where she said she'd be, and he'd been working on easing up on her. He longed to hold her close to him, believing that if he did, he'd keep death away. However, he knew all too well how that worked out. At the height of her best year ever as a corporate lawyer, cancer struck and left a gaping hole in their lives. He hadn't been able to stop death then, and couldn't now.

Heading down the produce aisle, he picked up a package of fresh mushrooms then put some vine-ripened tomatoes into his basket. Next stop cheese.

***

Glad to be in the warm store, Sheryl pushed her cart with Mattie's carrier in the basket down the aisles. She'd already picked up a box of cereal. But had skipped the milk because of the cost. *I hate going without, but for my daughter, I'd give up anything. Even without milk, the cereal is a healthy alternative to fast food. The store brand of Raisin Bran is still cheaper than a breakfast value meal at McDonalds, and it'll last longer.* A bag of apples and a bag of pretzel rods filled her needs. Only Mattie's baby food, diapers, and formula were missing. As Sheryl turned the corner to head down the next aisle, she thought she saw James. Not watching where she was going, she bumped into a young girl, sending her crashing to the floor.

Tears fell down the child's face, but Mattie's cries echoed in the store.

"Oh my God." Sheryl reached down and brushed the

hair from the girl's face. "I'm sorry. Are you okay?"

Sniffing, the girl sat up and reached over to collect the fallen book from the floor. "What'd you do that for?"

"Again, I'm so so sorry. I wasn't watching where I was going." She reached out her hand. "Let me help you up." With the girl's hand in her own, Sheryl tugged her up.

"Hey, lady. Your baby's crying." She placed her book in the cart and peered down at the child.

Sheryl reached into the cart and unbuckled her daughter from the carrier. She lifted her into her arms and placed her on her hip, facing outward then gently rocked her back and forth. "I'm Sheryl, and this is Mattie. I think she was very upset you got hurt. Why don't you let her know you are okay? Again, I'm sorry. What's your name?"

"I'm Allie." The girl reached out. "I'm okay, Mattie. Don't cry." Mattie wrapped her hand around Allie's finger and settled down.

"You're great with babies. Do you have any younger brothers or sisters?" She smiled as Mattie cooed at the young girl. "Mattie doesn't usually take to other people."

"No siblings. Just me and my dad." Allie scrunched up her face, which sent Mattie into giggles.

Sheryl glanced at the book the young girl had been holding. "I love to read. That looks like the latest girl sorcerer book. Are you a fan?"

"Yes. I've read them all."

As Allie glanced over Sheryl's shoulder, she turned to see what had caught the young girl's eye. A man with dark wavy hair strolled closer to them. A smile lit up his face. The square jaw, which might have appeared harsh another man, gave him a strong appearance, yet the small cleft in the chin turned the severity into rugged handsomeness. But his broad shoulders and artist's fingers started butterflies dancing in Sheryl's stomach. A quick flash of instant attraction, and Sheryl longed to see how passionate his kisses were. But she knew where her impulses had taken her before, so she tamped it down, burying it away.

Her own daughter had become her focus. Not a man.

"Hi, Daddy." Her new friend ran into the striking man's arms.

CHAPTER FOUR

Tanner had been standing there out of sight, observing his daughter and the strange woman. When he noticed the accident, he wanted to jump in to defend Allie. But she'd done all right on her own. Throwing his shoulders back, he smiled at her newfound ability to make friends. This justified his reason for the move. Allie's confidence had blossomed in the small town.

Tanner studied the woman. Her strawberry-blonde hair slid around her shoulders like waves, colors a mix like the fall leaves on a tree: red, gold, and light brown. Her tresses were thick, with a little natural curl. She obviously didn't hit the salon to style it each week like his sister did. He glanced at her fingers. No wedding ring and no shiny high-end polish. In fact, her nails were uneven and short, as if she'd been chewing on them.

The woman's pain over the crash and then smiles at his daughter had his heart beating faster. It wasn't the practiced expression he'd often seen of the women he'd dated in New York, donned to make him think they were "good with children," but more of a shy, small-town variety. With the way she looked at the baby in her arms, he knew she'd never be a danger to his daughter. Love

233

radiated from her as she rocked the baby on her hip but still managed to discuss the book in his daughter's hands.

The woman's clothes dwarfed her body. Worn and out of style, they appeared more like hand-me-downs than her everyday fashion, but it was the contents of her cart that had him thinking she didn't have much money. Only generic store brands and minimal things. No splurges for coffee or soda. No treats of ice cream or steaks. The picture she painted was one of poverty, as if she lived on the streets, no place for a baby.

His sister's idea flashed through his mind. Maybe he'd run into a woman who could help him with his work schedule as well as caring for his daughter. Trusting his gut had gotten Tanner a successful Manhattan restaurant. Maybe he should trust it again. As he enveloped his daughter in a hug, he vowed to at least offer.

"Hey, bug. Did you find a book?"

"Yep. The new teenage sorcerer book. Can I get it? I really want to know what happens to Tina." She placed her hands together in supplication. "Pleasssseeee. I'll do extra chores. I'll clean the bathroom. Anything."

"Hmm." Tanner's gaze met the woman's. "Introduce me to your friend." He slid his arm around his daughter's shoulder and reached out his other hand. "I'm Tanner Watts, and you are…."

As her hand slid into his, a jolt jumped down his spine. "I'm Sheryl Wilder, and this is Mattie." She bounced her infant on her hip. "Your daughter has good taste in books." She nodded toward Allie. "I'm a fan of Shelby Susan's work as well. The series is wonderful for young girls, empowering them to reach for their goals."

"That's good to know. You sound like a teacher or librarian." He chuckled and reached a finger toward the baby.

"Goodness, no. Maybe someday. Right now, I'm just a mom. But I'm an avid reader." She kissed the top of her daughter's head.

Tanner ran his hand through his hair. "This is going to sound crazy. But I'm going with my gut, and it's never been wrong." He paused to take a breath. "I'm looking for someone to help with my daughter. I work full-time, am opening a new bistro in town, and well, I've seen you with her. You're great. Would you be looking for a job?"

Allie jumped out of her dad's reach. "Could you please? You're nice, and you could bring your baby, and we could play, talk about books."

Sheryl's mouth opened, but no sound came out. When Mattie started fussing, she returned her to the carrier in the cart and tugged a bottle out of her bag. Once her daughter got ahold of the bottle, she quieted down. Sheryl kept her gaze on her baby. "I did recently return to Amherst from out of state and am looking for a job. While it sounds almost too good to be true, I'd like to get more details."

Tanner pulled a card from his wallet. "This is my restaurant. It's got my cell number on the bottom. Please give me a call later and we can discuss rates, dates, times, and what I was thinking."

When she took the card, their fingers brushed again. Tanner smiled. "Please give me a call. You appear perfect for the job."

Allie leaned over the cart, staring at Maggie drinking. She ran a finger over the little baby's hand then turned back to her father. "You're getting the book, right, Dad? And don't forget, you promised ice cream."

A deep chuckle rumbled out of his chest. He rubbed the top of her head before pulling her close. "I guess, especially if it means you'll clean the bathroom."

Allie placed the book in his basket.

"We'd better get home if you want me to make pizza tonight." He turned toward the beautiful woman and baby. "It was nice meeting you."

"Nice meeting you, too, Tanner." She slid a cloth over her shoulder then lifted her daughter and burped her, gently rubbing her back. "I'll be in touch."

***

After getting a nice burp from her daughter, Sheryl laid her back into the carrier. She'd been gone long enough. Still not comfortable out in public, she feared running into someone who knew her. Quickly, she grabbed two jars of baby food, one can of formula, and one package of diapers. She mentally tallied the amount for the items in the cart. Should be under thirty dollars, certainly no more than forty. She tugged the remaining wad of bills from her back pocket and quickly counted them. After this, she'd have only about another fifty dollars left for the rest of the week—gas and more food. She was willing to eat the dry cereal and apples all week if it meant she'd have enough money for Mattie's needs. While she could have waited until she hid away more money, she doubted she'd have been able to find a more perfect opportunity to escape. Things were getting out of control with James's temper and his wife's demanding attitude. Seeing hatred in Karen's eyes toward Mattie had been the final straw. Either Karen would kill her daughter or get rid of Sheryl so that she could have Mattie for herself. Neither would she allow.

Sheryl quickly folded the money away, stashing it back in her jeans, and then pushed her cart to the checkout.

The snow had stopped falling when she returned to her car. After placing Mattie's seat in the back, she loaded the two bags of groceries into the car. A tingle swept over her. Was someone watching her? Slowly, she brushed the snow off the car as she walked around it, casting glances about to see if James or anyone else had noticed her. The parking lot appeared quiet, with only about a dozen cars in the lot. She felt uneasy being out. With the snow brushed off, she ducked into the driver's seat.

Sheryl rubbed her hands over her face. Damp from the snow, her hands were chilled, although it was hard to tell how much since her face also was cold. She recalled the little girl and her father. The job he offered would certainly help with some of the money issues, but she didn't know what the pay scale was or even if she'd be able to bring her daughter. Safety for Mattie trumped money every time. She'd only find out once she called him. Besides, calling didn't mean she'd take the job. Sheryl needed to explore every avenue. She'd not realized how hard it would be to find a job with a baby in tow. After all, which retail store or bar offered free day care? Affording the day care would be a major deal…she'd been too frantic to get away to take everything into account.

She pinched her nose to stop the tears threatening to fall. Sheryl could always call her dad. He'd give her a place to stay, a warm home…but she didn't want to rely on him. Nor was she ready to admit her own her actions and face her family. Once they learned of James's wife, she knew they'd think even less of her than they probably did. Tugging her cross from under her T-shirt, she ran it over her lips. A gift from her grandmother, her mother wore it all the time. She recalled the coolness of the metal against her cheek when she hugged her mother tight. Or how her mother would hold it in her hand when saying the nightly prayer with them. On Sheryl's eighteenth birthday, her mom had pulled her aside and kissed her cheek before sliding the chain around Sheryl's neck.

I never got to say goodbye. She wiped at the tears sliding down her face. She'd been so angry at not being able to be there for her mother. They'd been close. She'd been able to share almost anything with her. Tomorrow, she should go visit her grave. She'd never been there before. She could introduce Mattie. Maybe bring about some closure or peace. Her daughter cooed in the back seat then a brush of air slid over her cheek, almost like a caress. Could her mother have been there? Showed she was watching over her? Sheryl lifted her chin. She'd always believed it.

Sliding the key into the ignition, she started the car and

headed back to the motel. She'd get Mattie off to bed then make that phone call about the job. She said a silent prayer for help making the right decision. *I've already made too many mistakes.*

CHAPTER FIVE

"Dad, why are we following that lady from the supermarket?" Allie asked from the back seat.

"I'm doing a background check. Following her tells me where she lives and helps me decide if she's someone I would trust with you." The slight fabrication sounded convincing to his jaded ears. "Don't you want her taking care of you when I'm at work?"

His daughter shrugged. "Sure. She was nice, and the baby was a-dor-a-able. But I'd rather help out at the pub."

A wave of sadness floated through him. "You were a great help this past summer. I couldn't have done so much work without your assistance. But now school's started, and I'll be working long hours, making sure everything runs smoothly. You can't be there as much with homework. Then, what if you wanted to join after-school drama or band? How could I get you there or get you home?"

She flashed the book she'd had on her lap. "I can sit and read. Never bother you at all."

"True but that doesn't answer the doing homework, after-school clubs, and what about those nights when I'm closing and don't get off until two a.m.? Where will you sleep? Under a table? Trust me, this is better." He paused. "Besides, I think your friend could use some help."

Tanner pulled his car into the parking lot of the motel. From a spot by the front edge of the building, he watched Sheryl park near the back and unload the groceries and her daughter. The lights in the lot illuminated the dingy motel. Loud music blared from one of the rooms, while two people sat on the concrete steps on the front part of the building, smoking and drinking.

"Is this where she lives?" Allie's voice squeaked.

"Yep. Looks like it." A lump settled in his stomach. In New York, he'd worked with a local women's shelter. Sheryl had the appearance of someone who'd been abused and might be in hiding. He longed to help her. Somehow, in the few minutes they spoke, she'd gotten under his skin. Was it because of his need to save and protect, or was it how she treated his own daughter?

"Why does she live in this dumpy motel?" Allie asked the question he longed to find out.

"She said she's new to town. Maybe she doesn't have an apartment yet." He doubted it but hoped it was the truth. His place was above the restaurant. The top floor of the corner of Park Ave and South Main. The apartment had three roomy bedrooms along with three full baths, a culinary kitchen, and wooden-floored living area, overlooking Main Street and the town hall. The loft featured a high ceiling and large windows. To be honest, the updated living space was half the reason he'd bought the building. The restaurant boasted the best location in town. The place was large enough for Sheryl and her daughter to move in with them, which would also give her better access to Allie's needs without compromising her own daughter's. *I don't know how I'll sleep tonight knowing she's in this hellhole. It's not safe, and I'd feel horrible if something happened, but I can't go charging in there and demand she come home with me. What a dilemma. I only pray I can convince her to come on board to my idea. And do it without making it seem like charity or pity.* He'd seen many women walk away from help when they felt pitied. Some even starved to death rather than take a handout. He couldn't let that happen.

Tanner turned and glanced at his daughter. "Are you ready to head home for some ice cream? I am."

Allie nodded. "Do you think we can have a little of each flavor?"

"Sure, but we'll have to think of a name for our new flavor. Cherry praline crunch? Caramel Cherry Nut?"

"I think it should be called Allie-ishousness." She giggled. "After all, I'm the one who decided on the two flavors."

"All right, bug. Make sure your seat belt is on. We're heading home."

***

It was almost nine thirty before Sheryl got Mattie settled and asleep. A bowl of cereal and an apple had filled her own empty stomach. As she rubbed her hand over her abdomen, she tried to recall the last time she'd eaten like a queen in a real restaurant. It'd been about five years ago. When James had wooed her with his good looks and charming personality. She should have known it was too good to be true. Her momma had always told her real things come with a price and hard work. Too bad she'd not been listening.

Sheryl stared at the card in front of her as she contemplated what to do. She held it between two of her fingers as if she held a snake and was afraid it'd bite her. Her thoughts kept returning to the wonderful little girl in the crib next to the bed. For her, she'd do anything.

She lifted the room telephone and dialed an eight plus the local number. Her hand shook as she waited for the guy to answer. One ring, two rings, three rings, four, five, six. She'd glanced at the clock on the nightstand. Was it too late? Had he gone to bed?

241

"Hello. Tanner speaking."

"Hello, Mr. Tanner. This is Sheryl Wilder. We met at the grocery store today." She knew she was talking too fast, but she was afraid if she paused, she'd hang up the receiver and forget about the job.

"Not Mr. Tanner, just Tanner. Or Mr. Watts. Naw, forget that. It sounds like my dad. Stick to Tanner."

She let out a soft snort as she tried to keep her giggle inside. With those few words, he'd helped with her fear.

"I'm sorry to call so late. It's Sheryl, the woman from the grocery store. I really shouldn't even consider this job, but, frankly, I need it." *Way to sound desperate, Sheryl.*

"Thank you for calling me. From the look of your shopping cart, I suspected you might. I made the offer partially for that reason. But, mostly, because you made my daughter smile and laugh. She lost her mother a couple of years ago and. other than family, I haven't seen Allie react so positively to another woman. You'd be doing us a favor by taking the job."

Her heart skipped a beat when he mentioned his wife's death. No young girl should grow up without a mother. Yet, too many did. His story made another chink in the armor around her heart. She glanced over at her daughter and recalled the smile on the young girl's face when she'd spied Mattie. Maybe this would be good for both of them.

"What are you needing in a nanny?" Her tone was cautious. Now, with hope inside, she didn't want to lose the chance at the job.

"My restaurant is due to open. I'm working long hours. The bar doesn't close until two a.m., and then we still have to prep things for the next day. It makes more sense to have you live in my apartment so you can be there during the evenings with Allie but not worry about having to take your own daughter home after I return. The middle of the night is not when you should be putting your daughter to bed."

"Do you have a place for us? I don't want to be in the

way." Could this really work out? Would this opportunity be the blessing she'd been praying for? Sheryl tugged her mother's cross out and twisted it with her fingers while she listened.

"Of course. Allie and I live above the restaurant. The loft is a little over two thousand square feet. You and Mattie will have a room with an adjoining bathroom. We'll share the living and dining rooms as well as the kitchen." The house she'd lived with James in Texas had been only a thousand square feet. With four people and only two bedrooms. Tanner's place sounded huge.

She took a deep breath. *Why am I still waiting for the other shoe to drop? Maybe because it sounds too good to be true. And I've learned about that the hard way.* "I want to be clear. Will I be expected to cook and clean? Or just care for Allie?"

"I need you to be at the apartment when Allie gets home after school, be sure she does her homework then all the other things she needs to do before bed. So you'll have to make dinner for her each night, unless you guys want to get some food from the restaurant, which is always an option for you. The only places you'll need to clean are your bathroom and bedroom…but I don't like a messy house. So, if you use the kitchen or living room, please clean up." His smooth, deep voice comforted her.

I could listen to his New York accent all day long. She found herself grinning like a fool when she spied her reflection in the mirror. She shook her head and concentrated on what he'd said. Groceries would be needed if she had to cook dinner. Would Allie like what she made? *I'm nowhere near her father's caliber if he has his own restaurant.*

Her voice came out with a squeak. "Of course. I'm glad to hear you like a clean house. What about money? Pay and incidentals like food."

"I'll pay you one hundred dollars per day and reimburse you for any grocery items you need, including your daughter's diapers and food. That's along with room and board. And if you need to drive Allie to after-school events or such, I can give you extra money for those expenses. Having you in the house, caring for my daughter, means I don't have to worry and can focus on my business. Knowing she's happy and excelling socially in this new town, returning to the happy young girl who she was before my wife died…that's priceless."

A gasp escaped her lips. "That's generous. Thank you. You can't possibly know me well enough to entrust me with your daughter, yet somehow you are. I vow to do everything in my power to make her a happy, well-adjusted kid." Tears filled her eyes. Tanner's offer seemed like a miracle. No more nights at the motel, worried about food. No more hungry tummies. "I'm happy to start tomorrow, if you need me to."

Tanner chuckled. "How about if you come by tomorrow for lunch and check over your room and my apartment? Allie will be at school. I don't want her getting her hopes up until you've made a decision. If you are still sure about accepting the job, you can start the following day. But, if you decide to pass, I will understand. You have to do what is best for you and your daughter. My address is 10901 Main Street. The door is off the side alleyway. I'll see you about noon. Will that work?"

"Yes. Noon is great. We can get lunch in then I can be back before her nap time. Speaking of her, I'd better get some rest. She likes to wake up early, and a crabby mom isn't a good mom. Again, thank you. You don't realize what your offer means to me…to Mattie and me. Good night."

"Good night."

Sheryl placed the phone back in the cradle then climbed off the bed and tiptoed over to her daughter. She leaned over and gave her a kiss on the forehead. "A chance for better things," she whispered.

As she stood over the crib and watched her daughter sleep, she smelled the scent of her mother's favorite rose soap. Her spirits rose even further. "Thank you, Mom," she spoke into the empty room then climbed under the covers and fell asleep.

CHAPTER SIX

Sirens and flashing red lights startled Sheryl awake. She jumped from the bed and peeked out the window, trying to discover the cause of the commotion. Two police cars and an ambulance were parked in the lot near the office area. Craning her neck, Sheryl only caught sight of the cars, no officers were visible. She hoped it hadn't been a robbery. When she'd grown up in Amherst, the only crimes she ever heard of were the drunk and disorderly type. The small town policed its citizens, making sure those who wanted to do real harm were run out by the police before anything dangerous occurred. But places change, and the world had become harsher. It appeared as if crime had found Amherst.

Glad to be getting out of the dumpy motel, Sheryl quickly glanced at her daughter who continued to sleep through the disturbance. Relieved to have a moment to herself, she hopped in the shower, wanting to look presentable for the lunch with Allie's dad today. After all, this job would mean the difference between staying here or moving somewhere safe.

As she dried off, she caught the sound of her daughter's cries. She wrapped the towel around her body then went out and lifted Mattie from the crib. Quickly, she tugged off the baby's sleepwear and wet diaper then used the warm washcloth from her own shower to wipe Mattie's body off. She laid her freshly diapered daughter on the bed then went in search of a clean bottle and some formula.

Knock. Knock.

Sheryl ran to the window and glanced at the policeman standing in front of her door. She left the security chain on but opened the door a crack. "Yes. What can I help you with, sir?"

She wasn't dressed and didn't want him seeing more than two inches of her face. And certainly not her daughter. It was safer for them to stay under the radar, even that of the police.

"Ma'am, there's been an incident, and we are asking everyone if they heard anything." The policeman flashed his badge. He wore a winter coat against the chill blowing through the air. Sheryl shivered as she kept her head down and stared at his dress shoes.

"I'm sorry. I woke up only about ten minutes ago. I was in the shower when you knocked. What happened?"

"The night manager was beaten and left for dead sometime early this morning. She's still unconscious, but we have footage of the suspect. We're just following up with all the hotel guests."

Her heart thudded. *I hope this doesn't have to do with me. It can't be James. He couldn't have found us.*

"I went to bed early last evening and must have slept pretty soundly. I didn't hear anything. I hope you find the person who did this. It's not safe for a woman alone. Thank goodness I'm leaving for Sandusky tonight." More lies fell from her lips. Even though she didn't recognize the officer, she didn't want the police looking for her again.

"All right, ma'am. Thank you for your help. Have a safe trip."

Sheryl closed the door and relocked the dead bolt. She leaned against the door and listened as the policeman went to the next door and repeated his questioning. Taking a deep breath, she pushed away from the door and got dressed in jeans and a sweater. She wound her hair into a bun on top of her head. A few tendrils escaped and framed her face.

"Let me get this bottle made, sweetie. Then I'll feed you. After that, we can go visit the cemetery before our lunch meeting." Her hands shook as she poured the powdered formula into the bottle while rattling off her plans to Mattie. The incident with the night manager had her frightened and desperate to leave.

As she shook the bottle, mixing the water and formula, she gathered up all their clothes and food. Sheryl was determined to not return to the motel tonight, just in case James was the man behind the attack.

***

"What did you think of the mom with the baby, yesterday?" Tanner asked as he flipped a golden-brown pancake.

"She was nice. I liked her baby." His daughter sat at the kitchen counter with a plate of pancakes and a glass of orange juice. She wore her favorite pink cancer support T-shirt and jeans. Her lunch was already in her backpack along with her homework from last night. It sat by the door, ready for the school bus's arrival.

"She's coming by today to talk about the job. I know you don't think you need a nanny, but I'd like you to be good if she takes it." Tanner removed the last pancake from the pan then laid the cast-iron griddle in the sink.

"I will." Her tone held the note of teenage rebellion he'd gotten used to hearing more of over the last two years. It'd been hard losing his wife, but harder for Allie losing her mom. She'd been shuttled with her grandparents and now with another new person.

"Anyway, I wanted to let you know. It's almost time for the bus. I'll see you after school." He leaned over and gave his daughter a kiss on the cheek. "Make sure you practice your spelling words before the test. You know them. Don't rush."

"All right, Dad." Again with the sassy tone then she was out the door. Tanner watched from the large window overlooking the street as the bus and Allie climbed in. His stomach rebelled at the thought of another bite. He shoved the uneaten into a plastic bag and put it in the fridge for tomorrow then rinsed and loaded the plates into the dishwasher.

He looked around the kitchen then ran his hand through his hair. Still so much to do before lunchtime and Sheryl's visit. He grabbed a rag and the spray bottle and set off to clean up the guest bathroom. At least the physical act of cleaning would keep his mind from nagging him about his decision to have a beautiful woman he was attracted to living under the same roof with him and his daughter.

***

After she stuffed all their items into the car, Sheryl loaded Mattie's car seat into the back. The police visit had her jumpy, and she'd skipped breakfast, so she munched on an apple as she drove up Route 58 toward town. She decided to visit the cemetery and introduce Mattie to her grandmother. The guilt of missing the funeral was sharp in her heart.

Sheryl studied the houses along the way. So much of Amherst had changed; new subdivisions blossomed along familiar roads. Yet, the town still retained its cozy feel. Giant leafless trees stood sentinel over sidewalks where families strolled during the warmer months. Sheryl could almost hear the children's laughter as she drove through town.

As she made the turn toward the northern outskirts, she recognized the family name on the local car dealership. It hadn't changed since she'd left town, although she supposed the daughter had probably taken over now. The old grocery store, near her great-aunt's home, closed and boarded up, saddened her. She'd gone there a time or two for treats while visiting Aunt Sally. *No matter how things stay the same, some things must change. After all, I've changed. I'm not the limp noodle I was—letting James dictate my life.* She glanced in her rearview mirror at her daughter. *I never thought I'd have kids, and look at me now. I can't imagine my life without Mattie.*

Soon, she drove past the large sandstone gate into the North Ridge Cemetery, her mom's final home. Many years ago, her mother had shown the girls where her spot was during one of the Memorial Day picnic and parade events. While cemeteries were often scary and depressing places, they never were for the Wilder sisters. Each year, the town began and ended their patriotic celebrations with a visit to the cemetery. As Sheryl drove past familiar names and family stones, she recalled the faces of all the loved ones resting here.

The place was almost entirely empty today. Only one other car drove the familiar lanes. Sheryl stopped when she noticed that the other vehicle had parked near her mother's headstone. An older gentleman and a young woman emerged from the dark sedan. His salt-and-pepper hair and stooped body marked his age, but it was the familiar walk that had her sitting up straighter. Her sister, Syn, helped her father walk over to his wife's stone then returned to lean against the car. He placed his hand on his wife's stone. She'd recognized Syn anywhere, the spitting image of their mother from the old photos. But her father had aged quite a bit. Gone was the man who had stood tall and firm against her dating James. *Where has the time gone? And how much more will pass before I can make things right?*

Quickly, she cut the engine and slumped in the seat, tears sliding down her cheeks. Too far away to hear what was said, she hoped he was sharing memories of happier times. She prayed he wasn't telling her about the failure Sheryl had become.

Seeing him sent the memories flooding back. Being carried on his shoulders, the tickle fights, and the many snowmen they'd built. She recalled the summer he taught her how to mow the grass using the riding lawn mower and how she hadn't been able to drive the car until she learned how to change the oil.

"That's your grandpa, Mattie. Someday, you'll get to meet him face-to-face and build memories of your own. But not yet." She'd vowed to protect her daughter but also her family. She didn't want James coming after him, either. Her father appeared frailer than she'd remembered. He'd never be able to handle the violence of James's anger. And she couldn't handle letting him know how she'd failed. Unmarried, with a child, and become a victim. She closed her eyes against the pain of imagining the pity in his gaze.

When she opened them a moment later, he'd returned to his car. She waited until they left the cemetery before starting hers and heading over to her mother's headstone.

CHAPTER SEVEN

Sheryl crossed another date off on the calendar. November twenty-second. Thanksgiving was in two days, but even with the new job as Allie's nanny, the approaching holiday had her melancholy.

"Don't forget your lunch, Allie. I packed a special treat," Tanner called out from the kitchen as his daughter sprinted out the door. He bent over Mattie in her playpen, giving her a goofy grin. Her giggle always made him smile. "You know, Sheryl, Mattie's going to be a stunner when she gets older. Those blue eyes and that pert little nose will have the boys falling all over themselves."

She turned away from the wall calendar. Her life should have been perfect, but something nagged at her emotions. "Just what I need, Tanner, a daughter who will probably be wilder than I was."

He placed a plate of oatmeal with blueberries in front of her spot at the kitchen table. "Come sit down. Something's been bothering you. Tell me about it." He tapped the chair before dropping into his own seat.

Sheryl shuffled her feet and sat down. As she stuffed a spoonful of oatmeal into her mouth, she thought about what she could, should, would tell him. After all, Tanner and Allie had been wonderful, her feel like a part of a family. She hadn't realized how much she'd missed it.

"Come on. You can tell me anything." He smiled. "Except that my cooking stinks." A chuckle escaped his lips.

"You know, if you have to laugh at your own jokes, they aren't funny." She side-eyed him.

"I've noticed you've lacked your usual bubbly self. What can I do to help? Has Allie been behaving? Is your pay too small?"

Her spoon clanked on the table. "No. no. You have been very generous, and Allie's super helpful. A delightful girl."

He laid his hand on her arm. "Then what?"

"With Thanksgiving, I'm feeling sad and missing my family." She placed her hand on top of his. "Holidays just get to me."

"I understand how it is being away from family over the holidays. While I didn't want to go back to New York and get sucked into the family deal, I did come up with an idea that makes me feel better about missing them." He spooned some oatmeal into his mouth.

"I hear you about your family. Did you know your sister has called twice this week to check on Allie and her grades? You'd think that woman didn't trust me."

He shook his head and bit down on his lip. "Want me to tell her off? I'm happy to do it. In fact, I do it once a week anyway."

She slapped him on the shoulder. "You can, but I understand where she's coming from. So I'll put up with it—for a while at least."

"If you're sure." He tilted his head toward her. "Anyway, back to my grand idea. This year I'm hosting a Thanksgiving event for the local Amherst firefighters and their families at the restaurant. Those men and women work holidays and don't get to spend the time with their families. I'll arrange it with the chief so they can leave the firehouse for the dinner. I'm sure it'll work out; the restaurant is only a block from the station. So I'll have a buffet set up for them, which will allow them to spend the holiday together. As a family."

Sheryl pressed her hands together. "Great idea. I'm sure they will appreciate it."

"There's only one problem." She felt her heart drop.

"Since I'm going to be working all day, in order to spend the holiday with my own daughter, I'm asking you and your daughter to come along, too." His sappy-eyed look did her in.

"Of course, I'll come. Please let me help in some way. Maybe it'd keep my mind off missing my own family."

"You know so much about my family, but I've not heard a thing about yours. Are they aliens from outer space?" he teased.

She ran her fingers over her cross necklace and then tugged it from under her collar. Twirling the charm, she considered exactly how much she'd share. *It'd be safe to share my childhood memories. Those he wouldn't question. I don't know how I could explain that I'm not in touch with my family today without telling Tanner about James.*

"Why don't you start with the necklace? You play with it when you're nervous or worried."

Sheryl studied his expression. The teasing had disappeared. His dark-brown eyes held her gaze. His forehead wrinkled as if he was puzzling out the meaning of life, but it was the way he leaned in and gently used his finger to trace circles on her arm which had her stomach tumbling. They'd developed a friendship over the last few weeks, and even though she was attracted to him, she'd kept her distance just in case James came back and she was forced to skedaddle again.

"I'm the middle of five girls. My poor dad didn't know what to do with all of us. Growing up, we learned many of the skills boys usually do from their fathers like ice fishing and hunting. Dad never held back just because of our gender. Before they passed, Grandma and Mom had taught us everything about cooking and sewing as well. Some of us more than others." She giggled. "You've tasted many of my extensive skills."

"Sisters...are yours as bossy as mine?"

She felt his finger still caressing her arm. Her body throbbed in time with the movement. As if the cross was on fire, she dropped the necklace and tucked it back under her shirt. Her palms tingled and goose bumps broke out on her skin.

She nodded. "Syn is the worst. She's the oldest and always decided what games we played or who could be which pretend character." She hesitated. "But she also looked after us. The first time someone made fun of me on the school bus, she stood over them with her scary face and demanded they apologize. Trust me, no one messed with one of us without taking on all of us. I followed her around like a little shadow."

"What about your other sisters?"

"The baby, Shevonne, was frequently the last one invited to do anything. While only two years younger than me, she was a baby in my older sisters' eyes. They would tease her and try to get her to do silly things that often ended up in us all getting punished." Sheryl rubbed her palm up and down her leg, trying to take her mind off Tanner's magical finger. She closed her eyes and took two calming breaths. *I hope he's not noticed what he's doing to me.*

"It sounds like an ideal childhood. So why haven't you seen them in a while? What are you hiding from them...and from me?"

"Excuse me." Jumping up from her chair, Sheryl sprinted to the bathroom.

***

Tanner watched her bolt from the room as if on fire. "So she's not immune," he whispered to Mattie. "She's more skittish than that kitten I found when I was ten. It took me two months to get it to come to me and let me pet it. Finally, by the third month, Sunshine was curled up on my bed, sleeping with me. I realize your mother's just as wary as Sunshine was, but I'm patient and determined."

He stood and picked up the dishes, rinsed and put them in the dishwasher. After he wiped off the table, Tanner picked Mattie up and laid her on a blanket on the floor in the living room. He changed her diaper and then made goofy faces at her. "Your giggle is the cutest thing." He bent over and blew a kiss into her neck, causing another giggle to escape her.

In the few weeks since they'd moved in, he'd come to enjoy the mornings at home. It felt like a family again. His daughter's smiles came more often, and she also doted on this little one. The couple of evenings when he'd bopped home to check on things, Allie had been holding Mattie and singing silly songs to her.

While his days had been filled with laughter, his nights were painful. As he tossed and turned in bed, Tanner couldn't stop thinking of the woman in the room next door. He dreamed of sneaking into her bed, peeling the clothes from her body, and loving her all night long. Because of this, he'd locked his bedroom door in an effort to provide her some protection, in case he wandered out of his room at night. Sleepwalking had never been his thing, but he'd woken each night this week with her name on his lips and given up wearing anything to bed. The sheets were irritating to his sensitive skin, but the rubbing of his rigid cock against his underwear left them soaked in the morning.

***

Crash.

Breaking glass and a car alarm. "Are you okay?" he hollered.

257

"What happened?" Sheryl bolted from the bathroom and stood looking out the front window. "It sounded like an accident, but there's nothing down there."

Tanner grabbed his cell phone and sprinted toward the stairs. "Thankfully, Allie's at school by now." Picking Mattie up, Sheryl followed him.

They opened the ground-floor door into the parking lot. This private spot was reserved for only their cars and the employees'.

"Oh no." Sheryl pointed at her old beater. The lights were flashing.

The early kitchen crew positioned themselves behind Tanner and Sheryl. Their voices sounded like mumbling over the screech of the alarm. "Anyone see anything?" she called out to them. When they shrugged and shook their heads, she realized they'd only come outside after the noise had started.

Approaching carefully, Tanner paused and looked under the car. "Stay there," he ordered and held out his hand toward Sheryl and the baby. "No telling what caused it. Could be as simple as a stray cat."

"I have to see." She shook her head when she finally got a look at the driver's side. It appeared as if the door lost a battle with another car. Scratches and dents marred the blue surface. She crept a little closer and glanced inside. Pieces of glass lay strewn over the seat and floor. A large brick lay on the driver's side seat.

Tanner slid his arm around her shoulders. "This was on purpose, but probably just kids messing around. I'm sorry. We'll find out who did this. Until then, you can use my car."

Her body shook, and she squeezed her daughter tighter. *He's found us.* "Tanner, I have to tell you the truth."

CHAPTER EIGHT

Tanner sat as still as a statue while she told him her story. His fists clenched tight against his thighs. The anger churned inside him, and he longed to lash out against the man who'd hurt Sheryl. *How could anyone go to such lengths to trap her and then smack her around? She should be treated like a cherished gift.* Thank goodness she'd run, taking Mattie with her. Tanner couldn't imagine what the poor child would have faced should Sheryl have stayed. "I understand why you did it. Frankly, I'm proud of you for taking the chance and escaping."

Her deep sigh echoed through the silent loft. He reached over and grasped her hand. "I thought you'd be angry," she murmured, her eyes finally meeting his.

"I'm angry but not at you. I'd love to get my hands on him, though. But why did you wait to tell me?"

"Shame." Her face pinkened.

Tanner released her hand and brushed his finger across her cheek. He loved the strength inside this woman.

"I should have listened to my parents. Then I thought it was love, but now I know the difference." Her voice had become quiet as she spoke. He'd hoped it was because she'd developed some feelings for him. A guy can dream.

"You have nothing to be ashamed of. James took advantage of you." He brushed a lock of hair off her face. "Have you filed a police report about the kidnapping?"

"I didn't. James threatened to take Mattie from me. He said he'd tell everyone I was a druggie and a neglectful parent." Her voice came out in a whisper. "Now, I'm afraid he'd tell them I kidnapped my daughter and she'd be taken from me."

Tanner stood and began pacing from Mattie's playpen to the couch. "I'm not going to let that happen. We can prove you aren't a danger to your daughter. As far as kidnapping, you weren't married to him. Did you put James's name on the birth certificate?"

She shook her head. "He didn't want to be named the dad at that point. It wasn't until his wife found out she couldn't have children that he became interested in Mattie."

Tanner stopped in front of her then tugged her to her feet. He enveloped her in his arms. "I'll protect you—both." He hoped she believed him.

***

Sheryl's hopes rose after sharing her story with Sergeant Jones first thing the next morning. She filed a report on the car vandalism and while the police couldn't pin the damage on James, the sergeant agreed to step up patrols in the area. He'd pulled the videos of the attack on the hotel clerk and had her study them, however, they were too dark to be sure it was him. Still, she felt it was, in her gut. *I wish my gut had been louder when I met him as a teenager.*

Tonight was the big firefighters' Thanksgiving dinner event. Helping out in the restaurant would keep her mind off the fear that seeped in when she was alone. Additionally, Sheryl fretted over her feelings for Tanner and his daughter. She'd become a member of the family but longed for a more personal relationship with him…if only she could forgive herself for the mistake she made years ago. She didn't believe she was worthy of love since being blinded by James.

It'd gotten more challenging to hide her feelings. Each brush of his fingers or smiling glance and she'd melt like a schoolgirl at her first dance with a boy. She'd taken to long, cool showers to help with her desire. Lately, she'd woken to find her panties drenched after wild sex dreams of the two of them, so steamy she could barely look him in the face each morning.

"Allie, we will be at the restaurant after your playdate. Come in there when Julia's mom drops you off." Sheryl gave Allie a hug. "Enjoy the first day of your break. I have some fun activities planned for just us girls this weekend." Sheryl watched Allie climb into Julia's mother's red minivan. With the last minute details for the event tonight, having her at a friend's house gave both Tanner and her a chance to get everything done. A little nervous about tonight, Sheryl was also excited. She wanted to make everything perfect for the firemen and their families who often spent the evening apart.

She'd talked Tanner into letting her make a special family Jell-O recipe to serve to the families. The lime-green concoction had been at every Thanksgiving table as far back as she could remember. Her mouth salivated. With Mattie in the baby swing, Sheryl started chopping celery. Usually her recipe made enough for a large family, but for tonight, she was quadrupling the ingredients. Luckily for her, Tanner's restaurant had a walk-in cooler to solidify the Jell-O.

With the ingredients on the kitchen counter, she began to mix the boiling water into the lime and lemon powders. Next she added the softened cream cheese that gave the salad its creaminess and texture. Finally, she dumped in the celery, crushed pineapple, and juice. Sheryl poured the mixture into four large baking dishes.

"It smells good in here. Are you ready for me to take the trays to the cooler?" Tanner lifted one dish.

"They need about four hours to solidify. While you are putting them away, I'll finish cleaning up then I can get Mattie fed and down for her nap." After Tanner took off, she loaded the utensils and bowls into the dishwasher.

While he made the trips, she got Mattie's bottle made. After checking the temp on her wrist, she lifted her daughter and carried her to the couch. She reclined on the end, with Mattie's head supported on the arm. "Are you hungry? You've been such a good girl, so quiet while I made the salads and a perfect angel at the police station. Why couldn't Tanner have been your father, rather than James?"

"It takes more than a sperm donor to be a father, and I'd happily be Mattie's."

Sheryl jumped. She hadn't heard him return. Her face heated. "I was just rambling. Never mind."

"Rambling? Or speaking from your heart?" His voice held a commanding note.

"That's very kind of you. But after my last disastrous relationship, I'm not ready to pick Mattie's father because he's been helpful." She glanced sideways at him. "A girl still wants romance, love, and a happily ever after." She lifted her daughter to her shoulder and patted her back until she elicited a burp. Cautiously, she stood then laid her baby on a blanket on the floor.

Now face-to-face with Tanner, she needed to get some things straight. She met his gaze. "I appreciate your generosity. You've made us feel at home. But I want a man who wants both of us, not just my daughter. I can't make a mistake again with Mattie's or my future…no matter how kind or cute you are."

Tanner pulled her close against his body as he held her in his arms. "Does this feel like a guy who is only interested in your daughter?"

His hardness pressed tightly against her core, making

her legs tremble. Having only dreamed of his hands on her, she suddenly felt awkward and unsure of herself. Reaching out, she brushed dark hair off his brow. But her gaze remained on his slightly open lips. She longed to close the distance between them. *What would his kiss feel like? How would he taste? Please don't make this only a dream.*

Before she could lean in and capture his kiss, the loud ringing of the phone jarred them from the moment. She stepped back then, unsteady on her feet, slumped down onto the couch.

Tanner tugged his cell phone from his pocket. "Yes." His voice sounded like a frog, deep and breathless. "All right. I'm coming." As he put away his cell, he stomped over toward the couch and placed his legs on both sides of Sheryl's.

Sliding one hand behind her neck and in her hair, he took possession of her mouth. His lips plundered hers as her core melted and her hands trembled. "Never doubt that I don't want you for you. I've been walking around for the last month with a constant hard-on, unwilling to hope you might have some feelings for me. I've got to get to the restaurant. Chef emergency. But we *will* discuss this later. Count on it."

As he strode from the room, Sheryl placed her palm over her heart in an effort to calm its out-of-control pulsing. Never had a kiss affected her so. She hadn't known his feelings, hadn't guessed his interest. She drew her arms around her body as shivers racked her frame. *If this is what one kiss from him does to me…what would a night of passion do?*

CHAPTER NINE

Keeping busy helped. After the scorching kiss, Sheryl couldn't think straight, so she jumped right into the preparations for the event. Down in the restaurant, he set up Mattie's swing while she folded utensils into cloth napkins. The noise from the kitchen staff did little to drown out her thoughts.

She envisioned Tanner and her entwined together, naked among his bedding. Her nipples peaked. Her face warmed. Not wanting to be caught fantasizing about him, she tried to change her thought process. Instead, scenarios played about in her head where they were one big happy family. Tanner rocking Mattie, while she and Allie baked cookies. Tanner and her standing and watching Allie as she headed out on her first date. Tanner letting go of the back of Mattie's bike as she rode it without training wheels for the first time. Dare she dream? She'd dreamed before and been burned. Now, with James targeting her, could she put the people she'd come to love in harm's way? After all, it was why she didn't go to her father's home. She didn't want him in the crossfire.

The smell of a stinky diaper wafted through the air. Sheryl glanced at her daughter. Mattie sat there with a silly grin on her face. "What'd you do, little one? Perfect timing. The firefighters and their families are arriving in thirty minutes. Let's get you changed, and I'll spruce up, too."

She picked up Mattie and headed back upstairs.

***

Tanner took one last look over the buffet. The food hadn't been put out yet, but the space was set up. A cornucopia of fruit, areas for the salads, rolls, side dishes, and main courses. A spot on the end for a carving station. Freshly sliced seasoned turkey would be the pièce de résistance.

The smells of bread, turkey, and pumpkin pie wafted from the kitchen. It certainly smelled like Thanksgiving. He only hoped that the firemen and their families would enjoy the food as much as he and his employees did making it.

The tables were ready for their guests. Gourds and Indian corn decorated the center of each. Soon families would fill the space with their smiles and laughter. He'd hoped all the work would keep his mind off the kiss he'd planted on Sheryl earlier, but it hadn't. Whenever he happened to catch a glimpse of her, instant hard-on. He recalled how she filled his arms and her special bond with Allie. His feelings had gone farther than sex; he'd fallen for the incredibly strong woman.

Dashing up the steps to the loft, he'd hoped to get a shower and change before the first guests arrived. He whipped his T-shirt up then bumped into something soft. His vision obscured, he reached out to steady himself and ended up with a towel in one hand while his other hand gripped skin.

"Oof. What are you doing?" Sheryl squealed.

Tugging his shirt over his head, Tanner stared at the beautiful...naked woman in front of him. Sheryl's damp hair hung about her shoulders. Small freckles dotted her shoulders. Her pink nipples hardened with his gaze. But it was the nest of light-brown curls between her legs that commanded his attention. He longed to bury himself inside her and show her the depth of his feelings.

As he raised his gaze, he met hers. Her eyes had a faraway, glazed look. Her tongue darted out and ran across her bottom lip. Sheryl's face was flushed.

Without taking his eyes off her, he brushed from her waist upward, gently running his fingers along the side of her breast. Her breathing quickened. He dropped his shirt and pulled her into his embrace, tight against his body. Her nipples brushed against his chest, making him even harder.

Sliding his free hand into her hair, he tugged her mouth to his as his fingers teased her nipple, tweaking and gently squeezing. Releasing her breast, Tanner slid his hand down her back and cupped her ass, shoving her curves against his hardness.

"Oh, Sheryl. I want you," he whispered against her lips.

"Please…yes."

At those two words, Tanner lifted Sheryl into his arms and carried her into his bedroom. Gently, he laid her on his king-sized bed and studied her lying among the pillows. How long had he imagined this happening? He quickly unzipped his jeans and dropped them to the floor. After stepping out of them, he hooked his thumbs along the waist of his boxer-briefs and slid them down over his erection.

Tanner lay down next to her and kissed her again. "Are you sure? I'm giving you one last chance to back out. Because once this happens, I'm not letting you go."

She smiled and pulled his lips back to hers then pushed him down against the bedding and rolled on top of him, silencing his doubts.

CHAPTER TEN

Sheryl stretched and rubbed her eyes. The warm body against her back felt wonderful. She'd dreamed of being with Tanner over the last two weeks, but her imagination didn't do him justice. Her body had come alive under his hands as she experienced her first orgasms with someone else. James had been her first and only, until today, but he clearly didn't know her body as well as Tanner. She snuggled back under his arm and relaxed against his body, feeling well loved. The afternoon sun had gone down, bathing the room in orange.

As she turned and looked at the clock on the nightstand, she gasped. "Tanner. It's late. The firemen are already downstairs. We need to get up."

Tanner rolled her onto her back and slid his leg between hers. Kissing his way up her neck, he appeared content to stay in bed.

"Stop. We can't leave. The firefighters and their families are coming soon. Don't you want to make sure your employees got all the food set up? What about Allie? She's due home soon." She shook his shoulders. "We can come back to bed later. Now, get up." She put some force behind her voice. Without giving him a chance to lull her back with kisses or other things, she slid off the bed and dashed for her own room.

Tanner called out. "You're right. I'm gonna throw some clothes on and head downstairs. I'll meet you down there when you're ready."

"See you in a bit. I've got to get Mattie ready, too." Sheryl darted back into his bedroom and placed a peck on his cheek.

"I'm holding you to your promise of later." He swatted at her ass. "Go get ready. I want to show you off."

Sheryl scooted back to her room and stared at the clothes in her closet. She hadn't brought much with her when she'd escaped James, but since she'd begun working for Tanner, she'd added a few cute pieces to her wardrobe. Just what to wear?

Her gaze caught on a wavy-black-print dress she'd picked up at Target. The knitted material would hug her body, showing off her curves, and the longer sleeves and scooped neckline would keep her warm, without needing an extra sweater.

After a quick wash in the bathroom, she dressed then, using a clip, tugged some of her hair up off her neck into a waterfall style. Adding a little blush, lipstick, and mascara to her face, Sheryl was ready. All that was left was Mattie.

Sheryl looked at her phone. Only a half hour late, even with getting Mattie fed and ready. *I'd call it a win.* As she entered the restaurant, the smells hit her first, causing her stomach to grumble. The soft lighting and fall decorations gave off a homey vibe, but it was the soft, happy conversations that truly made her feel at home.

She strolled over to where Tanner had set up Mattie's swing and placed her daughter inside. Sheryl laid a couple of toys on the tray and brushed an errant curl off her daughter's head. Tanner approached her, leaned over, and gave her a kiss on the cheek.

"I never did thank you. Today was everything I'd hoped it would be." The sparkle in his eyes had Sheryl's heart beating faster.

She wrapped her arms around him and hugged him tight. "I'm happy you made the move. If you'd have waited for me...it might be next Thanksgiving. I don't trust very easily, and you understand why."

"I do. And I want you to know, I'm serious about you. This isn't a passing fling. But I'm not going to rush you. Take all the time you need, until you believe I'll have your back."

Tears filled her eyes, but she blinked them away. "How did I get so lucky?"

"How did we? Even though you literally ran into my daughter?" he teased. "I want you to come meet everyone." He grasped her hand in his and led her off toward the tables.

Tanner took her to the first table and introduced her to the fire chief and his family. The older gentleman had his whole family there, including his first grandchild. Soon, Tanner had taken her to most of the tables, except for the larger one near the back.

"Hey, I have to dart into the kitchen to get some more bread started. Why don't you head back and see how that last table liked the food?"

"Sure. It was nice of you to introduce me to the others. But I hate keeping you from doing your job." She waved her hands at him. "I've got this. Shoo."

He kissed her cheek. "Have I told you how sexy you look? Maybe I'll just show you later." And then he ran into the kitchen.

Sheryl paused for a moment, stunned. She laid her hand on her cheek where he'd kissed her and knew she appeared to be mooning over him...but it was hard not to.

At the far back of the restaurant, a large family sat in

271

the dim lighting. Their laughter could be heard all the way up to the buffet. Sheryl longed to see her family again. Maybe, sometime, she'd be able to visit. Once things with James were done.

She strolled over. Two men in firefighter blues were the first to catch her eye. They looked handsome with their short haircuts and clean-shaven faces. A small child sat in a high chair at the end near an older gentleman.

"Thank you for coming—" All sound around the table stopped.

"Sheryl?" The man pushed back his chair and stood awkwardly. He gripped the table. His hands white against the dark tablecloth. But his face was immediately recognizable.

"Hi, Daddy." She bowed her head, unable to meet his gaze.

"What are you doing here? Is this a part of the event?" Slowly, he slid back into his chair with a thud.

Sheryl scooted closer and crouched next to him. "I'm here helping Tanner tonight with the event. I've been back in Amherst for a couple of months."

Joy, confusion, and sadness crossed his face. "Why didn't you come see us? Tell us you were here?"

She reached over and put her hand on top of his wrinkled one. "I'm sorry. Things were crazy, and I didn't want you mixed up in it."

"What do you mean? Crazy? Mixed up?" She could feel the warmth of her sister behind her. There was no mistaking Syn's bossy demeanor. As the oldest, she always told everyone else what to do.

Sheryl stood and faced her big sister. "Hi, Syn. You look good."

Her sister had her hands on her hips as daggers shot from her eyes. "You didn't answer Dad or me."

"Now's not the time. I'll come by and share, but enjoy your dinner. Tanner went to all this trouble to make sure the Amherst Fire Department and their families could have a wonderful Thanksgiving." She turned to hightail it to the kitchen to hide out. Maybe she could make it before the waterworks started. She didn't want to let them see her cry.

A hand grasped her shoulder. "Wait." Stacey held on to her. "You are family, Sheryl. Come eat with us."

Sheryl sighed. Tears filled her vision. She pinched the bridge of her nose to keep them from falling.

"Please. I'd like you to meet Mandy. And I'm sure you'd love to meet your nephew, Mackenzie." Stacey pointed at the baby gurgling in the high chair.

Sheryl nodded then reached out and wrapped her arms around her sister. Stacy, as second oldest, always seemed at odds with Syn. The two of them could be best friends or worst enemies. And when it was the second, the rest of the Wilder girls took sides. It was like being picked for Red Rover. You knew you'd end up on the ground with grass stains at some point.

A slamming door caught Sheryl's attention.

"Get my daughter over here, you bitch, or this girl gets it." James's voice sent shivers down Sheryl's spine. She looked over and froze. Just inside the door and by the kitchen, her ex stood with a large knife pressed to Allie's neck. The young girl shook with terror, and tears fell in rivers down her cheeks.

"I'm sorry, Sheryl. I didn't see him. He grabbed me," the little girl tried to explain.

"Shut up. Get my baby here, now. I'm not joking." A trail of blood trickled down Allie's neck, as she sobbed openly.

"I'm coming, James. Let her go, and we can talk." Sheryl's voice sounded stronger than she felt. She needed to buy some time. Soon, Tanner would be out of the kitchen and then anything could happen.

One of the firemen stood behind Sheryl. She felt his hand on her back. "Is there a back way into the kitchen?" he whispered against her neck.

"Yes, through that hallway," she murmured, pointing to the left, behind her. "Allie's father is in the there. Please don't let him do something that will get him hurt."

As she felt some people behind her move, Sheryl tugged her necklace from inside her shirt and began twirling it. "Please, Mom or God… Someone. Save Allie." Then she started forward.

CHAPTER ELEVEN

Tanner heard the commotion from the kitchen and peeked through the swinging door. His heart dropped. He ached to run out and drag his daughter from the madman's clutches, but he did the sensible thing first and called the police.

Leaving his phone on speaker on the prep station, he hoped the dispatcher would hear everything. It'd taken all of his patience to call for backup. Now, he needed to make sure James didn't hurt his daughter.

Two firemen and a curvy woman with short dark hair entered the kitchen silently. They motioned for the crew to leave the area by the other door, near where James was standing.

Tanner strode over. "Who are you? And what are you doing telling my people anything?"

The woman spoke softly. "Are you Allie's dad?"

He nodded. The woman spoke again. "Are you Allie's dad? You have to say yes or no. I can't see you. I'm blind."

He realized she'd never lifted her eyes to meet his. His face must be red. He felt like an idiot. "Yes. Who are you?"

"I'm Shevonne Wilder, Sheryl's sister. We're here to

help you get Allie away from that man."

"No offense ma'am. But you're blind. How can you help?"

"I lost my eyesight in a mortar explosion when I served a tour in Afghanistan."

Tanner grimaced. He still wasn't sure how that was going to help. The woman appeared small and defenseless.

"Trust us. She's good. Very good. She put my buddy in his place when he tried to get too grabby," one of the firemen bragged. He reached out his hand. "I'm Jackson Gambish, her fiancé." He motioned to the other man standing there. "This is Thom Johnson. He's Sheryl's oldest sister's fiancé. We're trained in some combat scenarios."

Tanner shook his head. Was this old family night? How did Sheryl's family think they could help? "I've called the police. They're on the line." He pointed to his phone. "They should be here soon. In the meantime, I'm not about to let this asswipe hurt my daughter, nor am I going to let him take Mattie away."

Sheryl's sister leaned in. "I have a plan."

***

"James. Please let Allie go. You're scaring her." Sheryl felt sick to her stomach. She'd been worried about bringing her family into danger but never thought James would do something like this to an innocent child.

"Just get Mattie, and I'll trade her for this girl." The crazed look in his eyes didn't bode well for Sheryl. She'd seen that look too many times to count, usually right before she felt a slap on her face or a kick to her abdomen.

She raised her hands and started toward him. "Please. This is silly. You don't want to hurt another child."

He glanced down at the child but didn't let go. "You shouldn't have taken Mattie. Karen's been out of her mind since you left. Mattie'd make her happy. I can't lose her."

She took another step closer. "I'm sorry about Karen. I know you love her." Sheryl wanted to scream at him about how he'd never really wanted her—or Mattie, until Karen had it in her head. Karen's mental stability had been in question since her last miscarriage a few years before. With each pause in speech, Sheryl took another step closer. "Karen wants a baby. Mattie's getting too big." She tried to explain what she'd seen happening with Karen. And another step closer. "James, I'm worried Karen's going to hurt my daughter."

James shook his head. "She won't. She loves her."

"But what's going to happen when Mattie starts walking? Or talking? She won't be a baby anymore."

A movement to the left caught Sheryl's and James's attention. He screeched, "Stop. Don't come closer."

Another bead of blood slid down Allie's neck. "Allie, dear, stand still. I'll get you," Sheryl mouthed.

Shevonne came out of the shadows with Mattie in her arms. Jackson stood behind her, as if guiding her. "I have your baby. Please let the young girl go."

"No, Shevonne. Don't," Sheryl shrieked as she reached out toward her daughter. "He'll take Mattie away from me."

Shevonne appeared to ignore everyone but the man in front of her with the knife. "Sir, I am happy to switch, but I'm blind and can't see you. Can you please let the little girl go?"

James withdrew the knife from Allie's neck but kept his hand bunched up in her hair and tugged, eliciting a scream of pain from her. "Just give her to me. Only you. Keep that man back."

Sheryl ran over to intercept her sister, but as she reached out to grab Mattie, Jackson held her against him. No matter how she hit at him, he wouldn't let her go. Tears fell down her cheeks. Would this be the last time she saw Mattie? Where was Tanner through all this? Why hadn't anyone called the police? It couldn't end this way.

Shevonne was within arm's reach. With one more step, Sheryl's daughter would be in her crazy ex's hands. Sobbing openly in Jackson's arms, she continued to struggle.

Sheryl's sister handed Mattie to Allie then tugged the two of them out of James's reach, pushing them behind her. Using her left foot, she kicked up at his arm, knocking the knife away. Jackson released Sheryl and grabbed Mattie and Allie then ran them to the far back of the restaurant where the remaining Wilder family waited.

Without Jackson holding her, Sheryl crumpled to the floor, her gaze fixed on her baby sister beating the crap out of James. A jab to the neck, and he collapsed facedown. Shevonne wrenched his arms behind his back and affixed them with poultry string. She remained standing over him until Tanner, and the police darted through the kitchen door and took James into custody.

**

Now that the excitement was over, many of the firefighters and their families had left. *I'm sure no one will forget this Thanksgiving. but I have so much to be thankful for.*

Tanner hugged his daughter tight against his chest. TJ had cleaned and bandaged the nick on her neck but she'd need time to deal with the events of the night. He glanced over at Sheryl who stood among her family holding Mattie in her arms.

"Mr. Watts. We will need a statement from you, Ms. Wilder, and your daughter tomorrow at the station. We've already gotten the other Ms. Wilder's statement." Sergeant Jones tapped his pencil on his pad then slid them both back into his coat pocket. "Mr. Dugan appears to be the same person who broke into the motel and beat up the clerk. We're running prints and using facial recognition software to be sure and help build a solid case."

Tanner reached out and shook the sergeant's hand.

"Thank you for getting here so quickly. Who knows what could have happened?"

"It appeared Ms. Shevonne had everything under control. And we're glad things worked out. Those Wilders are a pretty wonderful family." Sergeant Jones looked down at the floor. "I didn't say anything when Ms. Sheryl came in, but the wife and I used to play cards with her folks down at the VFW hall…that was before her mother's death." The policeman placed his hat on his head. "We'll see you tomorrow. Take care of your girls."

Tanner and Allie headed over to Sheryl and her family. As he approached, Mr. Wilder pulled away from the group and waylaid them. "Young man, I want to talk to you."

Tanner could tell where Sheryl got her strength. The older gentleman in front of him, who struggled to walk, seemed determined to intimidate him. Tanner leaned over. "Allie, go to Sheryl and meet her sisters. Can you believe she has four?" He patted his daughter on the shoulder and watched until she wrapped her arm around Sheryl's waist.

"Mr. Wilder, you wanted to talk to me?" He led the man to a chair. "Let's sit down and rest our weary bones."

"What do you know of weary?" He chortled. "I wanted to thank you for taking care of my little girl. She told us about her fears with James and how you took her in…made her feel a part of a family." He pulled a worn piece of paper from his pocket, folded it and unfolded it then tucked it back away.

"Sheryl rubs and twists the cross necklace she got from your wife when she's feeling worried or fearful. You two are very much alike. Only you fold and unfold paper." He smiled. "You know she loves you so much she didn't want to put you in harm's way. She's always suspected James would find her, and your safety was more important to her than her own."

"Silly girl. She could have come to us." He began to cough into his hand. Each motion appeared to rob him of his breath.

"Are you okay, sir?" Tanner reached over and patted him on the back. He filled a glass with water from the pitcher on the table. "Drink this. It'll help."

As he watched her father drink, Tanner recalled his own parents. He needed to reach out to them and share what had happened. He didn't want them finding out through another source like the papers or television. They deserved to hear it from him, and he had something special to talk about with them as well.

"I'm better. Thanks," Mr. Wilder croaked.

"I hope you'll listen to your daughter with an open heart. She's been through a lot over the years. James all but held her prisoner there, and her pride kept her from seeking help. She's been abused, but I plan to make sure the rest of her life is only magical."

Mr. Wilder placed his hand on top of Tanner's. "That's what I like to hear. All my girls settled and loved."

CHAPTER TWELVE

Christmas Eve

Tanner pulled into the Wilder driveway. Sheryl studied the house she'd left. Nothing much had changed, yet so much about her had. She let out a sigh. The sunlight glinted off her ring, which made her smile. "Why'd you do this today?" She waved her hand in front of his face.

"I decided our family needed to celebrate our future alone this morning. Besides, I knew you'd want to show it off to your sisters." He tugged her hand to his lips and placed a kiss on it. "Do you like it? I mean, even though it's not brand new?"

"The ring is gorgeous. Your dad was so sweet to let you have his mother's engagement ring to give to me." Another glance at the marquis-cut diamond with the two topaz triangular diamonds next to it, and her heart beat faster.

"Besides, I'm nervous enough, today. This is the first Christmas I've celebrated with my family since I left town." Tears filled her eyes. "Even though we've talked and visited in the four weeks since Thanksgiving, coming here again seemed like a dream." Syn had filled her in on all the news from Dad's Alzheimer's diagnosis to the miracle that happened last Christmas with Sherri's husband. She tugged her necklace from under her collar and played with it. *Will they be able to forgive me for missing out on so much?*

Tanner brushed his fingers across her cheek. "No tears. This is a time to celebrate. Let's go in and see everyone."

As he opened the rear door and helped his daughter out, Sheryl unbuckled Mattie's car seat. Tanner lifted the rear hatch and tugged out the baby bag and playpen. "Here, Allie. You carry the bag." He tossed it to her.

"Do you think that they made that special soup you told me about, Sheryl?" Allie skedaddled closer.

"My family always made it for Christmas Eve, but it takes days." Sheryl bent to whisper. "I never had it, though. I was always too scared."

"Welcome." Mr. Wilder stood framed in the doorway. His booming voice was in contradiction to his stooped frame. "Glad you all could come."

Allie stopped for a second then scooted and grabbed her dad's hand, still nervous about people, especially men, since her ordeal over Thanksgiving.

Sheryl sped up her gait. "Thanks, Dad." She swung the baby carrier to her left hip and reached out with her right arm to envelop him into a sideways hug. "I've missed you." She blinked quickly to stop the tears from leaving her eyes.

Tanner struck out his hand. "Thank you for the invite, sir. We've been hearing wonderful stories about you."

Sheryl released her father so he could shake hands with her guy then stepped around him and into the house. As she entered the home, voices called out.

"Give me that baby." Syn snatched Mattie's carrier out of her sister's hands. She set it on the floor and tugged the baby out. After divesting the baby of the pink snowsuit, Syn strolled into the kitchen. "Look, TJ. Isn't she adorable? We need to have a dozen!" TJ's groan floated out into the living room.

Sheryl took in the scene around her. A Christmas tree sparkled by the front window. On the couch sat her sister, Stacey and another woman. They had their heads together and fingers entwined. The other person had to be Mandy, her sister's wife. *I'm glad Stacey finally learned to live her life her own way and not worry about others. They are so cute together. Must be the newlywed thing.* She glanced down at her own ring and smiled. *Do Tanner and I look like that?*

"Sheryl, come meet my husband and our son." Sherri waved her sister over. A dark-haired man was seated on the couch with a toddler on his lap. His hair was cut very short, and a few scars were still visible around his hairline. He carefully set the little guy on the floor then pushed with his arms on the sofa to stand, a little unsteady. Sherri put her arm around his waist to assist. "This is my husband, Adam, and our miracle, MacKenzie." She lifted her son and kissed his cheek. "Wave to your aunt," she cajoled him, but he only giggled and stretched his arms out toward his father.

"It's nice to meet you, Adam. Congrats on your recovery. I understand it was touch-and-go." Sheryl waved at the little guy. "Hi, MacKenzie."

Adam dropped back onto the couch. "We had an angel watching over us." He smiled and wrapped his arm around his wife's leg. Sherri bent over and placed MacKenize back into his father's lap.

"I'd better go track down my own daughter. Syn ran off with her when we arrived." Still feeling nervous, Sheryl bolted from the room and ran into her sister, Shevonne, sending the glass of water her sister had been holding, flying onto the floor.

"Crap. I'm sorry." Sheryl held out her hand then realized her sister couldn't see it. Instead, she wrapped her arms around Shevonne as tears flowed down Sheryl's cheeks. "I'm sorry. I'm such an idiot. Syn told me about your vision but I forgot. Here I go making a mess of things. You don't need this. I'd better get my daughter and leave. I don't know how you could want me here. You've been a family without me for years. It was wrong of me to jump in here and expect to be welcome."

"Stop right there," Mr. Wilder yelled. Sheryl was stunned. She hadn't heard her father use that tone since the night she left. Everyone froze as her father approached her. He pulled her from Shevonne's arms and wrapped his feeble ones around her. Sheryl ducked her face into her father's flannel shirt and let her emotions go. After five minutes, she stepped back and wiped at her cheeks. "I'm sorry. I'm so sorry."

Her father lifted her chin so she met his gaze. "You have nothing to be sorry for. Let's sit at the table." He beckoned to the others. "Everyone. I have a story to tell."

Each of her sisters commanded a seat, their husbands and boyfriends next to and behind them. Sheryl grasped Tanner's hand in hers. She was glad for his strength and support. He'd put in a movie for Allie to enjoy and laid Mattie in her playpen. She hadn't planned on breaking down today, but being among her family had been a dream for so long. It had been polite of them to include her even if she'd messed up their lives by being gone and not around to help. She couldn't hate them for feeling like she'd deserted them.

Mr. Wilder tucked himself into his chair at the head of the table. He fiddled with his pocket then pulled a piece of paper from it, folded it, and shoved it back away.

"Dad. Is that the note you never let me see?" Syn blurted.

"Leave it. You can read it when I'm gone." He cleared his throat. "I'm so blessed to have my daughters and their loved ones under my roof this holiday. It's been so many years since we were all together." His glance passed over each and every one of them. "Each of you left Amherst and home shortly after graduating from high school. Syn was first and set off to find a way to mend her broken heart." He smiled at his eldest. "But she came home and soon reconnected with her first love." He paused and turned his scrutiny on his second daughter. "Stacey never trusted that we loved her no matter who she loved, so she ran. Good thing she did…because when she finally came home, she brought a wonderful young woman into our family." He nodded at Mandy.

"After a horrible accident last Christmas, I almost thought we'd lost Adam. But Father MacKenzie showed us how strong love and the power of heaven is. And, today, we have Adam and little MacKenzie celebrating with us." Adam pressed a kiss to Sherri's cheek.

"Then there was my baby, Shevonne. Always doing things her own way, she took on our country's safety by serving overseas. Like Adam, it took an accident for her to return, but she saw her disability as somehow making her less of a person. Luckily for me, she and Jackson were able to locate me after a battle with a skunk."

Shevonne cut in. "I see what's important now." She leaned over on her husband's shoulder. "Love and family."

"Now, this Christmas, Sheryl is home again. She left after we exchanged some harsh words. I never expected them to be the last things I said to my daughter. Evil took advantage of her big heart and hurt her in ways…" His voice broke. He pinched his nose as if he could stop the emotion from escaping.

Sheryl rushed over to her father and wrapped her arms around him. "I never meant to leave you all. James wouldn't let me come home, and when I spoke of family, he became enraged. Soon, it was easier for me to keep quiet so as not to anger him. But I never stopped thinking of you all. When I heard about Mom's passing…I wanted to come." She paused. "I…James…" She dropped her chin to her chest. "I wasn't able to stand for two weeks. He'd beaten me so badly, I thought I'd have the marks forever."

Gasps echoed around the table. Her father gave her a squeeze. "Your momma came to me in my dreams and told me she was watching over you." He raised his eyes and looked around the table at each person. "All of you. I know you think my mind is gone, dementia and all, but my sweet Yvonne comes to me each night. She made me promise to find a way to bring you all home, back here. Nonstop nagging to get her girls home, where they belong. One big family. I've done that. Now, together, you are stronger. You are family and will always have each other to support and care for. You are loved and never forget you are Wilders."

Mr. Wilder stretched then yawned. "I'm going to rest in my chair while you guys finish with dinner. After all, I've spent the last couple of days working on that soup." He rose and placed a kiss on Sheryl's brow. "You've always been closest with your mom. She gave you the cross because she somehow knew about your trials to come and wanted you to have the strength to get through them." He smiled. "And look at that beautiful family you have now."

He slowly shuffled to the Barcalounger and plopped down into it then leaned it back and studied the twinkling tree.

"Can I help with anything?" Sheryl called out as her family headed into the kitchen.

Everyone pitched in, and soon the buffet was laid out on the table. Glazed ham, sauerkraut soup, cheeses, lunchmeats and breads for sandwiches, pasta and Jell-O salads, spiced yams, fresh fruit, cottage cheese, 7UP punch, and cookies. It was a spread fit for a king. Each sister had a hand in the dishes. Some were family favorites, while others were new traditions. Even Allie helped by laying the napkins and utensils on the table. TJ and Jackson brought in the cooler filled with sodas and beers.

Sheryl's stomach had been grumbling as she swatted Tanner's hand away from the food. "You'd better wait. Dad's always first. He says grace."

"I'll get him, then. He's probably fallen asleep. We haven't heard much from him in over an hour." Tanner sprinted toward the living room but quickly returned. He pulled TJ aside and whispered to him. Shortly, the two of them left again.

"Don't tell me Dad's missing again?" Syn called out. "He's done this before during an episode."

"I didn't hear the door," Shevonne chimed in.

Sheryl lifted her necklace and twirled it between her fingers. "Tanner. What's going on?" she called out.

The women booked to the living room and found Tanner and TJ standing around Mr. Wilder. The older gentleman appeared asleep, a peaceful smile on his face.

Syn gasped then slid to the floor next to her father's chair. TJ enveloped her, pulling him against him.

Sheryl huddled in Tanner's arms. "What happened? He was fine an hour ago."

"What's going on? Tell me," Shevonne demanded. "You need to tell me. I hate not being able to see."

Sherri and Stacey ran into the room. They called out for Jackson, Adam, and Mandy. Soon, the girls each had their significant other as they dealt with their father's passing.

"Look." TJ grabbed a crumpled piece of paper from the floor by the chair. It looked like it'd been slept with. The deep wrinkles softened the note.

"What is it?" Syn pulled it from his hands. "A note. This must have been the paper he'd never let me see. Here. I'll read it." Her voice choked as she began.

My darling girls,

I've asked so much of your father. He's been the only man in this overly emotional home for so long. Yet, he taught you all the finer things in life—car repair, shooting, and how to cook a mean perch dinner. And I'm still going to ask a big favor of him. Cancer is taking over, and I don't have much longer. I never wanted to leave you so soon, especially when you all need me so much. But I don't have a choice. Often, when God calls, we don't have a choice.

I wish I could be here for you as you face the tribulations I know life will deal you, but know I'll be here watching over you, in your dreams and in the smiles of your children. Don't be too hard on your dad. He's got his own trials, and even as he's dealing with his own, I've asked him to bring you all together again—to be the five girls who played together as children in the woods across from our home. To be the girls who had each other's backs whenever anyone picked on one of you. You have drifted apart from home and from each other. Your dad can't come be with me until he accomplishes this. No matter how much we long to be together, he's had his own job to do.

If you are reading this, he's done it, and now we finally can be together as we were in life. Our love created the five of you, and through your children, our love will live on. Please don't be sad. We will always be with you… Be a family, love each other, and make us proud as you always have.

Look for us in the twinkling of a star or as the sun shines through a cloud…

All my love-
Mom.

Sherri hid her face against her husband's back. Stacey mumbled a prayer. Shevonne openly sobbed, wrapped in Jackson's arms. Sheryl reached out to her sister and pulled her close. "I've missed you." Soon, she felt her other sisters' arms envelop her. Their tears fell and mixed.

Syn spoke, "I'm glad to have all of you in my life. Sisters always."

"Always…" the rest echoed.

***

The funeral was a private affair with only the five girls. They stood among the dusting of snow on the cemetery ground, their arms wrapped around each other. Stronger together as their father was laid to rest next to their mother. Each woman laid a single flower on the casket. A sunflower, a lily, a rose, a tulip, and a daisy. As the casket was lowered, the clouds broke overhead and a beam of sunlight shone down on them.

Sheryl lifted her face toward the sky. "Love you, both. Thank you for bringing me home."

ACKNOWLEDGEMENTS

Writers don't create alone. Thank you to my supportive friends who give me plenty of chances to brag about my books and who enjoy the characters I write. I couldn't do this without your support.

To my family who loves me and understands when I'm keeping them awake typing into the night or burning dinner. Your commitment to my happiness is unfathomable.

Finally to my readers, thank you for taking the time to enjoy this story. I'd love to hear from you!

.

ABOUT THE AUTHOR

Melissa doesn't believe in down time. She's always keeping busy. Melissa is a wife and mother, an elementary school teacher, a radio movie reviewer, owner for a publishing company as well as an author. Her home blends two families and is a lot like the Brady Bunch, without Alice—a large grocery bill, tons of dirty dishes and a mound of laundry. She loves to write stories that feature "happy endings" and is often found plotting her next story.

Melissa loves hearing from readers!
www.melissakeir.com
http://www.facebook.com/melissaakeir
http://www.facebook.com/authormelissakeir(fan page)
www.twitter/melissa_keir

Other Books by Melissa Keir
Wilder Sisters Series:
Forever Love

Beach Desires

A Christmas Accident

Coming Home

**

Charming Chances:
Charming Chances (print of combined ebooks)

Second Time's a Charm

Three's a Crowd

**

Pigg Detective Agency:
Protecting His Wolfe

Protecting Her Pigg

**

Magical Matchmaker
Chalkboard Romance

One Night in Laguna

One Night Behind Bars

**

Crash and Burn (romance)

Redeeming Love (romance)

Musings of a Madcap Mind (memoirs)

**

Cowboys of Whisper Colorado
The Heartsong Cowboy

The Heartbroken Cowboy

Claiming a Cowboy's Heart

A Pigskin Cowboy

Broken Dreams

Broken Vows

Redeeming Dreams

Bidding for the Cowboy's Heart

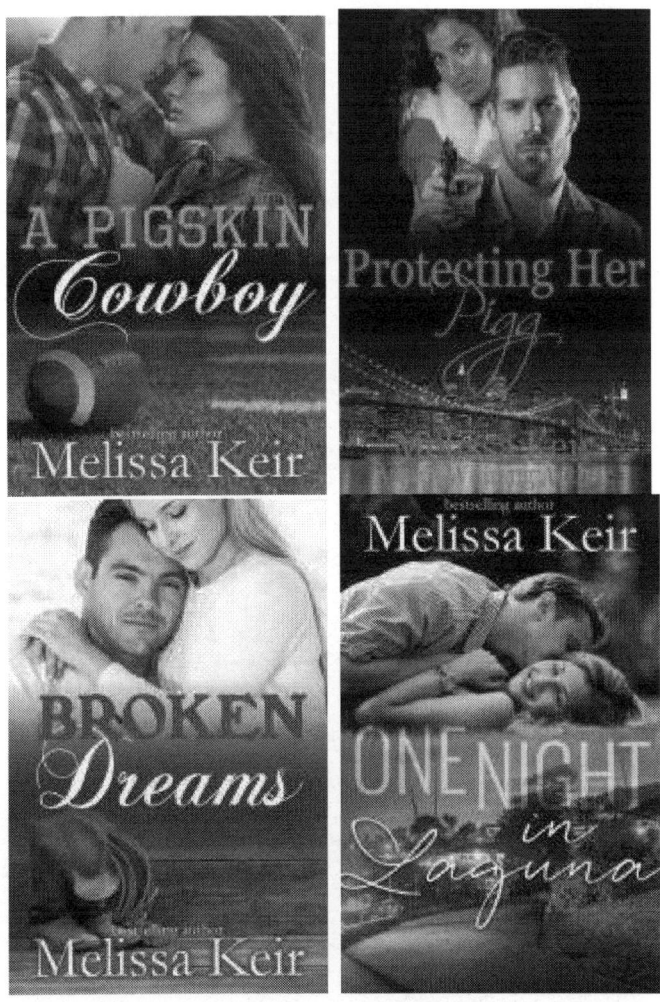

Fall in love with Small Town Romances
OTHER BOOKS BY MELISSA KEIR
www.melissakeir.com